Holiday Heart Strings

HARTBRIDGE CHRISTMAS SERIES
BOOK FOUR

N.R. WALKER

Copyright

Blurb

Englishman Braithe Branson arrives in Hartbridge, Montana, to take on a brief substitute kindergarten teacher position. His introduction to the sleepy town is being pulled over for speeding. Not an ideal start, but at least the deputy was cute.

Colson Price takes being a deputy very seriously. After all, his job is all he has. Disowned by his family ten years ago, he's vowed to stay closeted so it won't cost him everything all over again.

But the holidays are tough for Colson, and the new guy in town is far too tempting. With a promise of some very private no-strings encounters on the downlow, he can't resist.

Braithe is charmed by the handsome deputy, the gorgeous town, and the great group of friends he meets. But as the countdown to leaving gets closer, the more tangled the 'no strings' becomes.

Braithe and Colson have to hope that Hartbridge will find a way for this Christmas wish to come true.

HOLIDAY HEART Strings

N.R. WALKER

Chapter One

BRAITHE BRANSON

THE DRIVE from Helena to Hartbridge was beautiful. The mountains were glorious shades of autumn, like quilts of orange and browns and yellows. The sky was a perfect blue for late November; the air was clean and fresh.

A truly beautiful part of the world.

Also a far cry from the gloomy grey of my London home. Which was also beautiful, don't get me wrong. But this part of Montana was postcard perfect. Better than a postcard. No postcard could do it justice.

I made a detour to take some photos of Flathead Lake and have some lunch, taking my time to see the sights and experience everything I could.

The best part of my two-year working visa was experiencing the real America; not some whirlwind touristy trip but living as a local.

I was four months in and loving it.

With not much more than a suitcase, my laptop bag, and a crate of work supplies in my car, I uploaded my photos to Instagram, finished my lunch, and got back into my car for the final leg back down I-90 and into Hartbridge.

I was excited about this new town. What I'd read and seen on the internet had been idyllic and quaint, and I was especially excited to be spending the holiday period in a true American mountain town.

Turning off Montana Sky Highway, the road to Hartbridge snaked through the mountains, and the further I went, the prettier it got. Tall trees skirted the roads, there was hardly any traffic, and I had my music up loud, singing along, having a merry old time . . .

Until some flashing red and blue lights came up behind me.

Oh my days.

I might have screamed.

I checked my speed, and . . . Oh no, I was speeding!

Trying not to panic, I slowed to a stop, pulling off the road the best I could.

I'd never been pulled over by the police before. Not in England and certainly not in America. Did I put my window down? Did I get out? Did I reach for my wallet?

What was I supposed to do?

Oh, gosh, he's getting out . . . He's walking toward me . . . In his little brown outfit with his big hat and his black boots.

He knocked on my window and I let out a yelp, stabbing at every button on my door to get the window to come down, trying not to panic even more, which of course made me panic even more.

Finally, I got the window down.

"Hello, officer," I said with a smile. Maybe if he thought I was a dumb-blond tourist he'd go easy on me.

"Sir, licence and registration please."

His voice was gruff and no-nonsense. His shirt was decidedly tight, which was something I should not have noticed.

"Ah, yes, of course." I grabbed my bag on the passenger seat, and he reacted immediately.

His hand went to the gun on his hip. "Keep your hands on the steering wheel."

Oh my word!

I put my hands on that steering wheel so fast and made a high-pitched strangled sound that rang in my ears. I sat there, wondering if I was actually about to pee myself, breathing as if I'd just done a fifty-metre sprint. "Uh, how . . . how can I get my licence with my hands on the steering wheel?"

"You're not from around here, are you," he said. It wasn't a question. More a statement of gruff annoyance.

"No. I'm not."

"Where are your licence and registration?"

Oh my days.

My fingers were starting to hurt from gripping the steering wheel so tight.

"Uh, my licence is in my wallet. Which is in my bag. I stopped at Flathead Lake and grabbed some lunch and left it in my bag. The registration papers are in the glove compartment."

"Get them out, driver's licence first," he said. "Slowly."

I did as he asked and noticed his hand was still on his gun. Holy hell, I was terrified, trying to remember what else I'd stashed in my bag . . . Nothing illegal, of course. But incriminatory, maybe.

No, your lube and condoms are in your suitcase.

I found my wallet and held it so he could see what it was, opened it slowly, and pulled my licence out. I handed it over, then reached in the glovebox for my registration, and then passed that through the window, my hands shaking. Only then did he take his hand off his gun.

"London, England?"

"Ah, yes," I said, my mouth almost too dry to speak. "The good old motherland, except you guys claimed independence, which is understandable, honestly. I get it. I mean . . ."

Stop talking. Stop talking now.

He was quiet for a moment, and I risked looking up at his face for the first time. I couldn't see much, given his hat and the glaring sun behind him, but I think he smiled.

"Sorry, your gun makes me nervous."

Yep. It was a smile. "What brings you to these parts?" He read my licence again. "Braithe Branson."

"Oh, I'm, uh, I'm a teacher. I'm the replacement at Hartbridge Elementary. Maternity replacement." I put my hand to my stomach. "Not my maternity, obviously."

Oh my days, Braithe, stop talking.

He smiled again, this time enough to show his teeth. "Obviously."

I swallowed, my mouth now even drier than before. "Sorry. Nervous. Gun."

He tapped my licence. "Did you have a reason for speeding today, Mr Branson? An emergency?"

"Uh, unfortunately, no. Unless I can claim Kylie Minogue's *Greatest Hits* and the sunshine as an emergency?"

He was still smiling. Until he reined it in. "Ah, no. You cannot."

"I must have got a little heavy-footed. I have no legitimate excuse, sorry."

He looked up the road with a sigh. There wasn't any other traffic and I wondered what he was stalling for. He handed my licence back through my window. "I'll let you off with a verbal warning today, Mr Branson. But I won't be so generous next time."

"There won't be a next time, officer."

His eyes met mine. Brown like burned honey, his cheeks a little pink, a shadow of stubble on his jaw.

Oh, wow. He was really handsome.

He tipped his hat. "Drive careful now."

I shook my head to focus. "Uh, yes. Yes, thank you, officer. I will. You too." He smiled again, and I realised I'd just told him to drive careful.

Awesome.

But he didn't give me a ticket, so I counted my blessings and watched him walk back to his cruiser. In those brown trousers and his too-tight shirt.

Damn.

I drove five miles under the speed limit the whole way into Hartbridge. Not because I was mindful of speeding or because I was driving carefully . . . but because a cruiser with Sheriff written across the hood followed me all the way into town.

QUAINT DIDN'T DO Hartbridge justice. It was a gorgeous little town with its main street—aptly named Main Street— filled with stores with awnings and planters with flowers. There was a diner and a hardware store, a clothing store, a hair salon, and then there was Bridge Street—with a bridge, of course—over a picturesque river, all framed by the mountains and trees in the backdrop.

People smiled as they walked and chatted in the afternoon sun, leaves falling and kids chasing a dog in the park.

If they ever wanted to rename this town Perfectville, there'd be no objections. There couldn't possibly be.

I found the address I needed; given the very few streets in Hartbridge, it wasn't difficult.

It was a boarding house, of sorts.

My stay for only four weeks had made renting difficult. I'd tried the bed and breakfast first, and it was fully booked. Hotels were too costly for that length of time, even if they weren't all booked out for the holidays. And boarding houses were fine. The two other boarding houses where I'd stayed in my travels so far for my two other teaching stints, had been more than adequate. This one looked even better.

It was a white bungalow-style house with a porch on the front, complete with a small swinging sign hanging from the porch beam.

Parson's Boarding House.

I knocked on the door, and hearing a mumbled response and footfalls, the door opened. An older lady opened the door, perhaps late sixties, with short dyed-red hair. She gave me an up and down, seeing me holding a suitcase, and she smiled.

"Mr Branson?"

I nodded. "Please call me Braithe. And you're Mrs Parson?"

"That's me," she said. "Come inside, come in." She held the door for me and led me down the hall—while telling me how nice it was that I was a teacher—and through the kitchen toward the back of the house. "Your room's out here. It's more private, and you have access down the driveway if you don't want to come in through the house. Though you're more than welcome to do so, of course. Some folks just prefer their privacy. You have your own bathroom and a small kitchen. But you can use my kitchen in the house at any time. Help yourself to whatever you need."

What she'd led me to was what she called a mother-in-law suite. It was a small granny flat, or an annexe as we'd call them back home. Still part of the house but separate and self-contained. It was about the size of a large hotel room, complete with a double bed, a television, a small fridge, and a microwave.

It was perfect.

"This is great, thank you so much."

"As discussed, during the week I will prepare a hot meal, but you fend for yourself on the weekends."

"Oh yes, that's fantastic, thank you."

"But that includes tonight. I'm sorry, I already had plans. And tomorrow is Thanksgiving. I'm so sorry but I'm having dinner with my daughter and her kidlets, but I've enough leftovers—"

"Oh, you don't need to worry about me," I said with a smile. I didn't expect her to be fussing over me. "I can find something tonight, and Thanksgiving isn't something we typically do back home, so it's fine."

She blinked up at me. "Where's back home for you? You got a pretty accent there."

"England."

"Oh, how lovely." She gave me a two-minute rundown of her cousin who moved to England in the '80s, before she realised I was still holding my suitcase. "Heavens, look at me, taking up your time. I'll let you get settled in. Now, if you're looking for dinner, there's Carl's Diner on Main Street, and the pizzeria. Oh, and the Home Mart on Bridge Street."

"I'll be sure to find something."

"Make yourself comfortable. Turn the heat on if you get cold. Weather's been pretty mild so far, but that'll change soon enough. And you come find me if you need anything."

"I will. And thank you."

She left me to it, and I stepped inside, sliding my suitcase onto the bed. I looked around at the somewhat dated floral curtains, the white panelling, and I smiled.

It was bigger than I'd expected, and more private too.

Having my own fridge and microwave was a bonus, and I unzipped my suitcase to pull out my electric kettle.

Yep. I had my own. I didn't bring it with me from England. I'd seen one in a shop in Pennsylvania and couldn't resist buying it, because a good cup of tea was worth its weight in gold.

It tasted like home.

I unpacked my clothes and toiletries, tested the TV and the water pressure in the bathroom, and decided a quick trip to the Home Mart was in order. And given tomorrow was Thanksgiving and everything would likely be closed, maybe I could see if the diner had something I could bring back to reheat.

I explored a little, taking in the shopfronts along Main Street, with the cute awnings and fancy signs, the gorgeous flowers. When the sun had almost disappeared, the streetlights came on and made everything ten times prettier.

It really was the stuff of fairy tales.

I found Carl's Diner, and the bell above the door announced my arrival. There were some booths and tables, most filled with customers, and the waitress behind the counter offered a huge smile.

"What can I help you with today?" she asked.

I scanned the menu board and ordered the roast with a side of mac and cheese and greens. "Is it possible to get a second serving to take home?"

"Sure thing, sweetheart," she said. "Take a seat. I'll bring it out. Say, where's your accent from?"

Oh.

"England," I replied. I guessed they didn't hear many foreign accents in these parts.

The waitress turned to the cook and smiled. "Ah, Jayden. Got another import. An Englishman this time."

The cook, a handsome guy with brown hair and a stunning smile, came over, wiping his hands on his apron. "Hey," he said. "What brings you to Hartbridge? Visiting for Thanksgiving?"

He was Australian. So I'd misjudged the foreigner thing. "I'm here for four weeks or thereabouts. Substitute teacher at the elementary school. And, ah, this is my first Thanksgiving here." I cringed a little. "In America, that is."

"Nice." He nodded, still smiling. He held my gaze a beat too long, as if recognition passed between us. A gay recognition. Or maybe I'd imagined it.

Just then the door chimed again, and I turned to see a man walk in, wearing a brown sheriff's uniform. He took his hat off as he entered, revealing tufts of short brown hair and honey-coloured eyes. He was taller than I'd realised, and his shirt was still a tad too tight, and yet nowhere near tight enough.

He stopped when he saw me, then gave a nod to Jayden and the waitress before looking back at me. "Oh, hello again," he said. "Maternity replacement from the motherland."

I wanted to die.

"Hello again. I'm really sorry about that, officer," I said, pretending my face wasn't bright red. I knew it was. "I, uh . . . I, um . . ."

"It's deputy," he supplied. "Deputy Price."

"Deputy Price," I repeated, staring at him like I was in some kind of trance. Like I was an idiot. "Of course."

Jayden looked between us, back and forth, his smile now a grin. "Oh, this is beautiful. Hartbridge does it again." He clapped his hands together and yelled out to some guys at the first booth. "Hamish. We got another one."

Chapter Two

COLSON PRICE

I'D NEVER LET anyone off a speeding ticket before. If they broke the law, they were penalised. That's how it worked. It mighta got me out of favour with some folks, but the law was the law, and it was my job to uphold it.

So why did I let Braithe Branson off with a warning?

I was still asking myself that very question. I'd been asking myself that same question all afternoon.

Maybe it was his blond floppy hair and big blue eyes. Maybe it was his full pink lips or the blush that stained his pale cheeks. Maybe it was his cute-as-hell posh British accent or the way he rambled on.

Maybe because if sunshine was a person, it was Braithe Branson.

And I couldn't very well give Sunshine a speeding ticket now, could I?

I'd almost managed to stop thinking about him when I walked into Carl's Diner and found Mr Sunshine himself standing at the counter.

And as if that wasn't bad enough, he blushed when he saw me.

Damn.

Jayden, from behind the counter, yelled something out to his friends in one of the booths. They were a close group of men, all couples, all gay or bi, or whatever . . .

I envied them.

I envied them all.

I longed for what they had. That sense of belonging. That found-family closeness. I longed to be out, to be myself.

It burned inside me.

Right alongside loneliness.

Hamish came over to Braithe, took him by the arm, and led him back to their booth.

And just like that, another newcomer was included in their fold, and I was on the outside.

Again.

First Hamish, then Jayden, then Gunter.

All new to town, all gay, all happy and in love.

But not me.

Now, I didn't know if Braithe was LGBTQ+ or not. I'd have maybe guessed he could be. He was a little bit fem, very pretty, and he had asked if singing along to Kylie Minogue was a valid excuse to get out of a ticket.

But it didn't matter because I was not out. I was not—

"You okay?" Jayden asked quietly. He was now beside me, wiping the service side of the counter with a cloth. I must have zoned out because I hadn't noticed him come over. "You know," he murmured, his gaze meeting mine. "You're more than welcome to join us."

Oh.

"Oh, uh . . ." I couldn't think of what to say. Did he know I was gay? Was that what he was saying? Did he know? Did anyone else?

"Coffee, cake," he added casually. "Gossip, Hamish's bad jokes. Nothing crazy."

My heart was hammering against my ribs.

He had no idea how good that sounded to me. He had no idea how impossible it was.

"Another time," I managed. Which meant in another life, basically.

"Okay," he said with a smile that held more understanding than anyone else might have noticed. "Anytime you need." Then it was gone, and his business smile was back. "Now, lemme get your order for you. You phoned it through, right?"

I nodded. "I did, yes."

He went back behind the counter, and a few seconds later he came back with a bag full of takeout containers. "You feeding the whole sheriff's station an early Thanksgiving dinner with this?"

I tried to laugh it off as I paid the tab. "Something like that." I didn't want to admit the truth. That I'd be spending Thanksgiving alone, like I had for the last ten years.

"Someone's gotta work," I added, hoping not to sound too pathetic. The truth was, I *did* have to work. I volunteered so the others could spend time with their families and loved ones.

I didn't have either of those, so it was only fair.

"Ah, tell me about it," Jayden said, handing me the receipt. "The B&B is fully booked. I'm working all day tomorrow." He nodded to his table of friends. "It's why we're catching up tonight."

I looked over at the booth and saw them talking and laughing. Braithe now included . . .

"Nice," I managed.

"I'm about to take my break and join them if you want to stick around."

I swallowed thickly. "I, uh, I'm on the clock."

Jayden gave me a sad nod. "Remember what I said. You're welcome anytime. Doesn't have to be public if that helps. There's always a seat at our table."

Oh, yeah, he totally knew.

I gave a nod, put my hat back on, took the bag and walked out, the hit of cold air reminding me to breathe.

"Happy Thanksgiving, Deputy Price," Peggy Barton said as she and Ren closed up the hardware store across the street. She went to her car; Ren came across the street toward me.

I tipped my hat. "Same to you, Mrs Barton. You have a nice day tomorrow, you hear?"

Ren stepped up onto the gutter, gave me a nod. "Evening."

"Evening," I managed, hearing the familiar bell above the door as he entered behind me.

He was going in there for an early Thanksgiving dinner with friends and with his husband, Hamish. And with the new guy in town, the blond-haired, blue-eyed ray of English sunshine, Braithe Branson.

Where I was offered a seat at their table.

But it wasn't just a seat at their table. It was an offer of a place to belong. A place to be myself.

A place I couldn't sit.

I climbed into my cruiser, certain the bite of cold wasn't just from the chilly wind, and drove back to the station.

HARTBRIDGE'S SHERIFF'S office and the police department were in the same municipal building, and quite often, our jobs intertwined. It made sense. We worked together a lot, and given the small county, it was an effective and efficient way to pool time and resources.

So it was common to see the sheriff's sworn officers—myself included—communications techs, and professional admin support staff working alongside the police officers and their teams.

It was common for one of us to bring food and snacks for the breakroom, and tonight was my turn. I got off easy given it was the day before Thanksgiving and most of the staff had gone home.

I put the containers on the table, keeping one aside for my dinner tomorrow night, and called the others in. I stood beside my boss, Sheriff Ronny Parker, and shot the breeze in between mouthfuls of food.

It was kinda nice, like it always was. These law enforcement people were the closest thing I had to family, and we were a family of sorts. There was an unspoken camaraderie between us, one the badge and uniform provided.

It wasn't the family I longed for though.

God, my mood was so sullen today.

Thanksgiving was hitting me harder this year. Maybe it was because of the realisation back at the diner. Maybe it was because Mr English Sunshine was taking a seat at their table and I wasn't.

There's always a seat at our table.

That's what Jayden had said. That I'd be welcome anytime. As one of them. He definitely knew. How, I didn't know. Intuition, maybe? Or maybe from last year when I'd noticed Clay Henderson with another new guy in town, Gunter Zuniga, and I'd wondered . . . hoped . . .

But Clay wasn't out, not that I knew of anyway, and I thought maybe . . . I'd been a fool.

I'd been reckless.

That night I'd run into all of them at the pizzeria and they'd asked if I wanted to join them. I'd never wanted anything more . . .

"Colson," Charity said, snapping her fingers. "Base to C2, do you read me?"

I started but laughed at her use of my cruiser call sign to get my attention. She was the comms manager, after all. "Sorry, zoned out there."

She smiled, a half-eaten plate of lasagne in her hand. "It's just you and me tomorrow, and Officer Bouchard from the PD."

"And it's all we need," I replied, giving her a fist bump and a nod to Bouchard. "Bringing the A-team."

I figured making a joke of it would distract them enough for the reason I hadn't been listening to their conversation.

It worked.

Hartbridge was the largest town in Baker County. There were a lot of smaller satellite communities, a lot of ranches, and a *lot* of national parks. Our work was mostly community stuff and thankfully, very little crime, but our law enforcement teams were a good bunch of people.

I liked everyone I worked with. Some I got along with better than others, of course, but there wasn't anyone I disliked. And from what I could tell, they liked me just fine.

No one knew I was gay though.

Would their opinions of me change? I'd like to think not. It was always hard to tell.

Like how I never thought my family's opinions of me would change, and look where that got me . . .

I woke up on Thanksgiving Day and stoked the fire. It was a cold morning, with winter letting us know it was on its way. But it was nothing a hot shower and steaming mug of coffee couldn't fix.

I had a small two-bedroom house on Juniper Lane. It was old, like most houses in Hartbridge were, but it was cute and warm, sturdy as hell, and it was mine.

Well, mine and the banks.

Owning a house in my hometown of Billings was probably never an option for me, but prices in Hartbridge were more forgiving. And having my name on that title deed was the most rewarding thing I'd ever done.

I was proud of my little house.

With its original floorboards and tiled fireplace from the 1940s and the retro lemon-coloured kitchen from the 1960s. The bathroom was done in the 2000s. Not new by any stretch now, but good enough for me.

I did my usual spate of housecleaning, then raked the backyard, tidying up anything that needed it, and rolled into work by 1400. I did some admin work, nudged the never-ending piles of paperwork, and had most of Ronny's to-do list done when Charity, sitting at her desk with the phone pressed to her ear, raised her hand and beckoned me over.

"Okay, thanks again, we'll send someone over right away," she said, a look of concern on her face. She put the receiver in its cradle and her eyes met mine. "That was Mrs Linchardt. She said there was a young man on the bridge. Could be a jumper. They were driving down to their son's for dinner. She didn't want to interfere but didn't want to not say anything. And Bouchard is on another call."

I gave a nod. "On it." I collected my hat and pulled my coat on before I was even out the door.

The thing about the holidays was, be it Thanksgiving or

Christmas, they weren't always the happiest times of the year for some folks. For some, it was all about decorations and food, family and festivities.

For others, it was the very worst time of the year.

Emergency workers knew this all too well. Now, Hartbridge didn't have stats like the bigger cities, but we weren't immune. And if someone was standing on the bridge in the dark on Thanksgiving . . .

I hightailed it out of the lot and made a beeline straight for Bridge Street. No lights, no sirens. I didn't want a possible jumper to panic, and as the bridge came into view, I could see a lone figure standing on the bridge sidewalk.

Oh no.

I parked the cruiser, cut my lights, and got out. The person didn't even seem to notice me, just kept staring down at the water. They wore a white coat over jeans and a grey knitted cap, their elbows on the railing.

"Evening," I said calmly as I approached, my heart thumping.

They turned, startled, and I saw who it was then. Lit by only the streetlights, his pale skin looked translucent, and blond tufts poked out from under his beanie.

Braithe Branson.

He put his hand to his heart. "Oh, you frightened me," he said.

I gestured back to my cruiser. "You didn't hear me?"

He looked past my shoulder, surprised to see my vehicle. "I guess not."

"Is . . . is everything okay, Braithe?"

"Oh, yes," he said, smile wide. "This is such a beautiful spot. I was watching the water. It looks silver and . . ." His eyes went from the water to me again. He wasn't smiling now. "Is everything okay with you?"

"I'm fine. We just had a passing driver call in concerned about someone standing on the bridge."

"Concerned?" Recognition dawned. "Oh my goodness! Me? No, I was just watching the water. I didn't mean to make anyone worry. Gracious, that must have been awful."

I held my hand out, gesturing toward the grassy area near my cruiser. "Want to come off the bridge for me?"

He nodded quickly and came off the bridge and stopped. "I am so sorry," he said. He put his hand to his forehead. "I can't believe someone thought that I was . . . I mean, I'm grateful they called because if someone was . . . Ugh, I'm so sorry. I didn't mean to be a bother."

He seemed genuinely okay. Horrified, if anything. Embarrassed. But not distraught or upset.

Thank god.

"Want to tell me what you're doing on the bridge at night?"

"I was just watching the water. It looked really silver and it sounds like a waterfall over the rocks." He shook his head and licked his lips, then gestured toward the intersection. "I went for a walk down Main Street. It's so pretty with the fairy lights and the flowers, and all the pretty shopfronts. It's like a fairy tale. And I came to the intersection and heard the river. I didn't mean to make anyone worry. Those poor people who must have thought . . . I'm so sorry."

I nodded, relieved he was okay. "That's okay. You didn't mean any harm."

"Oh, heavens no."

"Just that this time of the year can be hard on some folks."

He nodded. "I know. But honestly, I was just out for a stroll after dinner. I ate too much and wanted to walk it off. I got some takeout from the diner yesterday to have as my first American Thanksgiving dinner, and he probably thought I was feeding four people." He grimaced as he patted his belly. "But it was so good, and I ate too much."

He had dinner alone?

"First Thanksgiving, huh?"

He nodded and blew out a breath. Wisps of steam billowed upward in the cold air. "Turkey with cranberry and creamy potatoes and beans. It was amazing. I need to walk another few miles before I can eat some more."

I found myself smiling at him, wanting more than anything to fix that tuft of blond hair sticking out from his beanie. "You made some new friends pretty fast," I said, then realised it sounded very much like I'd noticed. "At the diner last night."

"Oh yes. Fancy meeting two Australians on my first day. There were many jokes about cricket and rugby and Marmite. Though I think they mostly took the piss." He snorted. "But for real, they seem lovely. Nice guys. Hamish asked me to join them for dinner tonight, but I thought that might be a bit weird. Nice of him to offer though."

I gave a nod, not entirely sure I understood much of that. "Uh, he took your piss?"

Braithe gasped, then burst out laughing. "Took *the* piss. Not took your piss, or my piss. When one takes the piss, it means they're taking the mickey . . . they're laughing at you."

I let out a breath of relief. "Well, that's better than what I thought it meant." He laughed again, his blue eyes glittering in the streetlight.

But then my radio crackled. "Base to C2, please respond." I took the receiver from my pack, keeping eye contact with Braithe. "This is C2. Negative to the jumper. Just a sightseer. All good here. Over."

"Roger that."

I cradled my radio, realising my conversation with Braithe

had come to an end. "Well, if you're all okay here, I should get back to the station."

He smirked. "Roger that, C2."

I raised an eyebrow, trying not to smile. "Really?"

"Affirmative. Is that some special deputy nickname?"

Nickname?

"It's my call sign. We have two cruisers. My boss gets the C1. I get the C2."

"There's no C3? Because you could call them C3PO and paint it gold. Or C4. That'd be a banger." He grinned at his own joke. "Get it? C4, banger. It's a plastic explosive . . ."

"I got the joke. It was just terrible." I refused to smile. "Can I offer you a lift somewhere?"

He still found something funny, apparently. He was smiling when his eyes met mine. "Negative, C2, but thank you. I can walk. It's a beautiful night." Then he shoved his hands in his coat pocket. "I mean, it's a bit chilly but if I got dropped off at Mrs Parson's place in a sheriff's cruiser, she might evict me. Can't have the whole town thinking I'm a criminal before I start at the school on Monday."

"You're staying at Mrs Parson's?"

He nodded. "Sure am. She has a little flat out the back of her house."

"A flat?"

"Oh, sorry, a separate living space at the back of her place. A flat. An apartment. I'm still not used to the Americanisms."

I could listen to his accent all day long. "Right."

"Anyway, Mrs Parson," he went on. "I've only spoken to her briefly so far, but she was very nice."

"She is."

"Everyone here is," he said. "In this pretty little town, tucked away in the mountains. It's a shame I'm only here for four weeks, to be honest."

Four weeks.

A shame, indeed.

The wind picked up and he turned to face it, his cheeks and nose turning pink.

"I rather like it here," he added quietly. "So far, anyway. First day of school on Monday. It might all change after that."

"I hope not," I said, the words out of my mouth before my brain could stop them. "I mean, I'm sure it'll be fine."

He smiled again and shivered against the cold. "I should get walking again and let you get back to work. Sorry again, for making you worry." He looked back at the bridge. "I never meant to be any trouble. Next time I'll take photos during the day."

"Good idea."

He took a step back, still smiling. "Happy Thanksgiving, officer."

"It's deputy."

He gave a terrible salute and a beautiful grin. "Roger that, C2." And he turned and walked back to the intersection, his hands deep in his coat pockets as he disappeared around the corner of Main Street.

I stood there, smiling after him.

I had no idea if he'd been flirting or if I was so out of practise, I'd missed the mark. Maybe he was that way with everyone. But, regardless, it had been fun.

He was only here for four weeks.

Four weeks of that accent, that cheeky banter, and that smirk . . . My radio crackled to life. "Base to C2, come in."

I answered on my way back to the cruiser. "This is C2."

"Got a truck in a ditch on Oak Gully Road. Bouchard's on route. No injuries, but it's on a curve and we might need some traffic control."

I started the engine. "On my way."

Chapter Three

BRAITHE

I was a ball of nerves going to work on my first morning. Excited too, but mostly nervous.

Meeting the principal was always daunting—would they like me, would they not—but being early, dressed well, and with all my paperwork in order was always a good way to start.

I shouldn't have worried though. Principal Nancy O'Connor was a professional, no-nonsense woman, in her late fifties, perhaps. Short, thin, with greying brown hair pulled up in a twist. She was also welcoming, and happy to have me on board.

She showed me to my classroom, then the staffroom, and one by one as the other teachers arrived, I was introduced and included.

It was nice.

My last job in Bozeman hadn't been so warm. Still professional and pleasant, just not so inclusive.

Being loud and cheerful worked in my favour as a kindergarten teacher. Kids loved my fun approach to learning, my loudness, and all the bright colours. But adults tended to view my fun, sunshiny approach to life a little differently.

Most picked up on my gayness immediately. Others took a little longer. I didn't hide it. I didn't flaunt it. But my flair and use of my hands when I spoke was a habit I could rein in when meeting new people. My smile and accent were usually enough of a decoy, and shoving my hands into my pockets sometimes helped so I didn't flail them around too much.

I wanted these people to like me, sure. But I wasn't about to start wearing pride shirts to work on my first day. I worked with the youngest students, and I was a male teacher in a female-dominated industry. I wasn't naive enough to know that close-minded bigots wouldn't take issue with their teacher being queer.

So I reined it in around the adults, a practice most queer people were very well acquainted with. And met all my students with as much fun and flair as I wanted.

I had a class of eighteen.

Smaller numbers than I was used to, and I loved it.

The room was a typical kindergarten set-up. Tiny desks and chairs, a play area, a dedicated craft space, and lots of artwork on display. It was colourful and fun and smelled of paint and pine disinfectant.

I loved it already.

Principal O'Connor introduced me to the class to begin with, a brief on class-time structure and a syllabus, and the class roll, of course, and then I was left to it.

Of course, my accent was a hit, and I brought up a map of the world on the smart board and showed them where England was. Then I showed them red double-decker buses and telephone boxes, Buckingham Palace, and London Bridge.

Then we settled into the routine and the lesson plan, and before I knew it, my first day at Hartbridge Elementary was over.

Nancy found me packing up at the end of the day. "How'd you find it?"

"Oh, just wonderful," I replied. "What a great little group of kids."

She smiled at the newly coloured-in pictures hanging up on display. Red double-decker buses with the word *bus* and some cotton wool balls stuck on for clouds. "Ah, looks like they had fun."

"They loved the idea of a big double-storey red bus, so I thought I'd put it to good use."

"Well, I'm glad you had a good first day."

"I did, thank you."

I used the next few hours to plan for the rest of the week and to print off some more fun things for the kids to do, incorporating their syllabus into some fun ways to learn.

When I got back to my little granny flat, Mrs Parson came out to see me. "I'll have your dinner ready at six thirty if that's okay."

"Oh, you really don't have to cook for me," I tried.

She waved me off. "Nonsense, sweet boy. I don't mind one bit." I wasn't sure about having her provide meals for me. I was grateful, but I didn't want to impose. I feared it would be like sitting down to dinner alone with some stranger's grandmother.

But it wasn't like that at all.

She was just the sweetest thing. She was worldly, she'd travelled a lot, she was well-versed in current affairs, and she was a fabulous cook.

We talked about books and film adaptations, about her time in Europe and Asia, and of course, her love of Hartbridge.

She'd grown up here, lived in Seattle for a time, travelled

the world teaching English, and came back to raise her family here.

I enjoyed our conversation so much I almost didn't want to leave, but after I'd bit back a yawn, she ushered me out, telling me to have a great day tomorrow and that dinner would be at the same time.

I didn't dare argue.

And my second day was just as great. I met a few parents, their kids dragging them in to meet the new teacher. Glad I chose to wear my sensible knitted navy sweater and jeans; it was the straightest outfit I had. But I wasn't oblivious to the smiles and flutter of eyelashes from some of the moms.

I just pretended I didn't notice.

I also pretended not to notice how even more moms turned up to collect their kids from the classroom at the end of the day.

Clearly, the Hartbridge grapevine had sprouted new leaves during the day.

Day three was much the same.

I was sure some of them had now taken the time to style their hair and apply make-up, but I ignored that too.

Raeleen Ascot, grade four teacher and the one colleague who'd chosen to befriend me, even gave me a nudge with her elbow. "I see there's been a sudden interest in the new teaching faculty," she whispered with a smile. "We don't even see this many moms on campus for parent-teacher conferences."

"Oh shush," I mumbled with a laugh. I was going to add that they were wasting their time, but if she knew of any single dads . . . but decided to keep a lid on that.

"Ooh," she added. "The Christmas concert this year is the last week before break. Where the parents come to watch their kids . . ." She nudged me again. "I'm sure you'll have a full audience."

Oh, heavens.

I'd seen the concert on the class schedule and had run a few ideas through my mind but needed to think more seriously on it. I'd probably end up going with a nativity scene. Kindergarten nativity scenes were always cute.

Given tomorrow was the first of December, preparations would need to start. I could also begin incorporating lots of Christmas crafts and fun activities, and with that in mind, I found myself in the very quaint, very small Home Mart.

It wasn't exactly Harrods, but there was a small craft and haberdashery section. And by small, I meant it was one tiny section of shelving in aisle three.

But it was better than nothing.

I found a bag of ice-lolly sticks and some small multi-coloured fluff balls and had a reel of string beads in my hand when someone came around the corner, into the aisle, and stopped. A man, tall and broad, wearing jeans and a plaid coat, holding a shopping basket—who I did my best to ignore— until he sighed and walked toward me.

"Work supplies? Or do you craft in your spare time?"

I looked up at his face and did a double take. It was my favourite deputy. "Oh, C2! I didn't recognise you," I said, gesturing to his civilian clothes. "Without your hat and brown outfit."

"Outfit?" He smirked. "You mean uniform?"

I shrugged, because no, I didn't mean uniform. Outfit was so much cuter. "Off duty, I see?"

He gave a nod. Was he trying not to smile? I thought he was. "Something like that."

"Nice."

"How's your job going? Kids treating you okay?"

"Oh, they are just the best little humans ever." I held up the reel of gold string beads. "Just seeing what Christmas craft ideas I can come up with. I think I might need to make a trip this weekend down to Mossley. That's closer than Missoula, right?"

He gave a nod. "Sure is. Just over the bridge and follow Beartrap Road down the mountain." He swallowed hard and gave the kids colouring books a serious frown. "Ah, if you want—"

"Hello, Mr Branson," a little voice said.

It was Xander, a boy from my class. "Well, hello there!" I said to him, then noticed his mom, who was smiling, patting down her hair.

"Hello," she said sweetly. "It's nice to see you again."

Jeez.

"Same."

Suddenly Deputy Price felt like he was a six-foot elephant in the room. He gave her a nod. "Jenny."

"Oh, Colson. Nice to see you too."

He gave a look between us, finally landing on her. "Be seeing you at the lighting of the tree tomorrow?"

"Oh, yes." She put her hand on Xander's shoulder and they made their exit. Jenny's smile cut to me before she was gone.

Oh boy.

Like that wasn't embarrassing enough.

"Got yourself a fan, I see," he whispered.

"I think I have a few," I replied, also whispering. "I don't know how to tell them they're wasting their time. Not really my type."

"Single moms?"

"Women."

He turned to look at the jars on the shelf but his cheeks flushed pink.

Much, much more my type. And possibly interested?

"So," I hedged, "Colson. I like that name."

His eyes darted to mine then. "And there I was thinking you liked to call me C2."

"That too. But I think I like Colson better."

He smiled at that, but then suddenly seemed to remember where he was. He straightened up and took a small step back. "Well, then. I'll let you get on with your shopping."

"Wait," I said before he could run. There was definitely a flicker of interest there. I could feel it. "You were about to say something earlier . . . about me going to Mossley. You said if I wanted . . ."

He blanched a little, then scanned to see if anyone was around, and let out a breath. "I was, uh . . . I was just going to say . . ." He let out another breath, clearly flustered or nervous. "I have to go to Mossley on Saturday morning if you wanted a lift. It's not official business or anything. It's just before the Christmas rush. You know how it is."

He was asking if I wanted to go for a drive with him?

"Oh, sure," I replied, unable to stop from smiling. "I'd like that."

Colson gave a nod, his cheeks now a rosy pink. He looked around, at anywhere else but at me. "I'll be in touch . . . or maybe I'll see you at the tree lighting tomorrow night."

I was too stunned that I had a maybe-date with the sexy deputy that I forgot to ask him what the tree lighting thing was even about.

I was still standing in the middle of the aisle with my mouth open when another familiar face came around the corner. Hamish did a double take before he smiled. He came up and squeezed my arm. "Does the look on your face have anything to do with a certain red-faced deputy at the checkout?"

Thank god, he could whisper.

"Uh, maybe?" My voice was more of a squeak. "I, uh, I think I might have a maybe-date with him? I don't know."

Hamish made a very strange, excited buzzing noise as he squeezed my arm. "Oh my god, tell me everything."

I blinked a few times. "Shopping in Mossley on Saturday. But listen, you can't say anything. I'm pretty sure it's on the down-low, if you know what I mean. As in, not out. Or maybe he is, I don't know. The way he was looking around . . . Maybe it's not even a date. Maybe he was just being polite and offered the new guy a lift."

Hamish was still squeezing my arm, which we both seemed to realise at the same time. He let me go and patted down my coat sleeve, making it all better. "Let me tell you something about this town," he said. "I know you didn't believe us when we told you the other night about the Hartbridge Christmas thing. But it's totally a thing, I promise you. And you turning up and making Deputy Price blush like that only convinces me of it."

Yes, they'd joked about some love spell that only happened in Hartbridge at Christmastime. Some gay love spell, for that matter, and I'd thought they were joking . . .

The last three gay couples to find love had all found it at Christmastime. Something about the town, something about how the decorations and snow made Cupid crazy.

But it was a joke.

Right?

I shook my head. "That's nonsense. And it's just a shopping date. During the day. And I'm only here for four weeks."

Hamish raised one perfectly arched eyebrow. "That's the funny part. We all thought that. I wasn't even supposed to be here at all. I took a wrong turn and ran into Ren, and now we're married. Jayden took on a casual cooking stint, met Cass, and never left. And then Gunter moved here for a new start and he and Clay are so in love it makes me sick. So I dunno what plans you have for after your four weeks here, but I think you can forget them."

I snorted because this was all ridiculous.

"You have me married off already and I don't even know if —" I looked around to make sure we were alone. "—a certain someone is even interested. Let alone that way inclined. I've spoken to the man all of four times."

Hamish sighed as if he was tired of having to explain it. "And you already have a date."

I put another bag of fluff balls into my basket. "What is it with this shop? I've been here ten minutes and ran into three people I know already."

He snorted. "Welcome to living in a small town."

"Hey," I said, remembering something. "Colson mentioned something about a lighting of the tree?"

"Colson?"

"Uh, Deputy Price."

Hamish gave me an uh-huh look. "You know his name? I've been here for years and thought his first name was Deputy."

My cheeks ran hot and I hated that Hamish noticed. I rolled my eyes at his smile. "I learned it five minutes ago. I've been calling him C2."

He squinted at me. "C2?"

"Yeah, it's the call sign for his cruiser . . ." I knew I'd said too much because that arched eyebrow was back.

"And you know this how?"

"From the other night. Thanksgiving night. I was on the bridge and he thought I was about to jump or something."

"Oh my god."

"I was just taking photos for my Instagram. It wasn't anything like that."

He put his hand to his forehead. "Okay look, we need to have a little talk. I came here for some milk for Ren's store. Let me get that." He looked at my basket. "Is that all you're getting?"

Now that I was going to Mossley on the weekend . . . "Ah, yeah, I think so."

Chapter Four

COLSON

THE FIRST OF December marked the tree lighting ceremony in town. The huge tree was in the park down by the river, right off the intersection of Main and Bridge Street.

It was always a fun night. Great to see the folks and families turn up, sing a few carols, and wander home. It was a community thing, a way of saying hello to the holiday season.

Sheriff Ronny Harper always insisted we turn up in uniform, as a gesture of goodwill and trust. To show we were a part of this community too, to smile and say hello to the townsfolk so they'd feel comfortable around us should they ever need a reason to call.

Ronny Harper was a real good man.

Proudly told anyone he was born here, met the love of his life here, and raised his family here. He was old school, but he was an open man who prided himself on staying up to speed on what the younger kids were doing these days.

He understood the world was forever changing and how towns needed to roll with it or get left behind and die, all while trying to retain their sense of history. It wasn't always easy.

He was in his sixties now, but as fit and active as anyone I knew. Sharp as a tack too. And he'd probably be embarrassed as hell to know that I thought of him as a father.

And that was a fine line for me to tread. At the end of the day, he was my boss. But still . . . I respected the hell out of him. So if he wanted me to turn up to the tree lighting night, say hello and be a friendly face for the town, then I would.

There was already a crowd gathering. People walked toward the park: families, parents holding kids' hands, some pushing strollers. Everyone in coats and beanies with scarves and gloves.

The weather had turned, bringing a cold snap that promised snow. The beginning of winter. Kinda perfect for December in the mountains.

I wore my work jacket, a brown bomber style, padded and warm. I'd have preferred a knitted cap, but my hat would have to do. I climbed out of my cruiser, pulled my collar up against the cold, shoved my hands into my pockets, and followed the crowd.

I spotted Ronny and his wife almost right away and made a beeline for them, smiling at people, and deliberately not looking for a blond and very cute Englishman.

Don't know what possessed me to ask him to go to Mossley. Did I need to go? No. Did I even want to go? No.

But did I want to spend time with him?

Yes.

Would I drive him anywhere he wanted to go?

Probably also a yes.

Why?

Because my heart acted before my brain could engage.

It also didn't hurt that we'd be out of town, away from prying eyes where people wouldn't recognise us.

Where people wouldn't know.

Did I hate myself a little for that?

Also a yes.

I swallowed that down and plastered a smile on my face, holding out my hand for Ronny to shake. "Sheriff. And Geraldine, always a pleasure."

"Hello, Colson," Geraldine replied. "How lovely to see you again."

"Nice night for it," Ronny replied, looking up at the dark sky. Clouds were low, the air was cold.

"Perfect."

See, the thing about being next to Ronny in a community setting was that he was the star and I was the supporting cast, which suited me just fine. Everyone either came to say hello, tipped their hats, or shook his hand and said hello to me out of courtesy.

The mayor, Mr Howard Briner, was a stout ranching man with a big grey moustache and a Stetson. He was also a good friend of Ronny's, so his arrival and subsequent conversation was a public display of politics.

I understood that, and in a small town, it just was what it was.

But while they chatted and said hello to passers-by, it gave me a brief moment to assess the crowd and traffic.

And to look for a certain someone . . .

Who was standing closer to the bridge with his new group of friends. Hamish and Ren with their dog, Jayden and Cass with his kids, Gunter and Clay with Mr Henderson and Cordelia.

Braithe wore a white wool coat, his grey beanie, and the scarf he'd worn the other night. Just one of the memories I couldn't get out of my head.

The others, him in his car that very first day and then just yesterday in the Home Mart were the other memories that played on a loop in my mind.

I was so infatuated with him. It was downright scary.

Not in a creepy way. Just in an 'I can't believe how pretty he is' kind of way. And also an 'I can't believe he told me to my face that women were not his type' kind of way.

He'd leapfrogged timid flirting and landed feet first into categorical coming onto me.

So bold and forthright.

So hot.

The mayor announcing he should get proceedings started was my cue to focus, and after he did his spiel on his love for Hartbridge and how he wished health and happiness to everyone for the holiday period, they lit up the huge tree. Lights flickered and illuminated the faces of everyone, rousing loud cheers and applause. Christmas carollers began, and then, like it was all part of the show, it began to snow.

It was magical.

It always was.

It made me miss my parents and my brothers and my whole extended family. Even all these years later, it made me miss what I no longer had.

So damned bittersweet.

I missed my brothers the most.

"This calls for a nightcap," Ronny declared. He clapped my shoulder. "You're welcome to join us."

Maybe he'd been watching me. Maybe he'd seen the sadness that accompanied me at this time of year. He knew, after all, how hard this time of year was for me.

I gave him a smile, grateful for his kindness but not really in the mood. But he also knew I was on duty. "Another time, perhaps. But thank you."

His eyes met mine, serious and silently telling me he got it. "See you tomorrow."

"Shall do. Fourteen hundred." Then I stopped. "Oh, I'll

be heading down to Mossley tomorrow morning, so I'll be out of town until after lunch. Will have my phone if you need me, and the radio in the cruiser, of course."

"Okay," he said, giving another glance upward. "Now go and get out of this cold."

Most of the crowd had dispersed, cars making a steady crawl out of town. I did notice, however, Braithe had a small audience of excited kids and smiling parents, mostly single moms. And I understood the reason.

He was new to town, single and incredibly attractive.

Why wouldn't they be interested?

Except he'd told me women weren't his type, and he'd agreed to spend tomorrow morning with me.

It gave me a rush of butterflies . . . only they lost flight when I remembered I hadn't finalised anything with him and I'd hoped to catch up with him here.

Could I wait for him to finish talking?

Was that too much?

Shaking my head and inwardly cursing myself, hating myself, I started for my cruiser.

"Excuse me, Deputy?"

It was Joanne Colley. She stood beside her car, door open, with kids in the backseat. "My car won't seem to start. I think it's the battery. It's been playing up and my son left the door open. I'm sorry to bother you."

"Oh, it's no bother at all," I replied. "I have jumper cables in my cruiser. We'll have you started in a minute."

I pulled my cruiser up beside her car. She'd popped the hood for me, and with a quick link up, her car started just fine.

"Oh, thank you so much!"

"My pleasure," I said, tipping my hat. I unhooked my cables and lowered the hood for her. I gave the two kids in the backseat a wave and they waved back. I was glad to see they were wearing gloves and caps. "Get home safe now. Be good for Santa!"

The kids grinned and Joanne drove off. I recoiled the jumper cables and threw them in the back of my cruiser.

"Your good deed for the day," a quiet voice said.

I turned to find Braithe walking up. Almost everyone was gone, Main Street dark except for the huge Christmas tree in the park, the streetlights casting yellow halos around small flurries of falling snow.

It almost made Braithe look ethereal, in his white coat against the dark, his nose and cheeks pink against his pale skin.

"Just doing my job," I replied.

He grinned. "Why do I get the feeling you'd help people even if it wasn't your job?"

"Maybe because I would."

He was still smiling, studying me far too intently. He seemed to pick up on my nerves or how his scrutiny cut a little too close to home because he looked up at the sky. "Can you believe it's snowing?

"Pretty spectacular timing." I let out a breath, a puff of steam rushing out to meet him. "Can I . . . can I offer you a lift home?"

He smirked, and damn if he didn't flutter his eyelids. "Another good deed. Or are you being a gentleman?"

Lord, have mercy.

He was bold.

Embarrassed, I went to my cruiser and held the passenger door for him. "Yes or no?"

He walked over and, without answering, got into my truck. Heaven help me, he was something else.

He waited for me to get in. He sat with his hands under his thighs—so he didn't touch anything or because he was cold, I wasn't sure. I started the engine and cranked up the heat.

"I've never been in a police car before."

"It's not a police car."

"I've never been in a deputy's cruiser before."

I chuckled because, damn . . .

"I should probably hope not."

He sighed. "I was hoping to catch you tonight."

Oh boy.

Too scared to meet his gaze, I put the cruiser into drive and pulled onto the street, indicating to turn up Bridge Street. "Is that right?"

"Well, yeah. If the offer still stands to take me to Mossley tomorrow, I thought we might need to discuss times and whatnot."

I drove as slow as I could to prolong my time with him. "The offer still stands, yes."

He was grinning. I didn't even need to glance over to know that he was grinning. But I did, and he was.

"Any particular time suit you, Colson?"

Sweet mercy, the way he said my name.

"Um. I can pick you up around eight. If that's okay with you. I need to be back by one o'clock at the latest. I work at two."

"Oh, if it's an inconvenience, I can—"

"It's no trouble," I said, way too fast. "Like I said, I have some things to get, so it's no trouble at all."

"Okay, well, do you need my address or number?"

I nodded out his window to Mrs Parson's house.

"Oh," he mumbled.

"You said you were staying here," I added quickly.

"Right," he said, letting out a laugh. "I did. That's correct." He met my eyes. "So . . . my phone number?"

My heart almost came to a screeching halt, thrumming so fast it hurt. "Yeah. I'd like that. You know, in case something comes up. I mean, if something changes." I shrugged because apparently making sensible conversation with him was difficult.

When I looked over, he was holding his phone, but smiling at me. I fumbled for my phone and he typed my number into his phone. My phone beeped with a text a second later.

Hi

The way my breath hitched in the quiet of the car was embarrassing, but he had the good grace not to comment on it. "I'll see you at eight," he said, his voice soft and lyrical, and I only remembered to breathe after he got out and disappeared down Mrs Parson's driveway.

Mercy, I was in trouble.

I ARRIVED at Mrs Parson's at five to eight. It was bad enough I'd been up since six, so damn nervous I could barely stomach a few bites of breakfast.

I'd showered and shaved, changed shirts three times, brushed my hair so much I'd had to re-wet it so it'd stick down, and watched the clock for a good long hour.

I sent him a text.

Out front.

I was still contemplating whether I should have added a smiley face, or if that was a flying leap off the cliff of insanity when the passenger door opened.

"Morning," Braithe said, smiling as if the gods of sunshine and fresh air had blessed him. He wore the same white sweater from last night and his blue scarf. No beanie this time, but it gave the sunlight the opportunity to turn his hair to gold. "Have you ever seen anything so pretty?"

"Uh . . ."

It took me a moment to realise he was talking about the view out the windshield and not talking about himself.

I made myself look ahead. There was a dusting of snow on the ground; the morning was still and pristine. But he was right. "It is," I replied. "I forget what it's like to see this town through fresh eyes."

He grinned and buckled his seatbelt up. "Are you ready for shopping?"

I made a face. "Will I regret offering?"

That made him laugh. "Not at all. I'm very excited to see more of the countryside."

Oh, his accent was dreamy.

Get your head in the game, Colson. Jeez.

I started the engine and headed through town. "Wait till you see this view." There were a few folks already on Main Street, but I crossed the bridge, headed out on Beartrap Road, and as soon as I rounded the bend on the side of the mountain, the whole view opened up across the valley below.

"Oh my god," he breathed, his blue eyes wide, lips open in a smile. "You weren't kidding. That's amazing!"

It was a sea of snow-topped trees, white on green, and the sky a pale blue. The national park skirted the mountain, we were surrounded by nature in all directions, and it made for some spectacular scenery.

"Oh boy, that's one helluva drop," he said, peering out across the road. "And this road is so steep. I'm glad I'm not driving. On the wrong side of the car. With snow. Oh my days, are you kidding?"

"Doesn't it snow in England?"

"Well, yes. But you seemed to miss the wrong-side-of-the-car part. And also the wrong side of the road."

Oh. I guessed that was right. "You drive here okay, though, right? Apart from the speeding thing."

He gasped, his hand to his chest. "I told you that was Kylie Minogue's fault." I laughed, and we snaked our way down the mountain, the sun and filtered shade changing the colours every other minute. He snapped photos with his phone, and we rode in silence for a few miles.

Until he grinned at me. "So, Deputy Colson Price, call sign C2," he said. "Have you always lived in Hartbridge?"

Oh damn. Personal questions already . . .

"No. I grew up in Billings. Been in Hartbridge for five years, deputy for four."

"Ooh, I've been to Billings."

"You have?"

"Yep. I flew into the airport there. Only stayed a few days. Long enough to see some sights and buy a car. I was warned public transport was a bit sparse between all the towns in these big-sky states."

"Smart."

I was trying to think of ways to move the conversation away from my hometown when he did it for me.

"How old are you, Deputy?"

"Twenty-nine."

"Are you going to ask how old I am? Or did you already work it out from when you saw my driver's licence the other day?"

I smirked at him. "How old are you?"

He rolled his eyes, his pink lips in a grin. "You absolutely already know."

"It's habit, sorry," I admitted. "Name, age . . . though I'll admit, the English licence threw me a bit, and the address." I pointed up ahead at something I thought he might like to see. "Look."

It was the state sign for Idaho.

"Ooh," he said, quickly snapping a few photos. "I've now been to five states. No, six."

"Six? How long have you been here?"

"Four months. I arrived in New York, did the touristy thing for a little bit. After a tour up to Niagara Falls, I finished up in Pennsylvania. I had a four-week teaching gig in Harrisburg."

That surprised me. "Really?"

"Yep."

"And how was that?"

"It was fine."

"But?" There was definitely a but coming.

"But it's not Hartbridge." He smiled. "People are nicer in smaller towns. I've already made friends here. In Harrisburg, I didn't have that. I was welcomed, don't get me wrong, but..."

"But it's not Hartbridge."

He laughed. "Exactly. Then I did four weeks in Bozeman. It was fine too, but..."

He smiled at me, but we didn't need to say it again.

It wasn't Hartbridge.

The trees had given way to cleared land and we passed some ranches, and soon enough we were in Mossley. "Hamish said his sister lives here," Braithe volunteered.

So he'd mentioned to Hamish that he was coming to Mossley, no doubt mentioning he was coming with me. Goddammit.

Not that it was his fault. I hadn't told him not to say anything.

"He said it was a nice town," he added when I hadn't spoken.

"It is. Even though we cross state lines, we do confer with the sheriff's office down here. Let each other know what's going on."

"Nice. You come down here often?"

I half-shrugged, half-smiled. "Sometimes." I didn't want to tell him straight off the bat that I tried not to, not for any other reason than I didn't ever really need to do any shopping. "So, which stores do you need?"

He looked struck. "Oh. I have no idea. Let me google." A few minutes later I pulled up at Walmart, and he was ridiculously excited. "Oh, this is going to be so much fun."

Damn, his bright eyes and wide smile almost did me in.

There was no snow on the ground here yet, though I doubted it would be long till there was. So it made for a pleasant few hours. He brought as much craft stuff as he could carry, some Christmas decorations, for his classroom and his place at Mrs Parson's.

He looked at my distinct lack of basket or cart. "Didn't you need to grab some things?"

Jeez. I'd almost forgotten.

"Uh, yeah. Just some gifts for the office. Nice to get something they haven't seen in the Home Mart."

The office usually did a Secret Santa gift swap—which I'd never really partaken in—though I always liked to get a six-pack of Guinness for Ronny and a box of chocolates for his wife, Geraldine.

It seemed like the right thing to do.

It wasn't like I had to buy for anyone else.

Braithe picked up a shirt and read the logo across the front. "What's the Griz? Is that some Montanan slang for something?"

I chuckled. "College football." I nodded to the other rack, which had considerably less on it. "The Vandals are the Idaho team."

"Which one do you follow?"

I gave him a is-that-a-serious-question look.

He understood. "Okay. The Griz it is." He took one shirt and added it to his cart. "I'll get one of these and send it to my dad back home." And then he stopped. "Do I need one for me? I think I do." So he added another one. "If I'm sending Dad one, I'll have to find something for everyone."

He found the most souvinerish gifts he could find, and thankfully he was a fast shopper. But then he stopped at a display stand of potted plants. At a glance, they looked like mini conifers.

"Hm," he said, tapping his chin. "I think I'd prefer one of these."

"Ah, okay. Can I ask what for?" It seemed kinda odd wanting a plant that he'd have to leave behind in four weeks.

Jeez. Four weeks . . . Less than four now.

"For my Christmas tree, silly," he replied, making room in his cart to add a whole damn potted tree. "And when I leave, I can plant it. It's better for the environment than buying a plastic one."

I found myself smiling at him. "That's very true."

He hefted the pot into his cart with more ease than I'd given him credit for. "Have you put your tree up yet?"

And just like that, my smile faded. "Uh, no."

"It's supposed to be up on December first," he admonished.

I could have lied and said I'd been busy. I could have lied and said it was up and perfectly decorated. But for some reason, I didn't. "I, uh, I don't usually put one up."

His eyes met mine, and when I expected him to be horrified and maybe even to ridicule me a little, he didn't. He didn't look at me with sadness or pity. It was more gentle curiosity.

"Do you not celebrate Christmas?"

"I do," I said with a shrug. "It's just not a big thing for me."

He nodded slowly, as if he understood something. "Well, I'm buying you one of these. As a thank-you gift for driving me down here."

"You don't have to do that," I said, but he was already adding a second tree to his cart.

"And I'm guessing that also means you don't have decorations," he said, and then he was throwing in some mini ornaments and tinsel. He smiled at the look on my face. "You can plant it in the spring."

I got the feeling he didn't take no for an answer too often.

"Are we done?" he asked. "I think we need a coffee and maybe some brunch. How does that sound?"

Like I'd have ever argued with him. "Sounds good." The thing about spending time with him was that it was everything I'd hoped it would be. He was fun and cheerful—how he made me laugh, how he spoke with his hands, and god, his accent . . .

But it was also terrible because it was everything I couldn't have.

Down in Mossley, an hour from home, sure. We could go shopping and eat at a café together and take a walk along the river so he could take some more photos where the sunshine was warm against the chill in the air.

Strolling along the riverwalk with him and laughing, I could pretend he was my boyfriend and this was our life, and I could pretend I was living my fullest life. Living the life I'd dreamed of.

The life I'd lost my family for, yet still denied myself.

"Colson?" he said. "Braithe to C2, do you copy?"

I must have zoned out in my head again. I chuckled at his use of my call sign. It was cute. I shook off the sombre feelings and smiled for him. "Sorry. Lost in thought."

"Are you ready to go? I don't want you to be late for work."

I checked my watch. We still had plenty of time. "Okay. I want to show you something on the way back."

"Oooh." His eyes lit up with mischief. "Will I like it? Is it fun?" Then he leaned in and whispered, "Would Jesus approve?"

I snorted out a laugh, but damn, I was not prepared for that kind of innuendo. "Ah, well, it's strictly PG-rated, if that's what you're implying." God, did I just say that? "It's G-rated, even."

He let out a long sigh, but there was a twinkle in his eye. "Well, I guess." We got back to the cruiser and it just so happened that his side was closer, so I opened the door for him.

"Oh, you know I do like a gentleman," he murmured as he brushed past me to climb in.

I held my breath until I closed his door and walked around the driver's side, and we headed out of Mossley in a comfortable silence while my heart rate went back to normal. "So," he hedged, and I almost dreaded whatever he was about to say. "About your little tree."

Okay, well, I hadn't expected that. I shot him a look. "What about it? I can pay you for it if you—"

He snorted. "Heavens, no. I was going to ask about decorating it. If you needed a hand, or . . ."

"I'm sure I can manage," I said with a laugh. "I don't foresee it being a difficult project."

He couldn't hide his disappointment. I got the feeling he couldn't hide any emotion too well.

But then it dawned on me . . . he was offering to come by my place. "Oh." My face burned and I shifted in my seat. "Did you . . . were you offering . . . ?"

"I can come around to yours and help you," he said, his eyes big, and my god, did he just flutter his lashes? "If you wanted me to, that is. If you think that's a good idea."

Okay, so he was definitely offering more than just decorating a tree.

My brain scrambled, short-circuited. Because I *did* want that. Oh boy, he had no idea how much I wanted that.

"I, uh . . ." I let out a shaky breath. "Wow, okay, um. I would like that very much. More than you could probably . . ."

His smile was blinding. "Okay, then yes, it is." But then he stared at me and gave a slow nod. "Oh. There's a but coming."

My stomach was a tight knot.

"I'm, um . . ." My mouth was too dry to speak. I tried to swallow. "It's complicated."

He reached over and gave my forearm a gentle squeeze. "I get it. It's okay."

"I wish . . ."

"Braithe to C2, do you copy? I said it's okay."

I tried to smile but it didn't feel right. He needed a better explanation. "I'm not out." But that wasn't entirely true either. "In Hartbridge. No one knows. I can't risk my job."

He flinched, not for himself but for me. His big blue eyes were full of compassion and understanding.

"It's okay," he said. "I understand. Believe me. As a gay kindergarten teacher, I get it."

"I wish it wasn't like this," I mumbled.

He reached over and slid his hand up my forearm to peel

my fingers from the steering wheel, and he held my hand over the centre console.

He was holding my hand.

My god, that simple touch. Something so mundane and ordinary to most people, the feel of his hand in mine was something I'd remember forever.

And despite the lump in my throat and my heavy heart, I felt better for even saying as much as I did, or as little as I had. Sharing the burden, so to speak.

It felt good to tell someone.

The turn-off to what I wanted to show him was coming up soon, but I feared I might have ruined the mood of the day, and I certainly didn't want to let go of his hand.

"Did you still want me to show you that thing?" I asked.

"Are you kidding me? Yes, I absolutely want you to show me that PG-rated thing. Whatever it is."

I laughed, a mix of humour and relief, because he was so forgiving. So understanding.

So perfect.

Reluctantly, I let go of his hand so I could pull off the road. It was no more than an access road, dirt, with tall pines on either side.

I drove past the no-public-access sign and as we started a steep incline, he shot me a wild look. "Uh, where are you taking me? That sign said no access, and I've seen enough *Dateline* to know how this ends. I have a smile that could light up any room, Colson, so hello, prime candidate for murder."

I snorted. "This is a fire trail," I explained. "The local fire departments use this to access the national park in case of wildfires. The public isn't allowed up here, but I am." I patted my dash. "Sheriff's vehicle."

"Is that abuse of power?"

I couldn't tell if he was joking or not.

"Probably. But I can tell them I was doing a spot check for teenagers who like to go camping out here."

Now he looked horrified. "People go camping in there?" He pointed to the forest of trees outside his window. "Like, on purpose?"

I laughed again but needed to concentrate on driving for a bit. The road had some pretty big holes in it, and I made a mental note to let the state forest guys know to get a grader up here in the spring.

But after another minute or so, we crested the top of the ridge and came into a clearing. It was used as a passing lane for trucks, but it also made a pretty good lookout.

I parked on the grass and cut the engine. "Come on," I said, opening my door. "You should see this."

He followed me around to my side and I led him up to a rocky ledge. He stood beside me and gasped. "Oh my," he said. "Colson. I can see everything!"

The view coming down the mountain from Hartbridge was spectacular, yes. But the view from the top of the mountain?

Mind-blowing.

Almost 360 degrees, and on a clear day, you could see for miles. The mountain range, the peaks, the valleys, the patch-work of trees and pastures below.

It was amazing.

Braithe took photos and a quick video, keeping me out of it, thankfully.

But then he took a shot of me, leaning against my cruiser, smiling at him. "This one isn't for Insta," he said. "This one is just for me."

I don't know why that made me blush.

He walked slowly over to me, a devilish smile and intent in his eyes. He stood far too close and gently raised his finger to tap a button on my chest. "We're all alone here," he whispered. "No one would know."

My pulse was kicking, my nerves were frayed. "No one would know what?"

He slow-blinked, seductive and sexy. "If I kissed you right now."

Oh, damn.

I couldn't speak.

"Can I kiss you right now, Colson?"

My god, when he said my name like that? I'd agree to anything. Somehow, I managed to nod.

He ran his hand up my chest to my neck, my jaw. He thumbed my chin, my bottom lip, then slid his hand around my neck, pulled my face down to his, and ghosted his lips over mine.

It almost buckled me.

He smiled but kissed me again, opening his lips and tilting his head, leaning against me . . .

My body reacted without my brain.

I snaked one hand down over his ass, one arm around his back, pulling him flush against me, and slipped my tongue into his mouth.

It'd been so long . . .

Far too long.

Since I'd held a man, kissed a man.

Like I'd been drowning for years, and he was air.

Pure oxygen.

He snaked his arms around me and groaned into my mouth, and it set fire to my blood. He was everything I wanted, needed. And he was as into this as me.

He mighta looked like an angel but he kissed like the devil.

I knew I had to stop this. I had to break away or I wasn't sure how it would end. Well, naked, probably.

Not here. Not like this.

I broke the kiss, panting. I cupped his face in both my hands and held him close, my mouth at the side of his head while I tried to catch my breath and get some rational brain-thinking words . . .

"Oh my days," he whispered, panting like me.

"Ah, yeah." It was all I was capable of. I'm sure he could feel the thrumming of my heart. "Wow."

Braithe laughed and leaned up on his tiptoes, making me look at his face. At his dreamy blue eyes and swollen pink lips. "So that happened."

"It did."

"And it should happen again." His teeth dragged along his bottom lip. "Often, preferably."

Mercy, I wanted that. So much.

But did I have to say it again? Did I have to keep bringing up how I couldn't— His eyes focused on mine and he booped me on the nose with his dainty fingertip. "I know what you're about to say," he said. "No one has to know. I can walk to your place when it's dark, or we can meet somewhere secluded, like this. Just you and me."

Could I do that?

He saw me hesitate. He watched me trying to calculate risk assessments in my head, and he knew I was failing. "I'm here for another four weeks. Four weeks of sex. Nothing more. No strings attached. Just sex. All the sex you can handle." He saw his wounded prey and struck the final blow.

He pouted.

Like a minx sent from hell to torment me, he pouted.

"Unless you don't want to, Colson."

Aaaaand he said my name.

I turned him around, pressed him against the cruiser, my nose to his. "Starting when?"

Chapter Five

BRAITHE

SEE, here's the thing. I hadn't intended to proposition the good deputy like that. I hadn't even meant to kiss him.

And oh boy, did he know how to kiss.

But up on top of that mountain, after the great morning we'd had, it felt right.

It felt good.

I knew he was guarded, and for good reason. But nothing was stopping us from having a sordid, secret love affair for the duration of my stay.

No one else had to know.

"You what?"

Hamish almost shrieked, the whole diner turned to stare at our booth, and I didn't miss the way Jayden smiled from behind the grill.

"Shh," I said, leaning across the table. "Keep your voice down. I shouldn't even be telling you."

Hamish gave me a serious glare. "Oh, but you're going to tell me. Everything. Spare no detail. The details are my favourite part."

"He drove me to Mossley this morning," I began.

He waved his hand. "Yeah, yeah. Not those details. The good details."

I rolled my eyes at him. I really liked Hamish. He was a good ten years older than me, but he was fun and kind. We were a lot alike, personality-wise.

"He took me to a secret lookout on the way back, and I kissed him."

Hamish shivered. "And? Keep going. You can't just tell me you propositioned him and then start from the beginning." He shrugged. "I mean, I'm sure the secret lookout was romantic and all."

I laughed. "It was. But anyway, I kissed him. And it wasn't some sweet, innocent peck either. It was filthy."

He fanned his face. "My favourite kind."

I kept my voice down. "And then I asked him if he'd be interested in a four-week, no-strings sexfest."

Hamish stared, looking me up and down. Hard to tell if he was proud or appalled. "You little slut."

Yeah, he was proud.

I laughed and sipped my coffee. "I don't know what possessed me to ask. And it was possible there might have been some coercion on my behalf."

He gasped. "What?"

"The power of the pout and eyelash flutter."

"Oh no, you didn't."

"Oh yes, I did."

He put his hand to his heart. "Be still. I'm too old and eat far too many cookies for this kind of cardio. I'm assuming he said yes."

I laughed. "He sure did. I'm going to his place tomorrow to help him decorate his tree."

"Mm-hm." He nodded. "Sure you are."

"I have to walk to his place so no one sees my car there," I added, a reality of it all. "And you can't tell anyone. Not a soul, okay? I shouldn't have even told you."

He gave a nod just as Gunter and Clay came in. Gunter pulled off his scarf and sat next to me, Clay next to Hamish.

"Who are we gossiping about today?" Gunter asked.

Hamish's eyes met mine. "No one. Braithe was just telling me he bought a truckload of Christmas crafts for his students."

"Ah," Clay said. "Making ornaments and decorations at school at Christmas time was my favourite time of year."

Jayden came over with a plate of scones and a pot of fresh coffee. "Oh, Christmas decorations. Braithe, did you find what you were looking for?"

I smiled up at him, ignoring Hamish's smirk. "I sure did." Afternoon tea with this group of guys was awesome. Ren came across the road when he shut the hardware store, and the only one missing was Cass. But the bed and breakfast was busy, and Jayden didn't stay long, clocking off and, after a quick chat and a round of goodbyes, he went home.

We didn't stay for long after that, and walking out into Main Street, I couldn't believe how much it had changed from just yesterday.

There were now Christmas trees in planters lining the street—Courtesy of Clay, as a proud Gunter announced—and there were Christmas lights on awnings and in shop fronts.

"Can you believe this place?" I asked. "It's just magical."

Hamish smiled, leaning into Ren a little. "It never gets old. It's as pretty today as it was the first day I got here. And each season is prettier than the one before it. Wait till you see it in spring. And autumn . . . I mean fall."

Ren snorted and I found myself smiling at them, admiring them, a little jealous. In a good way, of course. I wanted what they had.

One day.

"You'll have to send me a postcard," I said. "I won't be here come spring."

Hamish laughed. "Oh, sweet summer child. What did I tell you?" He clucked his tongue. "You're not leaving."

I snorted. "You make it sound like a horror movie."

Hamish tapped Ren's chest. "Tell him, babe. Tell him what happens to single gays who come here at Christmas time."

Ren chuckled and shook his head. "Well, the last few years have swayed the statistics on people moving into town. People who just happened to be queer." Then he winced. "Who moved here, fell in love, and never left."

Hamish nodded very seriously. "They get shot by Cupid and Santa. Tag-teamed, even."

Ren, clearly shocked, looked at me. "I'm so sorry. Hamish, you can't say that."

But all I could do was laugh. "It's fine. It's not going to be like that." I leaned in, knowing Ren would hear but figured Hamish would tell him, given they were married. "It's just sex. No strings attached."

"That's what they all say." Hamish looked me right in the eye. "But it's never just sex, is it? There are always strings. More strings than a yarn shop."

I smiled at that. But I could keep it real. I wasn't staying in Hartbridge—as gorgeous as the place was, and despite what nonsense they went on with about Cupid and Santa making me stay—and I'd had plenty of casual sex before. Well, okay, like five one-night stands, max. But still, they were fine, and I never wanted anything more.

I could do that with Colson.

I was sure I could.

Hamish gave my arm a squeeze and offered a small smile

that told me he thought otherwise. "Have fun tomorrow with the tree decorating," he said with a wink. "And I want all the details. All of them."

Ren put his arm around Hamish's shoulder. "Okay, leave him alone. We have to go." He grinned at me. "Take care."

"Bye, guys."

I fixed my coat collar up, wishing I'd brought my beanie, and decided a stroll along Main Street looking at the Christmas decorations was in order.

Saturday afternoons in Hartbridge were quiet, apparently. And oh-so lovely. The word picturesque didn't do it justice.

I thought back to the guys telling me about the Christmas curse of Hartbridge, how single men found themselves here, by choice or by accident, met the love of their lives, and never left.

Not really a curse though.

Nope, nope. Get it out of your head, Braithe. My home is in London, close to my family and old friends. This is just a working holiday. Two years of travel, and work and life experience, and some wild oats sowing before my thirties when I could find someone and settle down with . . .

Yes. The sowing of wild oats. That's what I was doing. Wild oats and no strings.

By dinner time, I'd decorated my little tree, packaged up a parcel to send home, sent my mum and dad an email, uploaded a few pics from the day to my Insta . . .

And spent a good twenty minutes staring at the photo of Colson leaning against his cruiser, smiling and squinting at the sun.

He was so handsome.

Yep. I was gonna sow oats with no strings with him so hard tomorrow.

I ARRIVED at the address Colson had given me a little before ten with a bag in my hand and a belly full of nerves. And a semi that hadn't quit since I woke up.

His house was cute. A green detached bungalow with a built-in porch at the front and shutters on the windows. His gardens were immaculate, his lawn mown with precision. His cruiser was parked under the carport at the side.

It was so him.

Even his address was perfect.

Eight Juniper Lane.

I walked up the path to his front door, my tummy now hosting a disco to a full kaleidoscope of butterflies. His door opened before I had even climbed the first step, and he stood there in jeans and a sweater, socks on his feet, and a nervous smile.

"Hey," he said.

"Hey."

I walked up the steps, brushed past him, and stood on his little enclosed porch. I took my shoes off and followed him inside. His lounge room was cosy and warm. Light yellow walls with white hang-rails, two leather couches forming a square with the corner to face a TV. A wood heater was open to the kitchen that filled the back wall, with a glass door that looked like it led to a mudroom and the backyard.

Simple and charming, inviting and very lovely.

"Your home is beautiful."

He let out a breath, smiling as he looked over the room. "Thanks. I like it." Then he looked at the bag I was holding. "Whatcha got there?"

I walked over to the kitchen counter and pulled out the first thing. "Morning tea," I said. "It's a pastry from the diner.

I only got one because it was so huge, I thought we could share. I will gain a stone while I'm here, I'm sure."

He stared at me, clearly confused, maybe horrified. "A stone?"

"In weight, sorry. It's a unit of weight measurement." I snorted. "From the look on your face I'm not sure I want to know what you thought I meant."

He grimaced. "Well, there's the geological kind, obviously, which in context didn't make a lot of sense. But here, if you have stones, you have balls. Or significant gallbladder problems."

I laughed. "Right."

He was embarrassed, and it was kinda cute. "Did you go to the diner this morning?"

"Yesterday and this morning. My daily strolls tend to lead me to wherever there is a cup of tea and food, apparently."

His smile faltered. "And you had to walk here . . . I'm sorry—"

"I like walking. I walk everywhere if I can. I've been on walks every day since I got here, sometimes twice, even three times. And believe me, with the calories I've been eating, I need to."

I didn't want him to feel bad about me having to walk here. That it wasn't a good idea to have my car parked at his place.

I gave his arm a quick squeeze. "Not having my car seen at your place is as much for me as it is for you." I put my hand to my chest. "New kindergarten teacher in town, remember?"

This seemed to placate him because he nodded and gave me a smile. "Do you want coffee? To have with the pastry?"

"Do you have tea?"

He stopped. "Uh, no. I don't . . . sorry."

Reaching into the bag, I pulled out a small box of ten teabags and handed them to him. "Now you do."

His eyes widened as he laughed. "You come prepared." I laughed because, oh boy, he didn't know what else I'd brought with me yet. "Speaking of prepared . . ."

I pulled out a white paper bag and put them on the counter. "Condoms and lube."

Colson's grip on the teabags made me think he was about to crush them. "Oh." I took the box of Twinings from his grasp and set them down. I took his hand. "It's okay if you don't want to, or if you're not ready. I just thought it best to have supplies should we need them."

He blinked a few times and breathed out a laugh. "I, uh. I want to. I'm just . . . I'm just not used to this. You're very bold."

I rubbed his knuckles with my thumb. "I know what I want, and I have no issue in asking for it. I apologise if that comes across as pushy or intrusive."

"No, no, it's fine. I'm just out of practice. Normally I . . ." He winced. "Normally you what?"

"Normally I meet in a bar and it's dark and talking about what we want is easier in the dark."

Oh, this sweet, sweet man.

"Do you meet in dark bars often?"

He shook his head. "No. Just a few times in the last few years, I . . ." He swallowed hard and looked down between us. "I'm not very good at this."

I dropped his hand so I could press my palm to his chest. "I think you're kinda great at this," I whispered.

His eyes met mine, honey-brown with flecks of gold. "What do you want?"

"A cup of tea."

He barked out a laugh. "Right. Sorry, I'll get right on

that." I was glad to lighten the mood. I didn't want him to be nervous or feel bad. This was supposed to be fun.

"Then we can decorate your tree, and then," I added, "you can take me to bed. There are ten teabags and ten condoms. Let's see which ones we run out of first."

Chapter Six

COLSON

I WAS PRETTY sure Braithe Branson was going to kill me.

Death by heart palpitations with a hard-on. Yep. The coroner was going to laugh about this for years.

Braithe was so forthright. So bold.

So damn cute.

He was small. Maybe five foot ten with shoes, but thin and fine-featured, with his blond hair and big blue eyes. He looked dainty and innocent.

What he was, in reality, was a sexual imp sent from England to torture me.

He'd brought condoms and lube with him. A pack of ten, no less, and wanted to play a kind of game to see how many we could use.

I mean, how presumptuous and assuming.

How hot.

And I was supposed to have morning tea with him? Sip coffee and eat half a bear claw with him while he laughed and licked his lips, catching sticky glaze from the corner of his mouth?

All while a white paper bag sat on the kitchen counter with a New York drugstore's name stamped on it.

Small blessings he didn't buy them from Hartbridge, I guess.

"Tree time," he said, putting our plates in the sink and taking my hand, leading me to the living room.

The little tree he'd bought me sat in the corner beside the TV and the box of decorations next to it.

He pulled me over to the tree, his hand so warm in mine, and he plonked himself on the floor. "Come on then, sit."

I couldn't fold myself up as small as he could, and I hadn't sat on the floor since . . . I couldn't remember when.

"I have to sit on the floor all the time," he offered. "One of the perks of being a teacher of tiny humans."

"A perk? This is a perk?"

He laughed. "Sitting on the floor, reading books, painting, colouring in, singing the alphabet song. Everything I do is a perk."

There was that sunshine again.

How could someone be a devilish sex imp trying to kill me one minute, then so sunshiny the next?

He pulled the tree over a little and opened the box of small ornaments. He took a few out and handed me one. "You have to put the first one on. It's your tree."

Oh, how his words, his kindness, warmed my heart.

"I can't believe you don't normally put a tree up," he mused, adding an ornament after me.

"It's just me," I replied, adding another gold ball. "Never seemed much point." He nodded slowly, and I was sure he was about to ask about my family. But he didn't.

"You're allowed to do things just for you too," he offered instead. "In fact, it's the best reason there is."

I couldn't help but chuckle. It was odd how him saying

that seemed to wrap itself around my insides. "You're right. I should do things for me."

Braithe nodded. "'Today you are You, that is truer than true. There is no one alive who is Youer than You.'"

"Is that Dr Seuss?"

He grinned. "Another perk of being me. I can quote any kid's book off the top of my head."

I laughed. "That's a pretty good perk." After a few more ornaments, I asked, "So, why kindergarten teacher?" I knew we weren't supposed to do the conversation thing. He'd said just sex, no strings attached. But a little conversation felt right.

"I love kids," he replied with a smile. "I love seeing their little minds learn and the looks on their faces when they understand something. I get to, hopefully, instil a love of learning." He added another ornament. "It's not always fun and games. Some kids don't have great homes and so I try to make school their happy place, you know. The classroom is a comfort and safe place and something to look forward to. They're so little and vulnerable, and I try to protect their little innocent hearts. Sometimes there are tears, and sometimes they're mine."

I stared at him, unable to find the words . . . God, how was he this wonderful?

"That's . . . that's pretty great." I swallowed down the lump in my throat. "I'm sure the kids love you."

He laughed. "And their moms. There's been a line."

"Oh, dear."

He sighed. "Maybe I should have worn a wedding ring."

I smiled and added the last ornament. "You didn't have a line at the last place you worked?" I hadn't meant that to sound so bitter. Or if I was asking if he'd had any men in his town, but it must have come across that way.

He knocked his knee to mine. "No. No line of single

moms. No dads either. No anyone, actually." He pulled out the small string of tinsel. "There was one guy in Montreal when I did that scenic tour. And before that, back home, my last boyfriend was months before I left England. He didn't want me to go, told me he wouldn't wait and didn't want to do the long-distance thing, so he ended it."

"Oh, I'm sorry."

"I'm not. He did us both a favour. We weren't a great match from the start, and I'm pretty sure he was banging someone else the next weekend, so, you know." He shrugged. "It is what it is."

"No great loss."

He shook his head. "No loss at all. What about you?"

"Boyfriends?"

"Yeah, or whatever." He shrugged like it was no big deal. "You don't have to tell me if you don't want."

I took a breath to steady my nerves. "There's not much to tell. I had a boyfriend in Billings many years ago. But he wanted me to come out. And it . . ." I made a face, pretending it didn't hurt to remember. "And there's been no one since. No one longer than a mutual exchange, if you know what I mean."

I put his hand on my knee and gave it a squeeze. "It's not easy. It rarely is. But here we are. Two single guys who haven't had nearly enough sex in the last however long, and we have four weeks to remedy that."

He really could just talk about casual sex as if he was discussing the weather.

At least he'd lightened the mood.

"Okay, the final touches," he said, handing the small tree-topper star to me. "You can do the honours. But you have to christen it first."

I was confused. "Christen it? With what?"

"A name, silly."

"You want me to name the tree?"

"Yes. Look at how cute he is."

"Uh . . ." I tried to think. "I don't know. What did you call your tree?"

He grinned. "Spruce Willis."

I burst out laughing. "You did not."

"I did!" He put his hand to his heart. "I swear to you, I did."

I looked at the tree. "Well, I think it's actually a conifer."

Braithe gasped. "Conifer Aniston." He gestured to the tree. "Look at how pretty she is."

I was still laughing. I couldn't remember the last time I'd laughed so much. Braithe jumped up to his feet and held out his hand, helping me to mine. "Now, about making up for all the sex we haven't had."

Oh, god.

Trying not to panic, I checked my watch. "I do have to work—"

He pulled on my hand, leading me toward the hall. "Then we need to be quick."

I snorted. "Considering how long it's been for me, I don't think that'll be a problem."

He laughed, stopped only to grab the paper bag off the counter, and continued down the hall. "Uh, which door?"

I dropped his hand and went to my bedroom door. I turned to face him, smiling but certain the blush on my cheeks told no lies. "I, uh . . ."

"It's okay if you don't want to. I just thought—"

"Oh, I want to. Like, I really, *really* want to. Too much, is what I'm trying to say. This is going to be over so fast, so if you have any expectations of this being drawn-out, mind-blowing—"

Smiling, he stepped in close, leaned up on his toes, and kissed me softly. He also reached behind me and opened the door, then pushed me backward with his body.

For a small guy, he could push me around so easily.

Boss me around, too.

Not that I minded. Not at all.

I wrapped my arm around his lower back, and he walked me backward until my legs hit the bed. We fell, him on top of me, his blue eyes dark with desire and mischief. The moment he pressed his arousal hard against mine, he crushed his mouth to mine.

Open lips, warm and wet, and his tongue, so good . . . so very good.

He certainly liked to be in charge and it was a rush, a turn-on to feel so desired, wanted. He was as desperate for more as I was.

I hadn't felt this alive in so long.

God, it felt so right.

And it was more than I'd had in forever, but I needed more.

I rolled us over and hefted him up into the middle of my bed. He laughed, his tongue swiping the corner of his mouth, and when I spread his thighs wider, he pulled me by my sweater to come closer. I fit against him so perfectly, his legs wrapped around me.

"Much better," he murmured before I kissed him, delving my tongue into his mouth, tangling with his.

He moaned.

Obscene.

Delicious.

I was so hard already, my cock desperate for contact.

There was no way sex was going to happen today. I was too turned on, and it had been far too long.

But there was something I could do . . .

I pulled back onto my haunches, his thighs over mine. He was panting, his lips kiss-swollen and wet, his eyes wanting.

I pulled my sweater over my head and tossed it to the floor, and he hummed, his fingers skating up my chest. "You're so hot."

I pushed his sweater and shirt up to reveal his slim, pale torso, pink nipples, and hairless chest, his tiny waist.

Lord have mercy.

He was so beautiful.

I unbuttoned his jeans, and he lifted his hips, eager as I reached in and freed his cock.

Oh, hell yes.

My cock pulsed, my balls drew down and I knew I'd made the right choice. "I'm too turned on," I admitted. "You're too fucking hot." I popped the button on my jeans and unzipped, pulling my erection out and moaning at the relief.

Braithe eyed my cock and he sighed. "Oh yes. Yes, please."

I leaned over him, my left hand by his head, taking us both into my right hand. So silky, so hot, and almost too much to bear.

"Oh my god," he said, his voice tight. He leaned up and kissed me, grunting into my mouth as I worked us both, and when that was too much, he fell back on the bed, his eyes closed and mouth open, rocking his hips, driving upward into my fist.

Then his eyes shot open. "Oh god, Colson. I'm gonna . . . I'm . . ." His back arched, he gripped his own hair, his cock pulsed against mine, and he came, taking me over the edge with him.

I came in thick spurts on his belly, waves of pleasure too big to contain rocketing through me, and I groaned.

I didn't recognise the noises I'd made.

Never had it ever felt like that before.

I convulsed, racked with aftershocks, and Braithe pulled me to him. The mess smeared between our bellies, but I did not care. His arms around me, his body underneath me, my face in his neck . . .

I never wanted to move.

I wasn't sure I even could.

"You alive in there?" he murmured.

"Negative."

He laughed as he traced patterns on my back. "That was pretty hot."

"I was too turned on, sorry."

He chuckled. "I don't know what you're apologising for. I came before you."

I pulled back, and resting my head on my palm, I met his eyes. "I wasn't gonna last. I did warn you that it'd been a while."

He laughed and traced his finger down my cheek. "I also jerked off this morning because I didn't want to come the second you saw me."

I snorted, hardly believing we were having this conversation. "I did too. Hot shower and anticipation."

He laughed, his eyes sparkling with humour. "Next time we'll do better. We can't let the teabags win."

I laughed too, our bodies shaking with the effort, and it made the mess between us all too apparent. I rolled off him. "I'll get us a cloth."

I'd expected him to stay on the bed, but no, he followed me to the bathroom. He leaned against the sink and let me wipe him clean, then he helped me clean myself.

There was no shame, no hiding, and even though I wasn't used to that, I really liked it.

"So, about next time," he mused. "Is tonight too soon?"

I laughed and fixed the button on my jeans. I was still shirtless though, and Braithe put his palm to my chest and slid it down to my abs.

"You know, I don't think I've ever touched abs like this," he said, studying every inch of me. "I've seen it in pictures and movies of course, but not in real life. I mean, I've seen some that are close, but nothing like this." He ran his hand up to my pec and gave me a gentle squeeze. "Damn, C2. You are jacked. And this?" He gently fingered the fine hair on my chest, sending a rush of goosebumps over my skin. "Hot as hell."

My cheeks burned with embarrassment, despite what we'd just done in my bedroom. I met his eyes and, with my finger under his chin, lifted his face so I could press my lips to his.

Soft and sweet.

Damn.

"Uh, tonight? I finish after midnight, so it might be too late." He pouted and gave a sad sigh. "I have to be at work at seven."

"I'm off tomorrow," I said. More of an offer, really. "Next two days. I have Mondays and Tuesdays off, actually."

That earned me an immediate smile. "Oh, really? So tomorrow night, hypothetically, I could go for an evening stroll and find myself walking along this adorable lane, and then find myself naked and face down on your bed, totally by accident, and then you'd be like 'oh no, what do I have here' and then you'd have to rail me. Say, around seven o'clock?"

My heart knocked against my ribs and, damn, if I didn't have to readjust myself already. "Hypothetically, I think that sounds like a plan."

He bit his bottom lip, still smiling, and he palmed my

crotch, giving me a decent squeeze. "May I suggest a lunchtime wank? Because I think I'm gonna need this for as long and as many times as possible."

I laughed, embarrassed, but given my dick was already half hard again at the mere mention of me railing him, it was probably a good idea. "Yes. God forbid the teabags win."

❄

I WALKED INTO WORK, trying not to smile like an idiot, and hung my coat and my hat on the hook, still trying not to smile.

I popped in some gum just to give my mouth something else to do.

And I stuck my head into Ronny's office. "Afternoon, Sheriff."

"Ah, Colson. Just the man I wanted to see."

I stepped all the way inside his office. "What can I do for you?"

He made a face at the planner on his wall. "Now, I know it don't feel right even asking because it's your scheduled day off and all, but I told my Geraldine I'd ask. And you can say no, no hard feelings."

I knew what he was about to ask me, and he knew I wouldn't ever say no.

I mean, it made sense that I work Christmas Day. I had no family, and he had an entire brood: kids, grandkids, his sister and her kids, great nieces and nephews.

"About Christmas Day," he began.

"It's fine, boss. But I'll tell you what." This was probably cheeky, but I was in a good mood, so I figured I'd try my luck. "You get that lovely wife of yours to make me an apple pie with that fresh vanilla cream just like she made for your birthday, and you got yourself a deal."

He eyed me, face stoic. "Are you bargaining with me, son?"

"I believe we'd call that a successful negotiation, sir." He roared, laughing.

"Deal."

Chapter Seven

BRAITHE

"He has no photos up in his house, his spare room has a weight bench in it—although that does explain his abs, because oh boy, does he have abs, and his biceps are like wow," I took a breath and gathered my thoughts because I was so easily distracted by memories of Colson's body. "But when we talk of family, he gets quiet and changes the topic. I'm telling you, he has a story. And I don't know if it's a good one."

Hamish, Jayden, Cass, and Gunter were sitting in the booth at the diner, staring at me.

"I thought you were doing no strings," Hamish said. "Because this sounds like it has strings."

"No," I said, shaking my head. "I'm just saying he's the sweetest man you could ever meet and I think he might need some kindness, that's all. He's not out, and he's all alone."

Jayden frowned. "That is a bit sad."

"What can we do for him?" Gunter asked. I liked Gunter. He was older, mid-forties at a guess, which was twenty years older than me, but he was a gentle soul. "If he's not out. And he's a bit of a public figure. People recognise him. If we invite him out for dinner at a table full of queers, people will assume he's queer too, right or wrong." He shrugged. "It sucks, but that's what happens. Remember that time we asked him if he wanted to join us at the pizzeria? He wanted to, you could tell. But he can't."

"Then we have a private dinner party," Hamish said. "At our place. Like an early Christmas dinner party, before Jayden and Cass get swamped at the B&B, and Clay's only gonna get busier up until Christmas Day."

Gunter nodded, Cass smiled, but Jayden put his hands up. "I'm not cooking for it. I have enough to do at my two jobs, thank you very much."

Hamish laughed. "Of course not. We'll all bring a dish. It'll be a potluck of whatever, and we'll play Christmas music and have a great time."

It sounded amazing.

I whispered so only our table could hear. "Colson has Mondays and Tuesdays off, if that helps."

"Monday night, but not tomorrow night, obviously," Hamish said. "It's too soon."

Jayden shrugged. "What about next week?"

Everyone looked around the table and kind of nodded. "Excellent! It's a date," Hamish said. "Now I just have to tell Ren."

I snorted. "And now, I just have to get a certain someone to agree to come along," I added. "And I have no kitchen to cook anything in, but I can bring some pizza and garlic bread from the pizzeria. If that's okay. If they're open on a Monday."

"Yes, that's okay, and yes, they're open," Jayden added. "Meat lovers is my favourite, if that information helps when ordering."

Everyone laughed, but Hamish was smiling at me. "Look at you, calling him Colson and knowing what days he has off.

And I think I put in a request for all the details and yet you hath not divulged."

"Oh god," Cass groaned. "Ignore him. He has no shame." Hamish tapped Cass's arm. "Oh shush. Who are you, Ren 2.0?" He might have been joking, but they were all kind of waiting for me to reply. I played with the napkin on the table. "We decorated his tree."

"And?"

I safely assumed they didn't want to know we called it Conifer Aniston. "And we ended up in his bed," I murmured quickly. "But we didn't, uh . . . complete the whole mission. It was more of a side quest. If you know what I mean."

They all laughed, and I felt stupid for blushing.

Goodness, I really liked these guys. And the offer to host a private Christmas dinner for Colson was just so lovely. I just had to get him to agree.

"Anyway," I added. "Hamish, let me know if you need me to bring anything for the dinner party. Not next Monday but the one after, right?"

He nodded. "Unless Ren already made plans that I don't know about, in which case, I'll let you all know, but I'm sure he'll be fine with it."

"Are you sure?"

Hamish patted my hand. "Of course. He sounds a lot like your man. When I first met him, he had no family, he was closeted and lonely. Believe me, if anyone will understand, it will be Ren."

"And Clay," Gunter added. "He wasn't out when I met him. Maybe it'll be good for . . . your guy . . . to hang out with us. He might just see that this little town will love him no matter what."

I hoped so. But still . . .

"I haven't spoken to him about any of this," I said. "About

his reasons, and everybody has their reasons. It's not up to us to force him." I sighed and sipped the last of my now-cold coffee. "I'll try to bring it up when I see him tomorrow night."

Hamish's eyebrow lifted. "Oh? Again so soon? How are those strings going?" he joked. "Not tangled up yet?"

I sighed, fighting a smile. "Oh, shush."

SCHOOL ON MONDAY was so much fun. The kids were so excited about all the Christmas crafts, and I told them of the Christmas concert and how we'd be putting on a show for all our grown-ups to come and watch. The school had some great costumes and props from previous years for our nativity play, but we would need some help with costumes, and given the steady stream of moms who came to collect their kids at the end of the day, I figured I'd ask for volunteers.

"Funny how they were all too busy once I told them it would be them doing the work at home and it would not involve spending time with me," I said to Raeleen in the staff room.

She laughed. "Yes, funny how that works."

I sighed. "It's fine."

She sipped her coffee and after a beat said, "So, not interested in any of the single moms?"

I snorted. "Ah, no."

She chewed on the inside of her lip. "The dads, perhaps?"

My gaze shot to hers, and I had to make a decision: lie and play it off as ridiculous or act as if it was no big deal. Thank god the staff room was empty because I went with the latter. "More my style, but no parent of my students." I pretended to shudder. "That's so wrong."

She laughed. "I thought it might be. More your style, that

is. Not that I was judging you or anything, because hell, I don't care either way. But it was mentioned a time or two that you've been having coffee and cake with the other gay boys in town."

There was a lot to unpack in what she'd just said, but I had to take it with a grain of salt. I believed she meant no harm, but it was a very blunt reminder that what Gunter had said was true and that Colson's fear was right on the money.

If he was seen in public with us, people would assume, right or wrong, that he was *one of us*.

It was bullshit and exhausting, but small towns were always gonna be small towns.

"The other *gay boys* in town are the nicest people," I said, keeping my tone pleasant. "They befriended me and made me feel so welcome."

"Oh yes, Ren grew up here. Nicest guy you could ever meet," she added. "He and Hamish held a big gay wedding and I saw the photos, and oh my gosh, it was so beautiful. Hamish is a hoot. He often carries their little dog around and it has little shoes for the snow. It's the cutest thing. And Cass? Can't say I was surprised, but Clay? Let me tell you, no one saw that coming . . ."

And so she went on.

Gossiping and giving me the rundown on the whole group and what the town thought.

I shouldn't have been surprised, but I was.

Small-town grapevines and rumours always ran rampant. That was never going to change. And she really didn't have anything negative to say. The truth was, no one cared or spoke about being queer negatively, but it was still a topic worthy of gossip.

And that hurt.

I liked Raeleen. I did. She'd been very nice to me and had

given me a warm welcome into the school. But after this conversation, she'd lost some of her shine for me.

And what's more, my heart hurt for Colson.

More gossip fodder. The grapevine would be sprouting new leaves. And with him being an officer of the law . . . I wasn't sure if him being the town deputy meant he had hurdles of different expectations to conquer. But I got the sinking feeling it might.

I got back to my place, feeling a little deflated. I'd explained to Raeleen that while my sexuality wasn't a secret exactly, it was no one else's business, and a fact some parents might not hold too favourably, so if she could please not divulge any private matters.

She'd given me a sad nod and said she'd understood, but the way she'd blabbered on to me made me think my plea fell on deaf ears. She clearly liked to gossip, so . . .

Yeah, deflated and a little worried if I was being honest.

I shouldn't have said anything. But the truth was, the town already assumed I was queer, so it was maybe a moot point.

I ate an early dinner with Mrs Parson. She'd had a lovely weekend with her grandkids, and we watched Jeopardy together. She was actually really good at it and we laughed a lot, and by the time I said goodnight to her, I was feeling a bit better about my day.

About to feel a whole lot better.

Physically, anyway.

I changed into some athletic wear so it wouldn't look suspicious should someone see me walking. I could pretend to be out for a jog or, more realistically, a brisk walk at best.

Thankful it was dark early, and grateful the streetlamps on Juniper Lane were few and far between, I found myself walking up Colson's steps right on seven o'clock.

I gave a gentle rap on the door and he opened it, looking like the definition of comfort come to life. He wore jeans and a brown knit sweater, the same colour as his hair. He had on black socks and a shy smile. "Evening," he said, his cheeks pink.

"Good evening." I stepped into the warmth of his house. His wood fire was crackling and the TV was on but the volume was low. Something smelled good.

Him.

He smelled good.

Was he wearing cologne?

"You look amazing," I said, looking him up and down. "And you smell like I want to crawl into your lap and stay there."

He laughed, blushing for good measure. "And you look cold. Do you want a warm drink? Or to sit by the fire?"

"Cold?" I pulled my beanie off, then my gloves.

He licked his lips. "Your cheeks are red, and your nose."

"The wind is a bit fresh out there," I admitted. "But I'm fine. I decided to dress up like someone who jogs." I gestured to my outfit. "In case someone saw me walking. Not sure I'd convince anyone that I could actually jog. If you'd seen me run, you'd understand."

Colson chuckled, his eyes lingering on mine for a long beat. "You look . . ." His gaze went to my lips before back to my eyes. "You look great."

Damn.

That look in his eyes . . . it kicked my pulse up a notch.

"Do you want to kiss me, Colson?" I asked.

His gaze hit mine, sharp and dark. "I do. But my manners are telling me to offer you something to eat first, or . . . I don't even know."

Oh, he was just too sweet.

Smiling, I stepped in close and took his hand. "I think it might be rude of you to not kiss me, Colson."

He looked so nervous, so stiff that he might shatter. So I leaned into him, his body strong and warm, and put my hand to his cheek before I pressed my lips to his.

It seemed to snap him out of whatever trance he was in, because he wrapped one arm around my lower back, pulled me in hard against him, and kissed me properly.

A kiss so good it made my knees weak.

The way he felt, the way he smelled, tasted. Strong arms, stubbled jaw, warm mouth, and a scent that was earthy and sweet.

He was mesmerising.

He broke the kiss, leaving me breathless and dazed, and he smiled. "Can I get you a drink? A cup of tea?"

I shook my head. "No. After, perhaps."

"After . . . ?"

"After you take me to bed," I replied, my voice a whisper. "And kiss me like that again."

He blinked in surprise at my demand, but he took my hand and led me to his room. I took more notice of it now. The soft and pillowy bed covers were dark green, the wooden floors covered with a fluffy cream rug. There were simple bedside tables with a lamp, the only light on in the room casting a warm glow.

"Ooh, mood lighting," I said. "I like it."

He turned to face me, half smiling, half nervous wince. "Are you sure you want to do this? It's been a long while and I don't want to hurt you."

I cupped his face and kissed him softly. "You won't. Just take it slow, and we'll do great. I trust you, Colson."

His eyes met mine, and something flickered there. Something that told me those were the words he'd needed to hear. And the thing was, I did trust him.

He was genuine and kind, and I doubted he'd deliberately hurt any living thing.

He slid his hand along my jaw and kissed me, opening my mouth and tangling his tongue with mine. Slow and measured.

Perfect.

He undressed me, pulling my hoodie over my head and running his big hands over my ribs and up my back, pulling me close. He kissed me again, moaning at the feel of my skin.

But he didn't hurry.

It was like we played a pass-the-parcel game, taking turns to slowly unwrap one layer at a time with slow and deep kisses between each one.

My sweater, then his. My shirt, then his. My trackpants, his jeans. Until the unwrapping was done and he laid me down on his bed under the covers. I watched as he rolled a condom down his hard length, anticipation curling around my insides, ready for what I longed for.

What I craved.

He took his sweet time getting me ready. Sure fingers, skilled and thorough, until I begged him.

"Colson, please. I'm ready. I can't wait another second."

Then he nestled himself between my legs, kissing me deep and hard this time. He pulled my knees up, positioned his cock where I wanted him, and slowly pressed into me.

His body trembled as he sunk in all the way, his breathing shallow and sharp.

Such perfect restraint.

Until I was accustomed and ready. I rocked my hips and he took his cue and began to move.

"Oh fuck," he moaned in my ear, slowly thrusting in and

out. His thick cock filled me, over and over as he held me, kissed my mouth, my neck, dug his fingers into my skin, his arms holding me so tight.

He knew every button to push, and he pushed them repeatedly, with attention to detail and precision. He was moulding me into a shape I'd never been, a shape to bring out the best of me, just for him.

This wasn't about his pleasure.

This was about mine.

Every touch was for me, every gentle push and pull, every thrust. Everything he did to me was for me.

He made love to me like the secrets to my body were written in a language only he knew.

He coaxed my orgasm from me, wringing every ounce of pleasure out of me before he let himself go.

And getting to watch his face as he came was the greatest part of it all. Knowing that I drove him crazy, feeling his cock pulse inside me as he filled the condom. The way he clung to me, held me tight, and groaned in my ear as he came.

I'd never had anything close to that before.

We lay together, tangled and panting, and it felt like an out-of-body experience. Dreamy and floating, it took a long while before I could form a coherent thought.

"Wow." I chuckled. "Just . . . wow."

Colson laughed. "Yeah."

"The lunchtime wank had been a great idea."

He laughed again, this time burying his face into the pillow. "It was more of a ten o'clock thing for me. I couldn't hold out till lunchtime."

I laughed and laughed, curling into him. He pulled me in close and held me so effortlessly, so comfortably. I settled in with my face on his chest and could have so easily dozed off.

"Have you eaten?" he asked.

"I did. Mrs Parson cooks me dinner on a weeknight, and we watch *Jeopardy*. Did you know she taught English in Japan and Brussels?"

"No, I didn't know that."

"She's very smart. And she might look small and sweet, but she kicks my arse at *Jeopardy*, and she shows absolutely no remorse."

He chuckled, rubbing my back, and when we fell silent, I wondered if it was my cue to leave. Should I go? Did he expect me to leave so soon? What was the protocol for a no-strings, sex-only affair?

I wasn't sure. I had no clue. What I did know was that I wasn't entirely sure I wanted to leave just yet.

But then his stomach growled. He chuckled. "Sorry."

"Oh, have you not eaten?" I asked, propping my head up so I could look at him, not realising his earlier question might have been more of a suggestion than an offer.

"I ate a late lunch, and I picked a bit when I was doing my meal preps, but I haven't had dinner, no." He made a face. "I can eat later, it's no big deal."

I sat up and tapped his chest. "You need to eat. Come on then, let's get you fed."

I pulled on my trackpants and shirt, leaving my hoodie off for now. Colson put on his jeans and sweater, looking more like a comfort snack now than he had when I'd arrived.

Maybe because his hair was ruffled from me running my hands through it, gripping it.

I stood in his kitchen, watching as he took some containers from his fridge. "Can I get you anything?" he asked. "A cup of tea?"

"A cup of tea sounds good, actually."

He took his kettle from the stovetop and filled it at the sink, then set it going before returning to his dinner. "Today's my weekend, so I do all my shopping and meal prep. Makes it easier to take meals to work," he said. Then he shrugged. "And it's not like my days off are action packed."

He dished up a small plate of rice and vegetables. "Are you sure you don't want any? I promise I'm not a terrible cook."

"That looks decidedly far too healthy for me," I replied. "Looks delicious, though."

He nuked it and put the containers back into the fridge, and what he'd said about his days off not being action packed made me remember . . .

"So," I hedged, wondering how to broach the subject. "About your weekends, do you have mates you hang out with?"

He gave half a shrug. "Sure. I mean, there are some guys at the station I can hang with. Ray goes hunting and fishing, so it's fun to tag along with him sometimes. And other times the boys will have a few beers at the bar." He gave me a bit of a sad smile. "It's tough, doing shift work and being in law enforcement. We tend to stick together. Not because civilians are bad or anything," he added with a smile. "Just the way it is."

I nodded because I understood that. I really did. "What do you do for fun? To wind down?"

The microwave beeped and he took his plate out. "I work out. Keeps me fit and it's good for clearing the mind."

I gestured to his body. "It's good for a lot of things."

He chuckled as he took a forkful. "I don't mean to be rude, eating in front of you."

I smiled at him. "You're too polite. Please eat it. It actually smells really good."

He raised his eyebrow and offered me his fork. "Wanna try it?"

I stepped in close and he gently fed me a forkful of rice and vegetables. I hummed as I chewed. "That's amazing!"

He seemed pleased by this. "Don't act so surprised."

I laughed. "You just might have to cook dinner for me one night."

His eyes met mine. "I just might."

The kettle began to whistle and I stopped him before he could put his plate down. "I'll get it." I found the mugs and, using one of the teabags I'd brought and helping myself to a dash of milk, made myself a cup of tea.

He watched as I took a sip. "Good?"

"Perfect."

He ate a few more bites of his dinner and while there was a beat of silence between us, my mind kept going back to what I had to ask him.

The dinner party.

But it didn't feel right. And after my conversation with Raeleen earlier today, maybe Colson was right to keep his truth to himself. It wasn't up to any of us to decide what was right for him. And the truth was, I had a week to broach the subject.

"So," I said. "Did you want to watch some TV, or do you want to draw up a tally sheet of the condom versus teabags game?"

He almost choked on some rice.

I patted his back and chuckled. "Because, with this cup of tea"—I held it up a little higher—"we're now down two-one. And as much as I absolutely love a good cup of tea—and I will always advocate for tea in the hot beverage debate—I just don't think this is a game tea should win."

Colson laughed, but he ate his dinner a bit quicker, washed it down with the last of my tea—grimacing at the taste —and he took me back to bed.

Teabags, 2. Condoms, 2.

Chapter Eight

COLSON

I woke up late on Tuesday. Braithe left my place around ten the night before, so it wasn't exactly a late night, but holy hell, I'd used some muscles I hadn't used in a long time.

Which probably also explained why I woke up, looked over to the very unkempt side of the bed, remembered him being face down and gripping the sheets, and smiled. Laughed, even.

I should have stripped the bed last night, but after two absolutely mind-blowing rounds of sex, I was too tired, too spent, and too damned happy.

Sex without strings had its benefits. I had no doubt of that. But I also liked him. It wasn't as if I didn't like the guy or that we had a deal where he'd walk through the door, we'd take care of business, and he left.

He stuck around a bit. We talked and laughed, and he really was a great guy. It was a shame he was only in town for a limited time.

Not that I could have anything more with him. But damn, what a thought. What a dream.

An unrealistic and unobtainable dream, but it was nice to

pretend. It was also kinda depressing, and it killed my buzz. I rolled out of bed, pulled the bedding with me, and made myself some breakfast while the washing machine did its thing.

Braithe was also coming over tonight; it was my last night off, after all. So maybe washing the sheets would be an effort in futility.

Maybe I should have waited until after.

Or maybe I could leave the scent of him over my sheets to keep me company all week . . .

Which was kinda gross and creepy. But damn, I half-considered it. After I'd lifted some weights, I took care of myself in the shower. What did Braithe call it? A lunchtime wank. With his cute British accent and even cuter smile.

But yes, I took care of that.

Despite the two rounds of sex last night, I was ready to keep going. Just thinking of Braithe, his lips, how he kissed me, how he tasted. His body and how he took me inside him, the sounds he made. Whimpers, groans, begging.

Yeah, a lunchtime wank was definitely in order. And again, like yesterday, it wasn't even ten in the morning.

How was I supposed to last again until seven o'clock tonight?

How I'd gone from a months-long drought to needing more than four orgasms in twenty-four hours was absurd.

I went for a jog, hoping the crisp air and blue skies would help clear my head. And it did, to some extent. I stopped to talk to old Mr Ling who needed some help covering some plants in his front yard to protect them from the snow that was coming.

And I stopped in the diner for some takeout, happy to chat with Christa and Carl behind the counter. I was a little disappointed Jayden wasn't there, but also kinda grateful he wasn't.

I considered heading to the hardware store, not that I needed anything, and I didn't need to see Ren, even if part of me wanted to reach out *just because*. For some kind of connection to the gay world I wasn't really a part of. So I bypassed his store and decided to go to the Home Mart on my way home.

I'd just gone shopping yesterday. But for some stupid reason, for some crazy foolish reason, I had a burning desire to buy some Christmas lights.

Why? Well, that was anyone's guess.

Maybe it was passing all the houses on my jog and seeing them all decorated. Maybe it was seeing all the stores on Main Street with twinkling lights. Or maybe it was just nice to feel festive after so many years of not letting myself celebrate.

I'd always thought I needed family to celebrate with, and after all, that's all I'd ever known.

But what did Braithe say?

You're allowed to do things just for you too. In fact, it's the best reason there is.

Yeah. I was allowed to do things just for me too. So you know what? Some Christmas lights sounded like a good idea. And maybe it was foolish, but I was ridiculously excited when Braithe turned up at my place just after seven.

"Good evening," he said, walking in and giving me a soft kiss. God, he smelled sweet, like honey.

"Hm, hey."

Braithe looked around then, only noticing the low light. "Why is it dark in here?"

"I wanted to show you something."

His eyes cut to mine, and he smiled. It was stupid that I felt nervous or even a bit like a kid again. But I went over and turned the kitchen light off and the hall light, then I flipped the Christmas light switch on.

Soft colours lit up my living room. I'd draped the string of lights across the front window and along the picture rail above the TV all the way over to the kitchen, and between the glow of the fire and the warm flickering Christmas lights, it looked pretty damn good. Even if I did say so myself.

It had taken two packs of lights, but it was so worth it.

"I was going to get the plain white lights, and maybe I could have left them up all year, but I thought the coloured ones were more Christmassy, and you probably think it's stupid, but I haven't really celebrated Christmas in a while and—"

He came and stood behind me, his arms sliding around to my belly, looking at the lights over my shoulder. "It's beautiful."

"Do you think? I don't know what possessed me today to get them, I just . . . I just wanted to. I haven't wanted to celebrate Christmas in a long time. But I wanted to do it. Today. I wanted to do it . . . today."

He turned me around and cupped my face. "Merry Christmas, Colson," he murmured before kissing me again. "It looks amazing. Everything is soft and glowing, and it's perfect."

I was just glad he didn't think I was being stupid. He didn't ask why I hadn't celebrated Christmas in a while, he just accepted it. He didn't push me, and I was grateful for that.

"I'm glad you decided today was the day," he said, his eyes glittering with kindness and honesty. "I mean, I'll try not to believe it was the amazing sex we had last night that had you waking up feeling extra festive."

I chuckled. "I woke up feeling some kinda way this morning. Not sure festive was the right word. Closer to horny, I think. Though I don't even know how I could still want more after all we've done."

He let out a warm rumble of laughter, sliding his hands down over my arse, pulling our hips flush together. He was already half hard and it sent a thrill through me. "I woke up much the same way." He sighed happily, smiling up at me. "Maybe we could leave the ceiling lights off," he murmured. "And we could lie on the couch by the fire under the Christmas lights, and you could kiss me all night."

I cupped his jaw and brought his lips to mine. "Hm, I have no objections to that."

He smirked and grinded against me a little. "Or you could take me to bed and do to me what you did to me last night. I haven't been able to think about anything else all day."

"Oh god," I breathed. "Don't make me decide."

Braithe laughed. "Okay, both it is. Those teabags don't stand a chance." He led me to the couch, falling back onto it and pulling me with him. He manoeuvred us a little, adjusting his hips and pulling one of the cushions out from behind his back with a laugh. But I settled in between his legs all too easily, and I tried to take my time kissing him.

I wanted to go slow, to drag it out, to enjoy every moment.

But as soon as our tongues touched, his hand found my hair, raking and pulling, and my self-control lost the fight.

It became a fever of desire and arousal, seeing which of us could kiss harder, dig deeper, moan louder.

I wanted him like this. I wanted him every way he'd let me have him.

And he did let me have him. Twice.

Once right there on the couch, still dressed, with mutual and impatient hands. And once later in bed with more patience and time to explore every thread of pleasure. Every inch of skin, every valley of his body, every touch that made him gasp and groan.

It felt like hours, but at the same time, it went by too fast. He left closer to midnight, and even that was too soon. I wanted to sleep next to him; I wanted to know what it felt like to hold him all night and wake up beside him.

I wanted to kiss him good morning and make him breakfast.

I wanted more than my life here in Hartbridge could allow.

And I wanted it far too soon.

I'd known him for a handful of days. Sure, we'd shared laughter and our bodies, but I didn't know him. Well, I knew some things. That he was smart and kind and that he never cussed or swore. I knew he had a great sense of humour and that he closed his eyes for that first sip of tea. He had a mole on his lower back and one on his hip.

I knew he was only staying in Hartbridge for three more weeks, and I knew I'd have a gaping hole in my life when he left.

A hole to remind me forever of what I so desperately want, and that I cannot have.

And it had been, what, ten days since I'd first laid eyes on him? Eleven? Yep. I was in way over my head already.

It wasn't him, per se. It wasn't Braithe, exactly. It was what he represented, what he could never be.

And it was that heavy, sinking feeling that I went to work with. Grateful for the distraction and for work to keep me busy. To take my ever-thinking mind off him.

"Everything okay, deputy?" Charity asked.

The office had gone quiet and I had no clue what I'd missed. A few people were watching me, so I'd clearly missed something.

"Yeah, sorry," I said, straightening up in my chair. "Just thinking." I gave her my best positive-attention face. "What were you saying?"

"I was saying," she went on, clearly having to repeat what she'd just said. "Secret Santa gifts this year. Limit of ten bucks. You in?"

Oh, thank god. I thought it had been something important. "Sure. Why not?"

It also didn't hurt that I'd grabbed a few gifts the other day when I was shopping in Mossley with Braithe. I hadn't needed to then, I just wanted him to think I had people to buy for.

Maybe this year I did.

Ah, jeez. Should I get him something?

I think maybe I should.

But what?

What on earth did I get for him?

I pulled out my phone and searched up *teabag gifts* and somehow mistyped it, then got a whole lotta pics and links for porn.

What the hell?

What the hell was teabagging?

Sweet heavens have mercy.

Thank god I hadn't searched for that on my desk computer!

Ronny coming through the door with a heavy sigh made me almost drop my phone. I fumbled with it before I could turn it off and slam it face down on my desk.

"What's up?"

He took off his coat and hung it on his hook. "Just had a meeting with the mayor."

His frown didn't bode well. "Oh?"

"I'm double-booked," he said. "Mayor wants to hold a town meeting. Late notice, but it's a small business thing and he wants to get it done before Christmas. I should attend."

I wasn't sure where he was going with this. "What can I do to help?"

"You know how I normally go down to the elementary school every year and give a talk to the little ones about fire safety with the fire marshal." He waved his hand. "And Doug brings the fire truck down and one of the guys dresses up as Santa. It's a whole thing, and the kids love it."

Oh.

He wanted me to go in his place.

Wait. To the school? Or to the meeting?

"I'd be happy to fill in for you, boss," I said.

Please be the school. Please be the school. Please be the school . . .

Ronny sighed again. "You don't mind? The kids get all excited and I love seeing their happy little faces. It'll be a shame to miss it this year."

Oh, heck yes. I was going to the school. I had to bite the inside of my mouth so I didn't grin. "Yeah, sure. I don't mind one bit. It'll be fun."

I was going to see Braithe in his classroom.

He grimaced. "It's tomorrow."

"That's fine," I said, trying to play it cool.

Ronny nodded. "Thanks. I'll go call the school now and tell them to expect you instead of me."

I tried not to smile too wide. "Okay. Let me know what I gotta do." I mean, how hard could it be? "Do I have to bring anything?"

Ronny's smile became a grin. "You got no experience in dealing with a bunch of five-year-olds, do ya, son?"

Uh . . . "No, sir."

Charity laughed from her desk. "Oh boy. I'd love to be a

fly on the wall." Their chiding and mockery aside, I was excited. Sure, getting to play deputy to a bunch of kids sounded fun. Better than desk work, that was for certain. But I was most excited to see Braithe in his classroom.

To see him anywhere would be a thrill, but at his work, in his element?

I gave Ronny a nod. "Already looking forward to it, sir."

JUST AFTER NINE O'CLOCK, the office was quiet, almost empty. Just me, Charity, and Bouchard. The cleaners had been and gone, and the night outside was dark and cold. Snow would be coming any day now, and it wouldn't stop for months.

The police scanner and our radios were the only sound.

It was a typical quiet night in Hartbridge.

I'd be heading out in the cruiser shortly, just for a dutiful lap through the streets, making sure the world was right. Just like I did every night when it was quiet like this.

My phone buzzed on my desk.

I snatched it up, not paying enough attention to the number. Half the town had my number. I hit Answer. "Deputy Price speaking."

"Oh, is this the Deputy Price of the Hartbridge sheriff's department, call sign C2?"

His voice was warm and smooth and very British.

I laughed, and hell, I think I even blushed. Thank god Bouchard wasn't looking at me.

"Why, yes it is."

Braithe sighed. "Oh, thank goodness. I'd hate to have called the wrong number." I was still smiling, still blushing. Which was ridiculous, but damn, just hearing his voice made me happy. I went into the breakroom and closed the door. It was mostly glass and I could still see Bouchard at his desk, but at least now I was afforded a little privacy. "And to what do I owe the pleasure?"

"Oh. You see, I thought I should speak to the very nice deputy who was coming to my classroom tomorrow." He sounded as if he was smiling. "Was it out of line for me to use this information provided to me in a professional setting? Because if you feel the need to reprimand me . . ."

I chuckled. "It's fine."

"Are you sure? Because if you feel the need to come by my place and serve me . . . with something . . . I won't mind."

Oh damn.

My dick was definitely listening.

"I'm at work," I said, half-hearted at best.

"What time do you finish?"

"I usually get home after midnight."

He sighed. "That's a shame."

I scrubbed my hand over my face, trying to convince my dick to calm down. "Did you call me to specifically torture me?"

He laughed. "I'm sorry. Is that a federal offence? Should you come by and issue an official warning?"

"Braithe," I said, half-warning, half-pleading.

"Hmm." Now it sounded like he was pouting. Which didn't help. At all. "Okay, sorry. I'll be good. I just wanted to talk to you, that's all. And then I was given your number to call if something were to change about tomorrow. I mean, I already had it because you gave it to me, but it seemed like a little birdie was dropping a gift right in my lap as a sign that I should call you."

"It's okay. It's fine, actually. I'm glad you called. I'm just on duty right now."

He was quiet for a moment. "You're glad I called?"

It felt like the hole I'd dug for myself was getting bigger and bigger, and yet, I couldn't stop shovelling. "Yes. You sound . . . comfortable and warm."

He hummed. "I'm in bed."

"Christ."

He laughed, and the sound warmed me right under the ribs. "I'm watching a frightful documentary. Did you know, on a small island in Japan, there's a crab that grows as big as a dog? Some are one metre across, from spindly toe to spindly toe. It's the stuff of nightmares."

I snorted. "You know I've never heard anyone use the words frightful and spindly in one breath."

"Is that what you took away from what I said? Not the part about there being a crustacean as big as a dog. On this planet, Colson. The very one we live on. Granted, I don't see myself going to this particular island in Japan in this lifetime. Or the next, now that I've seen what lives there. But still . . . a crab. As big as a dog. I think there may have been a glitch in the evolution matrix."

I laughed. I mean, I had no clue what to follow up with after everything he'd said, but boy, I sure did like the sound of his voice.

"I suppose I should let you go," he added with a sigh.

"I suppose," I replied. "I'm really glad you took the initiative and decided to call me instead of texting."

He laughed at that, but then he sighed. "I'm looking forward to seeing you at school on Thursday," he said. "Ten o'clock, don't be late. You have eighteen students and one teacher very excited for your visit. I'd hate for you to disappoint them."

"The kids, or the teacher?"

"I think there are valid arguments for both."

I was grinning like a fool, my heart thumping hard. "I'd hate to disappoint either."

He chuckled. "Good night, C2. I feel safer knowing you're watching the town tonight."

His words . . . That. What he just said burned right behind my sternum. "Night," I managed to whisper, despite the lack of air in my lungs.

I sat there, my ass against the table, trying to catch my breath, when Bouchard tapped on the door and opened it. He stuck his head through. "Everything okay?"

"Oh, yeah. Everything's good."

Real good. Best it's been in a long time.

He didn't seem too interested in my reply. "Okay. I'm gonna do a lap. You can stay inside where it's warm if you want."

Sometimes we alternated; sometimes he went, sometimes I did. It was no big deal either way. "Yeah, that'd be great," I replied.

He gave a nod, pulled his coat on as he walked out, and I sat my ass at my desk and did a quick Google search. I wasn't sure how to word it so I opted for the simple, honest truth. Surely, I couldn't be the only clueless person on the planet.

Gift ideas for someone you're not supposed to like but do.

Chapter Nine

BRAITHE

"No, I didn't ask him. It wasn't the right time," I said, ignoring the pointed look Hamish was giving me. It was agreed the dinner party wasn't solely for Colson, but for the whole group, still, I'd said I'd ask him. "But I'm seeing him tomorrow."

"You are?"

"At the school. He's coming along with the fire department. It's a fire-safety talk."

"They still do that?" Ren asked.

We were standing in his hardware store. I'd come in to find some things for the Christmas play my class was putting on. Hamish had heard me speaking with Ren at the counter, and he'd come out from the office with one very cute dog at his feet.

I kinda got the feeling going anywhere in Hartbridge without running into someone was a rarity.

Ren smiled with a sigh, clearly recalling a fond memory. "They did that when I went to school there, all those years ago. They bring down the fire truck and we all got to climb up on it. It was awesome."

"I'm looking forward to it," I said. "All the kids are very excited."

"But you're not interested in climbing the fire truck, are you?" Hamish murmured. Thank god there was no one else around.

"Oh shush," I scolded him. "Come and help me find the paint."

Hamish pointed the way and I followed him to one aisle in particular. "What do you need paint for?"

"For the backdrop of the Christmas play I'm putting on. I got permission to use the classroom on the weekend to get it done." I gasped and grabbed his arm. "Oh, thank you so much for volunteering to help!"

Hamish stared at me. "I did no such thing."

"It's really kind of you."

He rolled his eyes and let out a fake annoyed sigh. "What time?"

I grinned at him. "Nine o'clock?"

He narrowed his stare. "One condition. I want all the details—every single juicy one—of how hot things get with a certain deputy. Understood?"

I laughed. "Deal." I leaned in. "Because it's hot. And I mean hot. He has years of pent-up frustrations, and when it's a long time between drinks, a man gets thirsty. Know what I'm saying?"

His smile was wicked. "Oh my god, I love you."

I laughed and looked at the paint selection. Most of it was paint for houses and the like, but there was a small selection of other types. "Okay, which is non-toxic? And water-based."

He crouched down and found me a few bottles: blue, white, yellow, black. "What scene are you painting anyway?"

"What scene will *we* be painting?" I corrected. "A nativity scene. The stable, sky, a few palms maybe."

"Aww, how cute!"

"Kindergarteners are the star of the whole day," I said. "They are just as cute as buttons." Then I had an even better idea. "You should come to the end-of-year concert. It's like a Christmas fun day. There'll be cake stalls and crafts, and the class plays, of course."

Hamish smiled and patted my arm. "I'll let Ren know. I think Cass's kids are involved too, so they'll probably be there."

"Oh, of course. His kids are in grades six and four, right?"

He made a face. "I think so. That sounds about right. Jayden has told me, but you know . . ." He sighed. "When you don't have kids . . ."

Oh.

"Did you want kids?"

He stared at me as if I'd sprouted a second head. "Are you crazy? No. I have a niece and nephew down in Mossley and I adore them. I spoil them rotten, and I would die for them. But I like having a disposable income, free time, and a clean house. Thanks for asking."

I laughed because I got that. I saw what parents went through. Parents of the kids at school, but also my sister back in England. I saw what she went through, and being a teacher myself, I knew how exhausting it could be. Kids were hard work.

"Plus," he added, "we have Chutney. She's our baby."

"Chutney? As in the condiment, or the girl from *Legally Blonde*?"

Hamish gasped and gripped my arm again. "Oh, you are so one of us. Are you sure you don't want to apply for a permanent position here?"

I laughed. "Maybe. If there was one."

Would I? Could I?

It sure sounded nice. Great friends, gorgeous town, great school.

Great deputy.

As amazing as that sounded, it just wasn't possible. Even if I wanted it, if I wanted it all, it wasn't something I could have. My position here was for four weeks only. I needed to work to stay in the country, and that was the bottom line. I'd have to move on eventually.

As if he could see where my thoughts had taken me, Hamish's smile became a frown and he quickly changed the subject. "Now, what else did you need?"

THE KIDS WERE SO excited for the visitors, especially the fire truck, and sure, the sheriff's cruiser was going to be a hit too.

I was more excited for the deputy.

Not that I let on but seeing the kids bursting with excitement made me extra giddy too. And when Principal O'Connor knocked on the classroom door to announce two very special guests, my stomach was full of knots.

Until Colson entered in full uniform, and those knots turned to skittering butterflies.

Those well-fitting trousers and his tight shirt and his broad-brimmed hat. He wore his holster, and now, I was absolutely no fan of guns, but oh boy, did it make him look hotter.

He grinned at the kids, looking almost as excited as they were.

Principal O'Connor introduced him. "Okay, class, this is Deputy Price. Deputy, this is our kindergarten teacher, Mr Branson."

Colson's eyes met mine, and he chewed on the inside of

his lip to stop from smiling too wide. "Good morning, Mr Branson."

Oh-so different to how he'd said goodnight last night on the phone, all sultry whispers and longing.

Then he turned back to the class and gave a wave. "And good morning to everyone."

Oh, he was just the cutest thing.

Then Principal O'Connor introduced the man who was with Colson. To be honest, I hadn't even noticed him come in. Probably not good on my behalf—I should be aware at all times—but I'd been so distracted by a certain someone else.

"And this is fireman Sergeant De Silva."

He was about my age, maybe older, and wore a navy-blue uniform jumpsuit and a big fireman hat that the kids clearly loved. He was as fit-looking as Colson; his big fireman coat did little to hide the muscled body underneath.

He took his hat off, tucked it under his arm, and grinned at the kids. He was handsome, no doubt about it. He was well-tanned, had a crewcut of brown hair, blue eyes, and a square jaw.

But my eyes kept drawing back to Colson.

Were the tops of his ears pink?

Was he embarrassed or nervous?

It made me jump in and direct the conversation. "Okay, class, I know we're all very excited, but these two officers are here to talk about something very important. So, we're going to put on our best listening ears, okay?"

Colson smiled at me, taking a second to realise the kids were waiting for him to speak first.

"Okay, put your hand up if you have a wood fireplace at your home," he began.

Then he and Sergeant De Silva pinballed off each other about keeping safe around fires and what to do in an emergency. The way he spoke so animatedly, so perfectly, for a bunch of five-year-olds, just made me like him all that much more.

They made it fun while reinforcing danger and seriousness, and when it was question time, they showed patience and kindness.

And then it was time for all the kids to try on Sergeant De Silva's fireman hat.

Colson angled his way closer to me. He was smiling when he nodded to the row of painted red double-decker buses. "Not hard to tell whose idea that was."

Damn, if I didn't have to shove my hands in my back pockets so I didn't touch him.

"And the little Christmas trees." He pointed his chin to the windowsills where all the little popsicle-stick Christmas trees had been left to dry. "Did you make me one?"

I laughed. "Would you like me to make you one? I only have about a thousand ice lolly sticks left."

He snorted. "Ice lolly? What is that?"

"Ice lolly. Like a popsicle."

He grinned. "That's the most English thing you've ever said."

"Excuse me, mister deputy," James said. "Can I try your hat on?"

Colson took off his hat and put it on James' head. "You sure can. But that makes you an honorary deputy when you have it on your head, okay?"

James was most thrilled, and then his hat got passed around to all the kids, and when he went to save his hat from Declan and Gracie, Sergeant De Silva came over to me.

"Thanks for letting us come in today," he said. He had kind eyes.

"Oh, we're thrilled to have you," I said. "The children have been so excited all week, looking forward to seeing the fire truck, apparently."

His smile produced a dimple, and his eyes met mine, and . . . there was a look.

Oh.

"My name's Soren," he said. "Mr . . . Branson, was it?"

Yep. Definite interest.

Gee whiz.

"Right then," Colson said, suddenly appearing beside me. Much closer to me than he was to Soren, the sexy fireman. "Shall we take them out to the trucks?"

Yes, we absolutely should.

"Okay class," I said, using my teacher voice. "I need two very neat walking lines. Line up at the door."

And so we marched out of the classroom, down the hall, to the front doors of the school. And sure enough, parked outside was a big shiny red fire truck, and a very familiar sheriff's cruiser.

There was another fireman by the truck. He'd obviously been waiting all this time and probably had to stay with the truck. He was older, with grey hair, rocking a hot body, a huge smile, and a Santa hat. He introduced himself as Fireman Doug.

Was everyone in this town gorgeous?

We divided the class into two groups of nine. Doug and Soren took the kids to explore the fire truck, while I helped Colson with the kids and his cruiser.

They couldn't do much, but they got to sit up in the passenger seat and look at all the buttons on the dash, and they could turn the blue and red lights on but no siren, thankfully.

Colson was just so great.

He was fun and patient and answered all their questions, but admittedly, the fire truck was cooler.

Well, the kids thought so.

And I didn't even mind because it gave me a chance to chat with Colson while the kids overtook the truck like ants.

"Thank you so much for doing this," I said, keeping it professional.

"You're welcome. It's great fun. Better than doing paperwork." He helped one of the kids down from the step on the side of the truck. He came back to me and gave me that smile that made my knees weak. "And I got to see your classroom."

I was trying not to smile too much or give myself away. But it was futile. "I think you should come past my place when you finish tonight."

He made a serious face, as if we could be discussing the snowstorm they'd predicted for next week. "Won't be till after midnight. Closer to one."

I noticed then that Sergeant De Silva was watching us, so I gave Colson a nod, kept my face neutral, and my voice low. "I'll set my alarm."

I went to help Emily climb down, and I didn't get another chance to speak to Colson before their time was up. I made the whole class say thank you and goodbye, then stand in a line on the path, and much to their delight, when the fire truck drove off, Doug waved out the window, flashed the red lights, and gave a quick whir of the siren.

The kids all jumped and squealed, and then Colson put his lights on and flicked his siren on for half a second, earning more jumpy claps from the kids before they waved until long after both vehicles were gone.

It was much excitement, which led to a rowdy lunchtime and tired little minds before home time.

But all in all, a great day.

And it was going to get decidedly better, somewhere between midnight and one o'clock.

After dinner, when I was showered and snug and warm in my bed, I sent him a text.

I heard the stars are extra pretty at 12.30 a.m. I think I'll set my alarm.

His reply came through a few minutes later.

Stars?

I grinned as I replied.

The ones behind my eyelids. The ones you'll make me see.

A moment later, my phone rang in my hand. Instead of saying hello, he chuckled, warm and delicious. "Stars? Really?"

"Yes. It's a new constellation called orgasm. It's amazing."

He laughed louder. "Are you trying to kill me? I'm at work right now."

I hummed happily. "I'm sorry. Do you need to make a house call to issue a reprimand or something? I promise there will be no resisting arrest."

He groaned. "After midnight."

"Walk down the driveway at the side of the house. My light will be on, the door will be unlocked."

His half-strangled moan was all I heard before he disconnected the call. I set my alarm for midnight, giddy and ridiculously happy, and desire began to pool low in my belly; warm, buzzing.

I felt like I was a kid waiting for Christmas. Only this time I wasn't waiting for Santa.

I WOKE with a start at my alarm, disoriented and confused. I hadn't slept long enough, and it was far too dark and . . . then I remembered.

I shot out of bed and unlocked my front door, flipping on

the light by my door, and I was brushing my teeth when I heard a gentle knock on the door.

Hard to be sexy when you're smiling with a foamy toothbrush in your mouth.

Colson came in and closed the door, leaning against it. He smiled at me, shaking his head, and hit the light switch, casting us both in nothing but the muted light from my bathroom.

"Evening, officer," I said, taking my toothbrush out. "Anything I can help you with?"

He groaned out a laugh and ran his hand down to his crotch, gripping a rather large problem he had there. "Ah, yeah, I think so. Did you know giving an officer of the law a hard-on four hours before the promise of seeing stars could be construed as an obstruction of the law?"

I grinned, liking where this was going. "Oh no," I said. "Will the punishment fit the crime?" I looked down and eyed the offending hard-on. "I mean, we know it fits."

He took three long strides toward me, took my face in his hands, and kissed me, toothpaste and all. "You were sent to test me, weren't you," he murmured.

I laughed. "You started it by coming into my classroom this morning in your sexy outfit."

"Uniform," he growled.

I dragged my finger down the buttons of his shirt. "Being all cute and wonderful with the kids."

"I was just doing my job."

"And did I mention the uniform?"

His gaze met mine, and I realised I was still holding the toothbrush. I went into my bathroom and tossed it into the cup and rinsed my mouth, and when I turned around, he was standing in the doorway, leaning against the jamb, smiling.

"Why were you brushing your teeth at midnight?"

"Because I'd been asleep and I wanted you to enjoy kissing me."

He slow-smiled. "I already do enjoy kissing you." I walked over to him, trying to be seductive, even though I was in my pyjamas and had bed hair. He didn't seem to mind.

"Now, about those stars," I said. "I'm ready to see them whenever you are."

"I've been ready since your phone call at nine o'clock."

I chuckled and palmed his erection. "Then take me to bed, Deputy."

He hummed and slid his jacket off, letting it fall to the floor, then took my face in both his hands and walked me backwards to my bed. We fell on it, him landing on top of me, keeping me secure against him, and he crushed his mouth to mine.

The kiss was deep and demanding, sending jolts of electricity through me.

I widened my legs to accommodate him, and he fit so perfectly. I hooked my ankles at his back and he grinded against me, our erections rubbing through our clothes.

I needed more. I needed to feel him, skin on skin. I needed this feeling to never end.

I broke the kiss, gasping for my oxygen-deprived brain to think . . . *Trousers, idiot. Undo his trousers.*

Right, yes.

"Trousers," I mumbled, trying to get my hands between us, trying to get his belt undone.

He leaned up on his knees, undid his belt, and popped the button. He had a small wet spot near his hip, and god, it almost did me in. All I could do was watch.

"Condom?" he asked.

I snatched the foil packet and small tube of lube from the

bedside, and he only then seemed to realise he still had his boots on. "Shit," he said, pulling at the laces.

"Leave them on," I said, rolling over onto my stomach and sliding my pyjama bottoms down over my arse. "Do me like this."

He gasped and didn't move. "Are you . . . sure?"

"Colson," I said, short on patience. I slid my hand underneath me, raising my hips a little so I could get a proper hold of my cock. I began to stroke and that was all it took for him to move.

He was quickly between my legs, rolling the condom on and applying lube to us both. A slippery finger, then two, and before I could lose the rest of my patience, he leaned over me, his blunt cockhead pressed against my hole.

"I wanted to take my time with you," he whispered, hot and rough against my ear. "But you make me want you so bad."

"Please, just do it," I begged. I was getting desperate, aching with the need for it. I raised my arse, pushing against him, and he got the message.

He sank into me, pushing deep and breaching me in the best of ways. God, he felt so good, and knowing he was fully dressed, that he wanted me so bad he couldn't wait, was such a thrill.

I pressed my forehead into the pillow and arched my back, taking him in one long push. I tried not to groan too loudly, but then he was pressed against my back, his arm under my chest, and he drove up.

I cried out, trying to bite it back, and he groaned in my ear. "You're so tight," he said, his voice strained. "Feel so good."

My breath came out in a rush, and I relaxed into it, letting him set the pace and have full control. He began the slow glide, rocking us back and forth, so deep inside me, deeper with every thrust.

He kissed my shoulder, my nape, my ear.

"You drive me crazy," he murmured. "All I think about is you. Kissing you, being inside you. Like this." He moaned and shuddered with restraint. "God, Braithe."

The way he said my name . . .

Drove me crazy.

I raised my arse to meet him, gasping at the different angle. So I did it again and again, sparks igniting inside me.

But then he gripped my hips and angled me perfectly, driving into me over and over, scraping sparks along every nerve until they finally caught. Fire ripped through me, so exquisite, such ecstasy, it danced with pain.

I came so hard, like I'd never felt before. I cried, actual tears, overwhelmed and ruined in the very best of ways. I was only barely aware that he'd climaxed too. I was so consumed, so obliterated, I couldn't think . . .

He collapsed on top of me, holding me, his cock softening inside me. I almost wept when he pulled out and he was quick to roll us over and pull me into his arms.

"Are you okay?" He was concerned, holding me so tight, rubbing my back. I laughed and cried some more, my hands still shaking. "I am so good right now," I said. A tremor rocked through me, making me laugh and groan.

"Are you cold?"

I laughed, sounding a little hysterical. "Ah, not at all. That was probably the most intense orgasm I think I've ever had."

There was a brief pause, then he snorted. "Oh."

"I mentioned seeing stars before, but I think I just saw the whole galaxy." Another tremor hit me, leaving me shuddering and laughing. "I think you just gave me my first prostate orgasm."

He laughed, sounding surprised and a little proud. "Maybe I should leave my boots on more often."

"You can come around at midnight every night," I said. "If you'll do that to me."

He scoffed. "No pressure then."

I chuckled, feeling warm and safe, and once the tremors stopped, the boneless, spongy feeling crept over me. "Can't move," I murmured, suddenly not able to keep my eyes open. "So spent."

He sighed and rubbed my back, softly kissing the side of my head. "I can't stay."

I whined, actually whined, and snuggled into him. I knew he couldn't stay, and it wasn't fair of me to add my guilt to his own. "I have no bones," I mumbled. "Can't move."

He chuckled a little, kissed my temple, and rolled off the bed. He came back with the washcloth from my bathroom, cleaned me up a bit, then pulled the bed covers up and tucked me in. When I cracked my eyes open, he had his coat back on.

I mean, he hadn't undressed at all while he was here. It really was an efficient way to fuck.

Except my bed felt empty. I would have loved to have slept in his arms all night.

He brushed my hair back from my forehead and kissed my lips softly. "I'll call you tomorrow."

I smiled, not sure if I was dreaming, knowing I probably was, hoping I wasn't.

Still too obliterated to move, I slept like the dead.

Chapter Ten

COLSON

I WOKE up on Friday feeling kinda strange.

I'd slept well. After leaving Braithe's at almost one in the morning, I got home, had a steaming-hot shower, and fell into bed.

I'd wanted to stay with him. I'd wanted to, so badly. And leaving him in his bed and walking out was the hardest thing I'd done.

Okay, *not* the hardest.

But man, I ached to stay with him.

My chest still burned when I woke up at nine. He'd have been at work for hours already, and I couldn't get that heavy ache from my chest.

Sex last night had been different.

Not just the fact we were too keyed up to take our time, too fuelled by passion and desire to even take off my boots, I'd had my way with him fully dressed. Hell, his pyjama pants were barely pulled down over his ass before I entered him.

And I'd had plenty of rushed encounters with strangers where taking our time and general pleasantries weren't high on the list. There was nothing wrong with that.

But last night . . . it wasn't the rush or the desire. It wasn't the thrill of nailing him to his bed while I was still in full uniform.

It was how he'd shaken and trembled, how he'd cried and laughed, how I'd held him tighter than I'd ever held anyone. It still wasn't tight enough. I was *inside* him, and it still wasn't close enough.

I'd kissed him, tasted him, held him, fucked him, and it still wasn't enough.

And I knew, I knew all too well, that it wasn't the physical things I was craving.

It was the emotional things. It was the connection to another person. The closeness. The human contact.

I wanted it so bad.

And that was the cause of the heavy burning in my chest.

The longing.

I'd like to think it wasn't Braithe in particular. It was just *someone*. But there was also that little voice in the back of my mind that told me no, it was him.

All him.

His blond hair that shone like spun gold in the sun. His pale skin that flushed pink on his cheeks and down his throat. His blue eyes and pink lips. His accent . . .

His laughter. How he talked with his hands. How he was in his classroom with his students.

Yeah.

The ache in my chest was my own doing.

I knew what I was getting into. I knew what he was offering—sex without strings—and I'd dived in headfirst regardless. I thought I could do the no-attachment thing.

But one taste of perfection and I doubted my sanity.

I couldn't have *perfection* because I couldn't come out.

Could I?

Would I lose my job?

Not directly. They couldn't fire me for being gay, but they could make me so miserable I left.

Wouldn't be the first time.

And the ache in my chest grew bigger, making it just that much harder to breathe.

I made myself go for a run.

Putting in a few miles between me and my problems had always worked before, and yet somehow, as my own feet betrayed me, I found myself jogging down Hickory Street.

Right past Hartbridge Elementary School.

His car was there. Because of course it was.

And just like that, the ache was heavier.

So I ran faster, ran farther. Pushed myself until my lungs burned and my legs were like Jell-O. It helped.

I got to work, feeling marginally better. Of course, Ronny called me right into his office.

"Heard you were great at the school yesterday," he said. "Might find myself out of a job soon enough."

I laughed it off. "Not likely, sir."

He smiled. "Not yet anyway. Got a few years left in me."

"I should hope so."

"The office staff tells me there's a Secret Santa thing on this year. I know you don't like to—"

"I already said I'll go in it," I said.

He was surprised to hear this, clearly. "Oh, good, that's good." His face softened with a smile. "Glad to hear that."

I nodded. "Felt right to . . ." Jeez. "To try and celebrate the holidays this year. I, uh . . . I even put lights up at home."

"Good for you, Colson." He studied me for a second. "Any particular reason this year's different?"

We'd never really divulged personal stories. He knew I never liked the holidays and that I had no family. He probably knew those two reasons went hand in hand, but he knew it wasn't something I liked to talk about. He also knew I could separate my work from my personal life, so he never had cause to question me. Just some things we talked about, some things we didn't. He might have been curious a time or two, but he never pushed.

Until now.

"No reason," I replied. "Just thought it was about time."

He managed a pained smile. "Well, I'm glad. Look, if you ever need to talk, you know my door's open, day or night."

"Yes, sir."

"The holidays aren't an easy time for everyone."

I took a deep breath, trying to calm myself. I really didn't feel up to this today. "I know, sir."

He'd always been adept at reading people, and I should have given him more credit. He'd started this conversation just talking about the school thing yesterday but clearly saw I wasn't in the right frame of mind.

"If you need a day off—"

"I need to be here," I said. "I need to be busy. So, if you have anything that needs to be done, filing or old jobs, or follow-up calls or visits that we've been putting off, I'm your guy."

He studied me again, maybe hoping his scrutiny would make me divulge more. Instead, I spread my feet a little, joined my hands behind my back, raised my chin, and remained silent.

I could do this all day.

Eventually, he conceded defeat with a nod. "All right then," he began.

"Uh, Deputy Price," Charity called out from across the office. "You got a visitor."

A visitor?

I never got visitors . . .

I went to the door, not knowing who to expect, maybe Mr Ling who promised me some pickled lemons at some point—not that I expected him to bring them to me—but there was literally no one else in my life . . .

There, at the counter, stood Braithe.

He was wearing his white knitted sweater with his grey scarf and an uncertain smile. But he was holding a Christmas tree made from green painted popsicle sticks with little pompom balls stuck on it.

"Hello," he said. "I hope I'm not interrupting. The students wanted to make a thank-you gift for coming to speak to them yesterday and bringing your cruiser and letting them wear your hat."

I'd been joking when I'd said I wanted one.

But now . . .

Damned if I didn't have to swallow back tears. "They made that for me?"

Braithe, who had looked about ready to apologise, finally smiled. "There are eighteen sticks; they painted one each. And there are eighteen little baubles. They each picked a colour."

Oh.

My nose burned and I wasn't sure I should speak.

Braithe stared at me, his smile now a look of concern. "I'm sorry," he said gently. "I should have called first. If now isn't a good time . . ."

I took the tree, my fingers brushing his. "No, it's fine. It's perfect, actually. I, uh—"

Ronny was suddenly beside me, his strong hand a reassuring grip on my arm. "Ah, I knew they'd like you more than me because I never got a tree in all the years I've been giving the fire-safety talk." He grinned at Braithe. "You must be the new teacher."

"Yes, Braithe Branson," he replied with a smile.

"Sheriff Ronny Harper," he said, his huge hand engulfing Braithe's when they shook hands. "Tell me, did Doug the fireman get a tree made 'specially for him too? Kids always like the fire truck more, and he never lets me forget it."

Braithe looked up at him. "Well, yes. Though it was Sergeant De Silva who did the talk, not Doug."

"Ah," Ronny said. "We're both passing the baton on to the next generation." He looked at me, though I didn't dare make eye contact with him.

God, why was I such a mess today?

Stupid emotions. Been bottled up so long . . .

Braithe gestured to the door. "I have another little tree the kids made in my car to take down to the fire station next. I thought I'd come here first." Braithe's eyes cut to mine. "So I better get going."

I swallowed past the lump in my throat. "Yeah, of course. Thank you. I, uh, I'm not quite sure what to say. Tell the kids I said thank you. Tell them it's the best gift I could have ever gotten."

He took a step backward toward the exit. "Right then," he said.

This wasn't good.

This whole day wasn't good.

I put the tree on the service counter. "Actually, if you have a second," I said, opening the door for him. I waited for him to say his goodbyes and I was probably way out of line, but I had to say something . . .

He walked the few yards to his car. "I'm so sorry," he said quickly, panicked. "I should have called first."

"No, it's fine," I said. "Look . . ." I took a breath, wishing I was still wearing my coat. "It hasn't been a great day. That's not your fault in any way; you just caught me off guard.

Actually, Ronny caught me off guard with some personal stuff a minute before you walked in, and I wasn't expecting . . ." I shook my head and tried to let out a long breath, hoping to start again. "I didn't want you to think it was you."

He shoved his hands in his pockets. "I'll tell you what. It's Friday night. I was going to grab some takeout from the diner and bring it home, but I think I'll grab enough for two and hang out at your place and wait for you to get there."

"Uh . . . what?"

"If that's okay with you," he went on to say, though I wasn't sure I was getting a say in it at all. "When you get home, no matter what time it is, your house will be nice and warm. We can eat dinner—I think today's special is beef stew and mash, and with this cold weather that sounds pretty good. And you can tell me what's bothering you because you shouldn't be alone."

"You don't have to do—"

"I'm the only one in this town who can, Colson," he said. "I'm the only one who you *can* talk to."

And damn if those tears didn't burn the back of my nose again, because what he said was true.

He gave a nod as if his suspicions were right. "You should go inside before you catch your death." He opened his car door. "Oh, and I'll need you to let me into your house. What time suits?"

He really wasn't taking no for an answer. I really didn't want to talk about it, but god, part of me did. Part of me really did, like maybe, just maybe, if I shared the weight of it, it wouldn't be so hard to carry all the damn time.

"I can swing by around eight," I replied.

He grinned. "Then I'll be there at eight. Text me if that changes." And he got into his car and drove away.

I stood there a moment, somehow feeling a little better already. Until I shivered and hauled ass back inside.

I put my little tree on my desk, with its perfect eighteen sticks and eighteen little pompoms, and smiled at it.

Charity came over for a look. "It's cute. You must have made an impression on the kids. Did I hear him say you let them wear your hat?"

I nodded and almost smiled. "They thought the fireman hat was cool. Couldn't let that go undefended."

She laughed and gently touched one of the little pompoms. "You doing okay?"

I swallowed hard and considered the tree and Braithe's concern, and knowing he'd be waiting at home for me, I nodded. "Yeah, I'm okay."

She clapped my shoulder. "Good. You know people here have your back," she said as she went back to her desk.

She hadn't said it as a question. It was a statement, and for now, it rang true. But would they still feel that way if they knew I was gay?

I wasn't sure.

With a sigh, I turned the little tree around so it faced the front, and I got to work.

"Just gonna go do a lap," I called out to Bouchard. "Gotta stop by my house and check something. Won't be long."

He gave a wave, not bothered either way. I pulled on my coat and my hat and drove home. I was nervous, excited but dreading it in equal measure, and it ramped up a notch when Braithe all but followed me up the front stairs.

I flipped on the light switch, and he put down a takeout

bag, tossed his backpack onto the couch, and before I could even say a word, he pulled me in for a hug.

A heart-fixing kind of hug.

A soul-mending kind of hug.

His arms went around my back, his face into my neck. He had to stand up on his tiptoes, but he held me so damn tight. Tighter than I would've guessed he was capable of.

It felt so good.

I'd never needed a hug more in my life.

"I wanted to hug you at the station," he whispered. "I could see you weren't having a good day." He pulled back and slid his hand along my jaw. "It's okay to not be okay."

All I could do was nod. I wasn't prepared to talk about everything right now. I was still on the clock, and I still had hours of work to go.

"When you get back," he said, "you can tell me as much or as little as you'd like. No pressure. You don't have to talk about anything that you're not ready to talk about. But I'm here to listen and to offer hugs."

I swallowed hard and managed a nod. "Okay. Thank you." He smiled and it made my heart feel better already. He grabbed his bag and pulled out a book before throwing his bag into my room. He was really staying the night.

That made my heart feel better too.

I stoked the fire for him and turned on the Christmas lights. "Help yourself to anything. Oh, your teabags are in the cupboard."

"Okay, thanks. Did you want to eat something? I got some of Carl's goulash from the diner."

"No, I'm fine. Maybe when I get home." I swallowed again, not sure where to look. "Are you sure you're all right to stay? I mean, I appreciate it, and honestly the idea of you being here when I get home is real nice, but I don't expect you to . . . I feel kinda bad, like I'm imposing . . ." I finished with a shrug.

He held up his book. "I have everything I need. A warm fire, a cup of tea, and my book. It's my idea of a perfect Friday night, to be honest." Then his smile softened. "And you're not imposing. I offered because I want to be here."

"Okay," I said, not much above a whisper.

"Now, you go out there and keep this town safe. I'll be right here. I might even use two teabags so we will have to have some catch-up sex at some point because of the teabag–condom tally." Then he made a face. "Ooh, but we did use one last night at my place, and that should totally count. I'll be damned if we let the teabags win."

I laughed for the first time all day. "Okay. See you sometime between twelve and one."

"I'll be waiting." He gave me a soft peck on the lips, then settled himself on the couch with his book.

It was absolutely something I could get used to. Something I wanted, longed for, even.

One day, maybe.

Though it would mean owning up to my truth and coming out.

Again.

It almost felt inevitable. That it had to happen if I wanted to be truly happy. The idea of being ostracised, knowing that there would be people I'd lose, twisted in my gut.

I drove around the quiet town until I felt a bit better. The night was pitch dark and cold. The lights inside houses looked cosy and warm, a stark contrast to the outside where I was.

A metaphor not lost on me.

I drove until small snowflakes hit my windshield.

And when it was quitting time, it was still snowing.

Normally, I'd have probably cussed at it but tonight was

different. I went home, knowing I had a lot to talk about. But first things first.

I came through the door and Braithe put his book down. "Oh, hi," he said. He'd clearly been absorbed in his book, and there was an empty mug on the side table. He got to his feet as I came around the couch. "What's going on?"

"Come with me," I said, taking his hand. "You'll need a coat and some boots." I led him to the back room, pulled my big coat off the hook, and helped him into it.

"Uh, Colson," he said, pointing his toe as I tried to help him into my snow boots. He had to lean on my shoulder so he didn't fall. "What are we doing?"

I fixed the last boot on his small foot, taking in how he was swamped by my coat and boots, looking extra cute as hell. I pulled a knitted cap onto his head, took his hand, and led him out the back door.

And into the falling snow.

"Oh my goodness," he said, his voice full of wonder. We stopped about halfway into my backyard. "Oh, Colson. It's beautiful."

I took in his smile, his eyes, how he looked up at the sky, and nodded. "It sure is."

He clearly guessed I was talking about him because he ducked his head. "Thank you for showing me."

It was romantic, for me at least, even if it was just my backyard and he was wearing a coat that was four times too big and my boots looked like clown shoes on him.

I'd never seen anyone look so perfect before.

He held his hand out, letting tiny snowflakes land. "It's magical."

"Do you get snow back home?" I asked. "I guess you do."

"Sure," he replied. "But does it ever stop being magical?"

Then his eyes met mine. "And no one has ever taken me out at midnight to see it before."

"I've never done this before either. I just thought it was pretty and I thought you might like to see it. I've never had anyone waiting at home for me before, so I got a bit excited."

He slid his hand into mine and looked up at the sky again. His pale skin looked almost blue, and his smile took my breath away.

And I knew. I knew right then that I'd tell him everything.

Chapter Eleven

BRAITHE

I HADN'T MEANT to come across as bossy or demanding. But when I arrived at Colson's work, he was very obviously upset and tense, and when I showed him the little tree, he'd almost cried.

He'd said it was just a bad day, and I believed him.

I also believed he needed to talk. He needed to talk to someone, and I was the only person in Hartbridge who he could talk to.

Sure, Hamish and Ren and all the gang knew he was gay, but Colson wasn't close to them. Hell, I didn't even know if Colson knew that they knew. He certainly couldn't talk about whatever was bothering him at work because he wasn't out.

And I was almost certain it had to do with being gay.

I was the only person he *could* talk to. And it would have been so easy for him to say he was fine, for me to drop it and pretend he *was* fine and let him go on never talking about it to anyone ever.

But I wasn't that type of person.

He clearly needed to talk, so I put on my best this-isn't-up-for-discussion voice and invited myself over to his place to stay for the night.

He didn't even try to argue.

The poor guy really just needed someone to talk to.

And I liked him. I couldn't deny that. I had feelings for this gorgeous man, and to see him hurting had made that abundantly clear.

So around half past midnight, once we'd stood in the falling snow—because he was so ridiculously sweet—we sat on the couch by the fire, my hand holding his.

He let out a deep breath and began.

"The holidays aren't a great time for me," he said. "I have no family. Well, I do. They kicked me out when I was eighteen. My dad . . ." He let out a shaky breath.

I squeezed his hand so he'd know I would wait.

"My dad threw me out of the house, and my mom took his side." He frowned at the fire. "I didn't even want to come out. I knew they wouldn't like it, but I didn't think they'd disown me."

"Oh, Colson. I'm so sorry," I whispered.

"I'd been with Stephen for about a year," he said. "My first real boyfriend. My first love. He was all my firsts, actually. First kiss. First time. First heartbreak."

Oh, man.

He sighed. "He was out and his family loved him, and he couldn't understand why I would want to hide it. We fought about it a lot and I'd tried to explain that my parents weren't like his. He knew they were strict and old school. But he thought they'd come around eventually."

"And he pushed you into it."

Colson nodded. "It came down to an ultimatum. He didn't want to date someone who wasn't out, someone he had to hide with. And I get it. It was hard for him, and me still being in the closet kinda made him go back in."

I didn't believe that, but now wasn't the time for my opinions. I was just here to listen, so that's what I did.

"And I wanted to be out so bad. I wanted to live like he did. We'd finished high school and the rest of our lives were just starting. I wanted my family to support me like his did."

"But they didn't."

He shook his head. "No. Not at all. I have two brothers I haven't seen in ten years."

"Oh, Colson," I murmured, taking his hand in both of mine. "I'm so sorry."

"They're both older than me too. They were twenty and twenty-three when it happened, living away from home in their own places. I had nowhere to go and they wouldn't let me stay with them. They all turned their backs on me."

This was horrible. I'd guessed his story wasn't a good one, but it was more awful than I'd imagined. I felt so bad for him, but I was angry too.

"And Stephen?"

Colson let out another sigh. "He was sorry, and he tried to be supportive, but in the end, it was too much. I think he felt guilty."

"He should have," I said. Okay, so I was trying not to let my opinions out but it got the better of me. "He shouldn't have pushed you if you weren't ready. No one has the right to force anyone out of the closet, especially when it could be dangerous for them."

His eyes met mine and he gave me a sad smile. "Thank you."

I brought his hand to my lap. "What did you do? Where did you go?"

"I couch-surfed for a bit, and I knew I needed to get a

stable job. So I applied at the sheriff's department in Billings." He shrugged, his face pained. "And basically put myself back in the closet. Not that I was ever really out. I told my parents and that went to hell. I lost my brothers. I lost my boyfriend who was also my best friend in one go. So all I learned from the whole experience was to shut up and play the straight game. Give nothing away and bury myself in work."

His eyes were glassy, but there was anger there too. "I'd come out when I wasn't ready and it had cost me everything. Now I've put myself back in the closet, not out and proud like I should be, because I'm terrified I'll lose what I have left."

"I'm really sorry," I said again, because really, what else could I say? "I'm sorry it was so hard for you. I'm sorry they treated you like that. You know you're better than that, right? You know you're worth more than the names they called you and all the horrible things they said."

He frowned at the floor again. "I know. It took me a long time."

"If it's any consolation, I hate them all."

That earned me a bit of a laugh, though his smile died off. "Then today . . ." At his work, when he'd become teary. "What happened today?"

"You happened."

I stared at him. "Me?"

He snorted out a laugh, but his eyes looked glassy in the firelight. "I woke up this morning feeling all tight across my chest." He rubbed his sternum with his free hand. "After leaving you last night, I wanted to stay so bad."

I rubbed the back of his hand.

"I wanted to stay. I wanted to wake up next to you. I wanted to sleep beside you."

Oh damn.

Like he could read my mind, his eyes shot to mine. "And

maybe it's not even you, exactly." Then he laughed again. "I mean, maybe it is. You're great and kinda perfect. But maybe it's because I've gone without this"—he gestured between us —"without the physical contact, without the closeness for so long. And I realised this morning when I woke up alone that if I do want this with someone—if I do want to date someone and wake up next to someone, come home to a waiting someone—then I need to come out." He let out a shaky breath and he scrubbed at a tear that began to roll down his cheek. "I can't have what I want if I don't come out. I have to risk everything all over again for any possible chance at happiness."

God, I hated this. I hated that this was still something people had to deal with. I hated this for him.

"You deserve happiness," I offered. "And you deserve to be loved. I hate that you have to choose."

He nodded and wiped away another tear. "Then today at work, I don't even know what happened. It was just all too much. I kept thinking that work is all I have. I can't afford to lose it too. I can't afford to get pushed out and made to feel unwelcome."

"Would they do that?" I asked quietly.

He swallowed hard and took a moment to consider. "I don't know. But it's . . . I can't take that risk." He let out a shuddery breath. "Ronny's great. My boss. He's a good man. He treats everyone fairly and he's reasonable. It's what makes him a great sheriff. But he has to look out for his department and what's in the best interest of the office. Public image is important. Right or wrong, we need to be seen as upstanding and exemplary." He put his hand up because he knew I was about to argue. "We know being gay doesn't change that, but the public doesn't always see it that way. Especially in small towns."

I sighed, hating that he could be right.

"And if he decides that I'm no longer a good fit for his department . . ." He frowned at the flames. "He can't fire me, exactly. But he can make it so I leave voluntarily."

"Would he, though?"

He thought about it, his forehead creasing. "Personally, I think he'd be fine with it. Professionally . . . ?" He shrugged, but then his eyes met mine. "I can't risk it. I can't risk losing everything again, Braithe. I wish I could. I wish I was strong enough."

"It's not a measure of strength," I said, putting my hand to his face. "It's about knowing exactly how sharp a blade is, knowing exactly what kind of wounds it will inflict, how long it takes to heal, and being asked to cut yourself on it again." I shook my head. "It's not strength. It's self-preservation, and I get that. I understand."

He fell against the back of the couch with a sigh, holding my hand tight. "I wish you were staying," he mumbled. "Longer than four weeks."

Oh boy.

I didn't have the heart to tell him it was less than that now.

Instead, I got to my feet and pulled him to his. "I'm staying tonight. All night. I can sleep in tomorrow. In your bed with you, and you can have your way with me when you wake up."

"Sounds perfect."

"I have to be at the school by nine tomorrow," I amended. "Just so you know."

"But it's Saturday."

"I'm painting the backdrop for the school play." I looked up into his eyes and smiled. "Hamish is helping me. You can help too if you want. It'll be fun."

He made a bit of a face.

"You don't have to," I amended, giving him an easy out.

"It's not that I don't want to," he mumbled.

"Hey," I said, making him look at me. "I know. Just know that you're invited but under no obligation to come. I heard everything you said tonight, Colson. And I get it. I won't pressure you. Ever."

He smiled. "Thank you."

"Thank you for telling me. Thank you for sharing your story with me, for trusting me."

His smile soured a little. "You weren't wrong when you said you were the only one I could tell."

"Do you feel better?"

He closed his eyes. "So much better."

I slid my arms around his waist and gave him a long warm hug. "I'm glad. Come on then, let's go to bed. It's late and we're running out of cuddle time."

I PICKED Hamish up from the hardware store and he got into my car and handed me a coffee. "Ugh, snow," he said, looking out the windshield. "I know it's pretty, and it's exciting now. But I can tell you, it won't be so much fun in three months' time."

I laughed and pulled out onto the street. "Morning."

He sighed and rolled his eyes. "Yes, morning. Sorry." He sipped his coffee. "So, did you ask Colson about the Christmas dinner? Ren's all excited for it, but he wants to sand down the front deck and re-oil it before everyone turns up. I told him no one will care. No one will even notice, and that it will be a complete waste of time, and it's winter! I told him this. But he said there's some new miracle product he got into the store blah blah blah," he held up his hand. "Look at my hands. I'm not cut out for manual labour."

I laughed. "Sounds fun."

"Painting with you today is a blessing," he went on. "I'm sure if I wasn't busy with you, Ren'd have me doing it by myself. I swear, he *knows* who he married, and yet he still persists."

I snorted, drove into the school parking lot, and pulled up alongside Principal Nancy O'Connor's car. "Well, don't thank me yet."

"You can buy me lunch at the diner as payment," he said. "And cake."

I grinned at him. "Deal."

"So did you ask him?"

"Uh, no, not exactly," I said, making a face.

"Why? Did something happen?"

I cut the engine. "Let's get inside. I'll tell you all about it." He followed me in, said a very quick hello to Nancy, and I cranked up the heating in my classroom.

"Look at how ridiculously cute everything is!" Hamish cried. "The little chairs and desks, oh my heart. And the paintings. Ooh, and *The Very Hungry Caterpillar*. I loved that book."

Hamish was such a ball of energy and I just adored him.

"It's a great school," I said. "The kids are a joy."

He took his coat off and hung it on one of the kids' hooks, grinned at it proudly, then sipped his coffee. "Okay, now tell me all the details of your man."

I wasn't sure where to start.

I pulled out the paints and brushes and laid the long sheet of butcher's paper over the desks. "Have you ever had a prostate orgasm?"

Hamish choked on his coffee, sputtering, and had to wipe

his beard. His grin matched his wide eyes. "This is the level of detail I'm here for."

I laughed. I probably shouldn't have led with that, but it was important to the story.

"We . . . we had ourselves a moment," I said.

He stared.

"It was amazing. And I don't know. It forged a connection between us. That sounds crazy."

He came over and gripped my hand. "No, it doesn't. It makes total sense."

"Not just a physical connection. It's not just the sex. He did me in a way I've never been done before, and I've never felt closer to anyone. I thought it was just me. I thought maybe I was beginning to feel things for him, totally one-sided, and that I was being a bit foolish." I shrugged. "I told myself it was just a physical reaction, ya know?"

He nodded. "But it's not one-sided."

"I don't think it is, no." I let out a sigh. "I called into his work yesterday after school. The kids made him a little Christmas tree as thanks for coming to the school for the fire-safety talk, and I thought I'd hand deliver it. Which I probably shouldn't have, but I'm glad I did. He was . . . kinda upset when I got there and giving him the tree made it worse."

"He was upset?"

I gave a nod. "I told him I'd wait at his place until he finished work, and we could talk. Hamish, he has no one he can talk to. So when he got home, after he took me out to see the snow—which was the sweetest moment ever—we talked. He told me his story, and it's not good. He has no one, and the people in his life were the worst."

Hamish frowned, the corners of his mouth pulling down. "Oh no."

I nodded. "Yeah. And he was sad when I turned up at his

work because what we did the night before and then him waking up alone made him realise he *is* alone, and that if he wants to be truly happy, he has to come out and he's not sure he can do that. And I don't blame him. I would never blame him, after everything he's been through."

Hamish deflated, still frowning. "The poor guy."

"I left his place this morning. We cooked breakfast and . . ." I smiled at the memory. "And went back to bed."

He laughed. "Mm-hm. Explains the good mood when you picked me up."

I chuckled. "And he was okay. He said he felt a lot better after he'd been able to talk to someone. And I'm glad I could do that for him, but . . ."

"But?"

"But I'm leaving." My stomach soured at the thought, and my heart thumped heavily. "And then he'll have no one. Again. God, it hurts my heart to think about."

Hamish's eyes met mine, as serious as I'd ever seen him. "I think your heart's trying to tell you something."

I sighed. "I know."

His whole face lit up. "So you'll stay?"

And my heart thumped even heavier. "I wish I could, but it's really not that simple."

Nancy popped her head through the door. "I'm heading off now. Be sure to lock the front door."

"Sure will," I said, holding a brush to prove that I was here to actually paint and not just chat. "Thanks again."

"Come on," I said to Hamish. "We better get something done." In no time at all, we had the basic nativity backdrop pencilled on. It wasn't that difficult. Just a stable and a palm tree, and a bit of sky.

Then we began to mix some colours and paint, our

conversation centring around what we were painting, the upcoming play, dinner party, and Hartbridge Light Festival.

He didn't mention me staying again, and I was kinda grateful.

Leaving hurt to think about.

I almost had the nativity stable done when there was a soft knock on the door. I certainly wasn't expecting anyone and just presumed it would be one of the other teachers or even the cleaners. "Come in," I called out.

Colson stuck his head in. "Hey."

He was the last person I expected. "Oh, hey," I said, unable to hide my surprise. I gave a pointed glance at Hamish so Colson would know I wasn't alone. "Come in, come in."

He stepped through the door, clearly very nervous. He was in his running gear, and he'd worked up quite a sweat despite the cold outside. "I, uh, I saw your car in the parking lot," he said, wiping his hands on his trackpants. "I hope it's okay . . ."

I'd told him Hamish would be here, so he knew. And yet, here he was. As if he was making a statement of some kind. Pushing himself and testing the waters, maybe?

Oh my days. My heart was fluttering.

"Come in," I said, taking his arm and pulling him. "Let me introduce you properly. This is Hamish Brooks. Hamish, this is Colson Price."

Hamish, being Hamish, took it all in stride. He didn't act surprised or shocked; he simply stuck the paintbrush he was holding into a cup of water and held his hand out for Colson. "Ah, Colson. It's so nice to finally meet you."

Colson swallowed hard and shook his hand. He looked a shade pale and as if he might turn and run, but he managed a smile. "Likewise. You said Brooks? I thought, uh . . . I didn't realise . . ."

"That I took Ren's last name?" Hamish grinned. "I sure

did. I mean, you've seen my husband, right? I'd take his babies if I could."

Oh, good heavens.

Colson blinked, stunned, but Hamish wasn't swayed. He just picked up a paintbrush and handed it to him. "Can you paint the sky? The sooner we get this done, the sooner Braithe has to buy me lunch."

"And cake, apparently," I added.

"The cake is the best part," he said, going back to painting the palm tree. "Don't tell Jayden I said that."

Colson was kind of smiling, so I handed him a small tub of blue paint. "For the sky."

And he helped us paint.

It wasn't anything extraordinary or decidedly gay. We weren't painting a pride poster, after all. But he was *here*. He'd come here knowing Hamish would be here with me. He knew Hamish was aware that he and I were sleeping together, so he was, in a way, here as a gay man.

The first time he'd done this in Hartbridge.

I didn't know what it meant for him, but I thought it was huge. It *was* huge. I was so proud of him.

I stood next to him as he painted the sky so I could do the roof of the stable. And I wanted so badly to reassure him, to touch his arm or rub his back. I wanted him to know his bravery didn't go unnoticed.

"Uh, Braithe," Hamish said. "Can you point me in the direction of the bathrooms?"

"Sure." I showed him to the hall and pointed to the sign.

"I don't really need to pee. I'm giving you a few minutes," he whispered.

I snorted. "Yeah, I figured."

He made an excited *eep* sound and grinned at me before he shoved me back into the classroom. I almost fell through the door and when I righted myself, Colson was watching me, paintbrush in hand and a shy smile.

"So, uh, Hamish is just giving us a minute," I said.

His cheeks ran pink. "I, uh, I heard."

I laughed and went up to him, leaned up on my toes, and pressed a soft kiss on his lips. "I'm proud of you. For being here."

He let out a rush of air and half-laughed. "I didn't plan to. I, uh, I remembered you saying you'd be here, and when I went for a jog, my feet just brought me here. I saw your car . . ." He shook his head. "I made myself come in before I could lose my nerve."

"You knew Hamish would be here," I prompted.

He nodded quickly. "This morning, at home with you, was probably the best morning of my life. I know that sounds crazy. But getting to sleep next to you, wake up next to you. Then cooking breakfast." He dropped the paintbrush into the water pot. "It's stupid because it's just mundane shit. It's everyday life for so many people, but I've never . . . I didn't think I'd ever . . ."

"It's not stupid. It's not stupid for people who can't live their truth."

He frowned and picked at his thumbnail before he shook his head and sighed, shoulders dropping. "But that's just it, isn't it? That's what it comes back to every time. I need to start living my truth."

I rubbed his arm. "Only if you're ready. Only then."

"I didn't think I ever would be," he whispered. "Not after last time."

Because he was looking down, I had to duck so I could catch his gaze and make him look at me. "It'll be different this time. You're different this time, older and stronger. You know you're worth the fight now, right?"

He smiled sadly and fixed his gaze out the window. "I think I'll have to be."

"There are some great guys in this town," I began. He looked at me then, confused and somewhat horrified. *Oh, jeez.* "No, not as a hook-up or potential . . . whatever. I mean Hamish and Ren, and all those guys. You know what they said? They said there is always a seat at their table for whoever needs one."

"Yeah."

Yet, he still looked so unsure.

"I get it," I added. "Sitting with a whole big group of queer men immediately makes people think you are as well. I know that. One lady I work with assumed as much about me because I have coffee with them. So I get it. It sucks that it happens, but you know what? Let them think whatever they want. Let them gossip, let them whisper. It says more about them than it does any of us." I took his hand. "Colson, you're better than them. You're better than any rumours or gossip fodder. It will only be for a short while and the rumour mill will move onto the next thing, and you'll be free to be yourself."

"You make it sound so easy."

"It's not easy. But it will pass, and you'll be free." He half-smiled, half winced, and let out a long breath.

"I tell you what," I said, deciding to strike while the iron was hot.

Well, now seemed as good a time as any.

"So," I began. "Hamish and Ren are having a Christmas dinner Monday night." His eyes cut to mine but I didn't lose hope. "It's just a casual potluck dinner between friends before everyone gets too busy."

He was still staring at me.

"They asked me to come along, and I wondered if you might like to join me."

He looked away, uncomfortable. "Oh, I, uh, I don't know . . ."

"You absolutely don't have to, I just thought it might be nice. Those guys are great, and they care a great deal—"

"Do they all know about . . . us. Or me? Do they know we're—"

I put my hand up. Bollocks.

"They guessed. In the beginning. Remember that first day in the diner? I said I'd already met you because you let me off a speeding ticket, and then they mentioned something about gaydar vibes, and I'd mentioned to Hamish that you'd taken me to Mossley, and then later on, about me getting nailed by someone—it was a whole conversation—and he guessed it was you because I can't lie . . ." I made a face. "But they kinda knew about you before I even got here."

He stared, then turned away and ran his hand through his hair. "The time I found Clay and Gunter skating on the pond. Last year. I saw his truck off the road, and . . ." He looked as if he'd tasted something particularly bad. "They knew all this time?"

"Never officially." I took his arm and made him look at me. "It's not an issue. They would never tell anyone. They know what it's like, Colson. They genuinely care that you're okay."

He sighed again, but he wasn't mad, he wasn't upset. He was just processing.

"So, about dinner Monday. It'll be dark, and we can take my car. It's at Ren and Hamish's place, so no one will see. It's just dinner, and we can leave at any time."

He didn't say yes, but he hadn't said no either.

"Don't decide yet," I pressed. "Think about it. No pressure." He relented a nod, that yes, he'd think about it. I considered it a win. "Now, speaking about gaydar vibes," I added with a smile. "I'm pretty sure our local fireman was looking at you."

His eyes shot to mine. "Me? He was looking at you. He didn't stop looking at you, and he tried to talk to you."

I barked out a laugh. "Is that why you kept coming over and interrupting?"

He scoffed. "I didn't interrupt."

I laughed, because yes, he did.

"I think he mighta liked the new kindergarten teacher," he said with a pout.

My eyes cut to his. "Uh, no. I saw him looking at us. To be honest, I think he might have been looking at you."

"Me?"

I shrugged. "I mean, he did ask me for my name, but then out at the truck, he was watching you."

Colson ran his hand through his hair. "Ah, no. He was looking at you." Then, like it got the better of him and he just had to ask. "So, did you give it to him?"

"Give what to him?"

"Your name."

I snorted. "No. I was too busy looking at a certain deputy in his cute little brown outfit."

"Uniform."

I laughed. "I know. I just like to see that flash of indignation in your eyes."

He faked a snarl that was mostly a smile. "And you dropped off the little Christmas tree for him the other day," he went on. "How was he then? In his fireman uniform, I suppose."

Oh wow. He was actually jealous.

"He wasn't there," I replied. "I left the tree with Captain Doug. He was most thankful."

Colson chewed on the inside of his cheek. "Well, good."

I laughed again. "Are you actually jealous?"

His gaze shot to mine. "No."

He totally was. I grinned at him. "I'll have you know," I whispered, "I prefer the deputy outfit over the fireman outfit."

He pressed his lips together and huffed. "It's a uniform. Uni. Form." I laughed, just glad that he was smiling again.

Hamish knocked and peeked around the door. "Everybody decent?"

I swatted at his arm as he came in. "Come and finish your palm tree. I've done nearly all the stable and Colson's done most of the sky."

"I gave you guys five minutes," Hamish said. "Please don't tell me you used it for painting. I'll be so disappointed."

I laughed, and Colson smiled. He was embarrassed and his whole face flushed red, but he smiled.

See, Colson? It could be like this all the time.

"If you must know," I said, "I was just telling Colson about the dinner party you and Ren are hosting next Monday."

Hamish's eyes lit up. "Oh yes! You must come. It'll be fun, and Ren's been making me sand down the merbau decking on the front veranda." He held up his hand. "Look at that. That's a blister. And can you believe I know it's called merbau and not timber or lumber or just boring old wood? I married a hardware store owner and look at where it got me. I know hardware things."

I laughed and even Colson chuckled. He seemed happier, more relaxed, even. And honestly, if anyone could do that, it'd be Hamish.

"I should get going," Colson said. "I gotta get to work."

Hamish got excited. "Ooh, does that mean we can pack up now? Is it lunchtime?"

"No. We need another palm tree." I pointed to the backdrop. "You keep going. I'll just walk Colson out."

"No smooching in the hallways," he said.

Colson's eyes went wide, and I dragged him to the door, where I did lean up and kiss him softly. "Thank you for coming by," I whispered. "I'll call you later."

His lip drew down. "Did you . . . did you want to stay again tonight?"

"Absolutely."

His grin was spectacular, and he slipped through the door and was gone. I walked back to find Hamish waiting, watching, smirking.

"Oh, he is just too adorable," he said. "Tell me everything."

Chapter Twelve

COLSON

SOMETHING in me changed that morning.

A realisation. An acceptance.

I was going to have to come out. I was going to have to tell Ronny, at the very least. If I wanted to experience what I experienced with Braithe that morning, if I wanted to find that happiness and inner peace, then I needed to come out.

And that's what it was.

Inner peace.

I'd never been happier. I woke up with his head on my chest, his leg over mine, my arm around him. The feel of his slender body curled into mine made my whole body sing.

Mostly my heart.

It felt so good.

As much as I'd wanted to devour him right then and there, his stomach rumbled, so we cooked breakfast. Together, both of us. Me on bacon-and-eggs duty, him on coffee and toast, and he fed me bites of toast while we waited, and it was just perfection.

Domestic and lovely.

All I'd ever wanted.

Then we'd ended up back in bed and that was perfection too. His body was perfection; the way he writhed, the way he groaned, the way he took me.

I reminded myself he was leaving. He'd been upfront from the start that this was a no-strings, sex-only thing. And as much as I didn't want him to go, he'd proven one thing to me: I wanted to live more authentically.

I wanted to have a life where I'd wake up next to a man, where we'd cook breakfast together and make love.

I had found myself jogging past the school by accident—that was no lie. My feet had betrayed me again. And I saw his car, and only his car, in the lot. I knew Hamish would be with him, and I knew that this was bold and ballsy.

But I wanted to do it.

Hamish was funny and he made no attempt to hide who he was. He knew that Braithe and I had been hooking up, and he made no big deal of it. He knew I was gay, and it was accepted as a simple truth.

No big deal.

Except it was. For me, at least.

I suspected Hamish also knew this, and him playing it down was entirely the point.

It didn't have to be a big deal.

This could be my normal.

If I ever found someone else after Braithe leaves . . . If I ever wanted to.

Did I want anyone else?

No.

Only him. For as long as he was here, I would never look at anyone else. And it wasn't like there *was* anyone else. Which made me second-guess myself. Should I tell Ronny and risk jeopardising my career when I may never find another partner?

Was I prepared to risk losing everything all over again for nothing?

I'd been so determined all morning. Especially after spending time with Braithe and Hamish. I thought maybe I could do it. But by the time I got to work, I'd convinced myself it might all be for naught.

So I figured it was best to say nothing. Not until I was completely sure. One hundred per cent certain.

No point ringing a bell that couldn't be unrung.

Until I got to work and barely got my coat off before Ronny called me into his office and asked me to shut the door behind me.

"Take a seat," he said.

Had someone seen something? Said something? My heart was thumping, painfully so.

It shouldn't be like this. It doesn't have to be like this. My mouth was so dry I could barely speak. "What's up?"

"I just wanted to check in with ya," he said. "Make sure everything's okay."

"Boss, I'm fine—"

"It's my professional duty to recognise when someone on my team might need some help. And there ain't nothing wrong in needing help."

Oh, dear Lord.

"I appreciate that," I tried.

"And it's not just professional duty, Colson," he said. "I consider you one of my own. How long you been here in Hartbridge?"

He considered me one of his own . . .

"Uh. Fi-five years."

"And my deputy? How long?"

"Four years."

He gave a nod. "You're a good officer, Colson. And a fine man."

My heart felt strangled, and my lungs couldn't take enough air. I didn't know where he was going with this, or why I felt like I was about to be hugged or fired.

"Sir?"

"And I know you find the holidays a tough time, and I ain't ever asked you why. It never did affect your work, so I considered it none of my business."

Oh no.

I tried to tell him I wouldn't let it affect me now, but I couldn't get the words out.

"Then this year you went and put up some Christmas lights for the first time, and just yesterday you were upset. I ain't ever seen you like that, and I can't help but think that's no coincidence." He looked at me with concern. "And then that nice teacher brought in that tree that the kids made for you and . . ."

I slow-blinked at the mention of Braithe; the world kinda tilted and his office felt far too warm.

"He took you outside and talked you down."

I opened my mouth to say something, but all that bravado I'd had earlier about speaking my truth was nowhere to be found.

"It's not easy for you to talk about," Ronny said gently. "It's okay, Colson."

I shook my head because it wasn't okay.

I wasn't okay.

"Your application to transfer from Billings stated you had no next of kin, no family," he murmured gently. "I'd imagine there's a grief to that which runs real deep, especially for someone as young as you."

"I have no family," I managed to say, barely a whisper.

"They're not dead, sir. At least I don't think so. I wouldn't know if they were."

I looked at him then and he was studying me, confused but listening intently. I expected to see pity on his face, but there was only concern.

And the words were out before I could stop them. The secret I'd managed to keep for years just spilled right out of me.

"They threw me out," I said. "When I was eighteen. Disowned me, renounced me from their family and their church. Told me to never come back, to never contact them."

I couldn't bring myself to look at Ronny now.

I had to wipe my cheek as it was. If I saw his face right then, I'd have lost it completely.

"What on earth for?"

"Because I'm gay."

The silence that followed was heavy and dark. I couldn't quite breathe right, the room felt hot and cold all at once, and it felt as if the world spun around me while I was stuck in place.

Before I knew it, Ronny was standing on my side of the desk. He leaned against it, his boots next to mine. "Look at me, son."

But I couldn't.

I didn't want to see it: the disgust, the goodbye.

He put his big hand on my shoulder. "Deputy Price, look at me." That made me raise my head. The rank, the official tone. He looked . . . sad.

"Don't you lower your head in shame, son. Not for no one."

I wasn't quite sure I heard him right. "Pardon?"

"I said don't lower your head in shame. You got nothing to feel ashamed for." He pulled his hand back and crossed his arms. "I'm sorry your family treated you the way they did. But that's their misgiving, not yours."

I couldn't stop the tear from falling down my cheek. "I, uh, I don't know what to say. I'm sorry for not telling you before, I just . . ." I finished with a shrug. Hell, I was too busy just trying not to cry.

"I'm sorry you felt you couldn't tell me," he said. "And that's a reflection on me, not you. Have I ever given you reason—"

I shook my head quickly. "No, Ronny. It's not that. You've been nothing but great. I just . . . I couldn't risk losing everything all over again. This job is all I've got. So if you need to pretend we never had this conversation, I'd appreciate that."

He shook his head, offering a sad smile. "Colson, I'm gonna tell you something. You know Ren Brooks at the hardware store, right?"

I nodded, not sure where he was going with this. "Ah, sure."

"His old man and me, shoot, we go back fifty years. Best of friends up until the day he died; that was just before you got here. We were both born and bred in this town, went to elementary school together, played high school football together. Got married around the same time, and Geraldine and Ren's mom would meet at the mother's group." He smiled at some far-off memory before it faded with a sigh. "Then when Ren was in high school, he came out as gay. And I'll tell you, it wasn't easy on his dad at first. People in this town talked. We'd play poker or go fishing, and he straight-up told me that he had a choice. He could love Ren as he'd always done, or he could lose him forever. But he couldn't change him, and even if he could, he wouldn't. He loved him just as much after he knew he was gay as he did the day before finding out. And you know what he said to me?" He smiled.

"He said imagine being a parent to a kid who's too scared to tell you something. Imagine your own kid being scared of you. And I remember looking at him, thinking that right there is parenting done right."

I had to wipe my cheeks again. Stupid damn tears.

"He told all those gossipers and all the folks who turned their noses up that there was nothing wrong with Ren, and there was nothing wrong with being gay. I'm sure a few of the old timers probably shook their heads at him, but all he did was prove he was a better father." He sighed with another sad smile. "And he raised a good kid. Everyone loves Ren, and he went and got himself married. You remember the wedding. It was a big shindig out at the B&B on Ponderosa Road."

"I remember," I said. How could I not? I'd sat in my cruiser down the road and watched the crowd gather on the beautiful lawns of the gorgeous house while I . . . while I wished it was me.

Ronny gave my shoulder a squeeze. "I guess what I'm trying to tell you is that it's okay. I can't guarantee no one in this town will have a problem with it—"

"I, uh, I don't know if I want anyone else to know," I said. "I'm glad I told you. I've been thinking it was about time. This year . . ." I swallowed hard. "This year felt different. Like it was time to move on and start living again. I was just thinking today, and yesterday actually, that I should tell you. As my boss. But I . . ." I glanced out to the main floor of desks, of cops and staff. "I don't know if I'm up for losing friends. Or causing any rifts in the team."

He looked me right in the eye and smiled. "That's what makes you a good officer, Colson. Because you think of them first. And it's totally up to you. But I'll tell you what. If and when you want to say something, be it today or a year from now, just know you got me in your corner, okay?"

Again, with the stupid tears.

"That means a lot," I said, trying to talk without blubbering. "It means more than you can know."

He gave my shoulder a bit of a shake. "You okay? Did you need to take today off? You never take personal time, so if you want some personal leave, it's fine."

Did I want to take the day off?

Did I want to find Braithe and tell him that I came out to my boss just now? Maybe I did want that.

I tried not to think too much about why he was the first person I thought of. Why he was the only person I had in my life to share this with.

A sharp rap on the door made us both turn, and I wiped at my face as Charity opened the door. She noticed the state of me but addressed Ronny. "Sheriff, got a tree down on Cottonwood Road out past McAfferty's. It hit a vehicle; single occupant of the pickup sustained minor injuries. Zanetti's on his way, paramedic en route."

I jumped to my feet and was out the door, pulling my coat on and getting into my cruiser before I could stop and think.

I had to tamp down any personal emotions and put my game face on. Emotions would have to wait.

Cottonwood Road was a good fifteen-minute drive down the end of Cedar Bark Road. It was partly dirt and gravel, and with the new snow on the ground, it was a slow fifteen minutes at best.

I put the time to good use.

With my phone in the dash holder, I dialled Braithe's number.

"Hello," he answered. It sounded as if he was smiling and in the diner. Probably with Hamish, at a guess.

"Hi, I can't talk for long. I'm called out to a job, but I just wanted to tell you that I told Ronny. I told him, and he was so great. I can't believe it, but he said he was in my corner, and—"

"Wait, wait," he said. "Let me take this outside." It sounded as if he was walking, and I heard the bell above the diner door chime. "Okay, I'm outside. You told Ronny what?"

"I told him. I came out." I barked out a laugh, getting teary all over again.

"Oh my days, Colson," he breathed. "I'm so happy for you! What happened?"

"He called me into his office and asked me about the other day and he wanted to know if I was okay. He knows the holidays aren't a good time of year for me, and I think all this time he assumed my parents were dead . . ." I still couldn't believe it. Even saying it all again now, it didn't seem real. "So I told him they weren't. Not that I'd even know if they were. And then I told him why."

"Oh, Colson. Where are you now?"

"I'm heading out to a job."

"I want to see you tonight. Can I wait at your place? Is that okay?"

I nodded before I realised I needed to say the words out loud. "That'd be really great. I'd like that."

I heard him talking to someone else, a muffle of voices, then he said, "Oh, Gunter and Clay had to leave. Clay's been called to clear a tree from some road in the mountains. Is that where you're heading now?"

"Sounds like it, yeah."

"Oh my," he murmured. "Please be careful."

I couldn't help but smile. No one had ever cared about me before. "I will. Uh . . . about tonight. There's a key to my mudroom at the back door. Under the mat. Use that to get in."

He chuckled. "Under the mat? Really? Isn't that the most

obvious spot? I thought a deputy would have a much better hiding spot."

"Base to C2," Charity's voice crackled over my radio.

"Braithe, I gotta go."

"Be careful!" he said quickly.

I ended the call and picked up the radio. "This is C2, over."

"Please be advised, fire truck and Henderson's are also en route for tree removal. Over."

I smiled because I already knew that Clay Henderson was on his way. "Noted," I replied. "Over."

I came upon the scene of flashing police lights, an old pickup on the shoulder of the road under the branches of a huge fallen tree. Police Sergeant Zanetti was out of his vehicle, speaking to the driver of the pickup. He appeared to be an older man with a cut on his forehead, and was being tended to by Chrissie, a local paramedic.

It wasn't a critical emergency scene but there were standard protocols that needed to be actioned.

I got out of my truck and walked over. "Sergeant," I said with a tip of my hat to Zanetti. "Chrissie."

"Ah, now Deputy Price is here too," she said, applying a bandage to the older man's cut. "See, Mr McAfferty," she said. "It's no trouble at all. We all like taking a drive."

I smiled at the old guy. I knew the type. Sorry to bother you. Didn't mean to inconvenience anyone.

"No trouble at all, sir."

Zanetti gave me a smile and we walked over to get a better look at the tree. It was big and blocked the road completely. "Fire department and Henderson's are on their way," I said. I wasn't sure if he'd heard.

He gave a nod. "Old guy was damn lucky he wasn't a few seconds slower."

So very true.

I looked at the far edge to see if I could get around it, but no. The tree was well and truly over the fence on the far side as well. "I'll climb through to the other side and put my beacon down the road a way for any oncoming traffic."

I mean, any traffic at all was unlikely, but still. Protocol was protocol. So I took my safety beacon, which was like a red flashing lantern, and began climbing through the fallen tree. I aimed for the thinnest part, which was closest to the fence but still, the tree was some kind of fir and was huge, and by the time I got through the other side, I'd been scratched and scraped by twigs and I was covered in sticky sap.

Gross.

Just as the fire department truck pulled up, Doug and his crew jumped out and all swung into action, hitting the ground running. Literally.

And of course, Sergeant De Silva was there, and of course he noticed me.

But not for long.

He was too busy pulling on his safety gear and clearing debris, assessing the damage. The usual. We'd all done this a hundred times. It happened a lot, especially in the winter. These were the tree-covered mountains of Montana, after all.

And then the old Henderson truck rumbled to a stop. Clay, his dad, Cliff, and Rusty all clambered out, and everyone got to work.

Mr McAfferty was fine, aside from the cut on his head. But Chrissie had assessed him and given him the all-clear. He was a tough old man: his words, not mine. Late seventies, mountain born and bred, and spent his life logging trees and working his land.

"Nothing a shot of whiskey at supper time won't fix," he said.

His pickup truck wasn't so lucky. The tree had done some damage. Zanetti made his report and offered to drive him home. We managed to get the pickup out from under the tree and I drove it, following Zanetti to Mr McAfferty's place not far down the road.

We left the truck by the side of his house, made sure he was inside, and after seeing Mrs McAfferty did as much cussing at him as she did fussing over him, we left them to it and went back to the scene.

Chrissie was gone, Zanetti left not long after that, and I said I'd stick around for traffic concerns until the road was cleared.

The thing about the mountains, on these back roads in particular, it got cold and dark early. I had my coat, but it made sense to help out rather than be sitting there watching.

It kept me warm and would get the work done quicker too.

Cliff Henderson assessed the trunk and the roots of the tree, and after seeing the rot, he said he wasn't surprised it fell.

Between chain sawing and trunk removal, Clay gave me a smile and a nod, and I was reminded that he knew about me and Braithe.

And then De Silva was beside me while I was sweeping debris off the road. "Might wanna be careful," he said, breaking a smile. "You might get yourself a job."

I snorted. "I'm good, but thanks."

He dragged a large branch off the side of the road to the fence line. "The other day at the school was fun," he said, wiping his brow with the back of his hand. "Pretty sure your boss and mine colluded to throw us under the bus and pass the baton over at the same time."

I laughed at that. "I think you might be right."

He looked over at what was left of the tree. He was good-looking, no two ways about it. Tanned and fit, sweaty and dirty. And the uniform wasn't exactly terrible. *Not as good as the deputy uniform* . . . I heard Braithe's voice in my head and remembered his wicked smile as he'd said it.

And like my brain was showing me option A in front of me, and option B in my head. De Silva or Braithe.

It was gonna be Braithe every time.

I was a top, and if my intuition told me anything, it told me De Silva was too. Sure, we could have some fun, maybe . . . but Braithe and I were a perfect fit.

"So," he hedged, still looking at the tree. "The, uh, the teacher—"

"He's taken," I said.

Now, I don't know what on earth possessed me to say that. Those words in particular or how fast they'd just rolled off my tongue.

But if he was interested in Braithe, he could back the fuck off.

De Silva's eyes flashed to mine and he nodded, a smile playing at his lips. "I figured he might be, yeah. The way he was lookin' at you."

Wait. Did I just come out to him too?

Without so much as saying so, I guessed I did.

But he admitted as much to me as well.

God, this was a day for it, apparently.

"He's, uh, he's not staying in town for long," I added, with no clue as to why. Then I thought about what he said. The way he was looking at me.

Had Braithe been looking at me? I wasn't sure. I was too busy watching the way De Silva had been looking at him.

Maybe De Silva was already out. Maybe he didn't have to hide like me. I tried to act cool like I wasn't a whole twisted knot inside. "Can I ask you something?"

"Maybe," he said. He wore an easy smile, and I felt bad for being so defensive. "Does the department know?" I gave a nod to where Doug was putting a chainsaw through some branches.

He clued in immediately. "Sure. What about you?"

"Not really. The sheriff does." I left out the fact that the sheriff had known for exactly one hot minute. "No one else, though," I added.

God, why was this so hard?

He gave a nod and squinted out across what remained of the tree. "Small towns, huh? Great in some ways, not so great in others."

I nodded, agreeing wholeheartedly. "Hm. Yeah."

"Listen," he began. "If you ever wanna hang out sometime . . ."

I put my hand up. "Uh . . ."

He laughed. "Not like that. Jesus. You're really not my type."

"Oh."

He found whatever my face did even funnier. "Just as friends. I've been in Hartbridge for a year, and with the shift work, it's not easy." He shrugged. "We can just hang out, shoot the shit. Watch football or hockey or whatever. It's just nice to have someone who gets it, and I'm guessing if you ain't fully out, then you don't have that either."

"Uh yeah, no. I don't. Having a friend who understands sounds good." Then, because I sounded like a loser, I tried for something funny. "And what the fuck do you mean I'm not your type? I mean, come on." I gestured to my body.

He chuckled. "My type seems to be the same as your type. The way you snapped 'he's taken' when I mentioned your little teacher friend with the English accent, I'm guessing we both like the twink-types. Right?"

Oh. Of course. I couldn't believe I was having this conversation. "I didn't snap, I just . . ."

"Staked your claim?"

I rolled my eyes, ignoring how my face felt like it was on fire, then I ignored the way he laughed at me.

Until Doug yelled at us. "You got time to laugh, you got time to learn," he hollered. "Learn how your damn broom works."

I snorted at De Silva because Doug was his boss, not mine. But then Doug levelled a stare at me that rivalled that of a pissed-off Ronny, and I got busy sweeping.

IT WAS WELL and truly dark by the time the fire department boys were done, and I stuck around while the Henderson Sawmill guys loaded up their truck.

Clay gave me another knowing smile and a nod, but he never said anything about knowing I was with Braithe, and I was glad.

I'd had all the coming-out talks I could handle for one day.

I got home right at midnight, and I'd almost forgotten that Braithe would be waiting for me, until I pulled into my drive and saw the Christmas lights were on, and the warm glow of the fire.

I sighed with relief, with pure joy that he was there, waiting for me.

I'd had one helluva day, and the fact he was concerned about me, that he cared enough . . .

I took the steps two at a time and couldn't get inside quick enough. He must have heard me pull up because he was standing up by the sofa and as soon as I had the door closed, he threw his arms around me.

His warm body against me, his arms locked around my neck, and his face buried against my throat. I slid my hands around his back and pulled him in close, breathing him in.

He smelled so good. He felt even better.

And this hug?

If I could find a way to inject how it made me feel, I would.

It soothed me, healed me.

I never knew how much I'd needed a hug until I met him. That human contact, that reassurance.

"Are you okay?" he asked.

I nodded, not wanting to let him go. "I am."

"And Ronny was okay?" He pulled back then but looked at his hands and grimaced. "Uh, why are you sticky?"

I chuckled. "I'm covered in sap." I showed him the arms of my coat. "I got most of it off."

"Did you want to have a shower? I can make us a tea, then you can tell me everything."

I slid my hand along his jaw and lifted his face for a soft, slow kiss. "I am so grateful you're here."

His expression softened. "Me too." Then he wrinkled his pretty little nose. "You smell like a car freshener."

I laughed. "Okay, hint taken. Quickest shower ever."

He was already on his way to the kitchen. "I'll make us a tea."

I was absolutely certain that I didn't like hot tea, but if he was making it, I'd drink anything.

A few minutes later, I came out wearing my long pyjamas and UGG boots, hair washed, and hopefully, free of tree sap. Braithe was on the couch, his legs curled up underneath him, two steaming cups of tea on the coffee table.

"Oh," he said, closing his book so he could look me up and down. "You look very good for snuggling."

I sat beside him, and he handed me a tea. "I am very good for snuggling." He sidled in a little closer, his legs still folded up and, half-leaning on me, he took my free hand. "Tell me what happened today."

I let out a sigh and told him everything that'd happened with Ronny, and he listened to every word, his blue eyes bright and full of concern and pride.

He told me he was proud of me.

And then I told him about my conversation with De Silva. "I just kinda blurted it out, because I thought he was going to ask for your number or something. I didn't mean you were taken, taken. I just meant that you were . . ."

Well, taken.

"Uh, taken?"

I ducked my head, resting my forehead on his shoulder. "I'm sorry. It wasn't my place to say, and if you do want me to give him your number—"

"No!" He barked out a laugh. "One hot and sexy man in uniform is more than enough, thank you."

I tried not to smile. "So you do think he's hot and sexy?"

He swatted my arm. "I told you I was too busy looking at you to notice him."

I laughed and an easy, peaceful feeling settled over me. "I came out to two people today. And De Silva said we should hang out sometime. You know, watch some football or something. He hasn't been in town long and he said it'd be nice to hang out with someone who understands, ya know? I told him that sounded good."

Braithe was quiet, chewing on the inside of his lip. "If you want to pursue something with him, you shouldn't wait until I leave . . ."

I laughed. "Uh, no. He said, and I quote, I was *so* not his type. And he said he could only guess that given a certain cute teacher with an English accent is my type, that he wasn't my type either."

He looked surprised. And flattered? "Oh." It was hard to tell if he blushed or if it was just the light from the fire. "Are you saying I'm your type? Or that you both acknowledged you're tops and you prefer bedding a bottom?"

I chuckled and swiped my thumb across his cheek. It was warm and delicious. I ghosted my lips across his, and god help me, that was delicious too. "Both." I kissed him. "You are my type. Exactly my type." I pushed him backward onto the couch and settled my weight on him, kissing him again. "Made just for me. Perfect in every way."

With a hand around my neck, he pulled me in for a kiss, slipping his tongue into my mouth. He tasted of tea and perfection. He wrapped one leg around my thigh and moaned.

Yep. He was made just for me.

I broke the kiss, trailing my lips down his neck and so god help me, I would have done him right there on the sofa.

"Take me to bed," he panted. "I need you inside me."

Oh Lord.

I untangled myself from his hold and got to my feet. I pulled him up but he jumped onto me, his legs wrapped around my ass and he laughed as he kissed me.

"To bed, deputy."

I carried him like that to my room and laid him down on my bed. It was a fumble of eager hands and desperate mouths but eventually, we were under the covers, naked, me between his thighs. He brought his knees up to our chests as I pushed into him, and he let out a soft whine until I was as deep as I could go.

He held my face in his hands and kissed me, gasping and groaning when I began to move.

I kissed everywhere I could reach, tasting his skin, his

desire. Rocking like that, we found our rhythm. Slow and deep, his hands in my hair, scratching my back and arching his as he begged for more. His cock untouched, sliding between us, I swallowed his scream as he came. I let go of the reins and gave myself to the pleasure, driving up into him over and over, his body luring me to the edge.

My orgasm detonated from somewhere deep inside me. My bones, my blood, my brain. He held me as if I were made of glass, and in that moment, I thought I might be.

He was everything. He was sweet, sweet perfection. And his fingers in my hair and the soft press of his lips to my forehead lulled me to sleep.

I woke up with him as the little spoon, my arm slung over his waist, my nose pressed to the back of his neck.

I smiled.

"Morning," he murmured.

"Morning."

"Been waiting for you to wake up."

I tightened my hold on him. "You should have woken me."

He chuckled. "What? Just so I can tell you I'm starving and you need to cook me breakfast?"

I laughed, nudging my nose along his nape. "Yes."

"I think it's a full English breakfast kind of morning."

I gave him a squeeze. "Hm, me too."

He laughed and swatted my arm. "I'm not on the menu." Then he hummed. "Well, maybe after breakfast."

I kissed his bare shoulder. "What exactly is a full English breakfast?"

"Eggs, bacon, sausage, hash browns, fried tomato, and baked beans."

I stilled. "Baked beans? For breakfast?"

He chuckled. "Yes. The British kind of baked beans, not the American kind."

I didn't even know there were various kinds. "Well, I can cook you everything else, but I don't have baked beans. Not sure I even want to know what your British breakfast ones are, to be honest."

He chuckled. "I'll make you try it one day."

Mm. One day . . .

He made it sound like *one day in the future* was something we had.

I peeled myself away from him. "Right then, breakfast time it is." I pulled back the covers from him. "And you're helping me."

Chapter Thirteen

BRAITHE

BEING with Colson for a lazy Sunday morning was possibly the best thing ever. Well, what he'd done to me the night before was also possibly the best thing ever, but the simple act of cooking breakfast and laughing, eating together, showering together, it was amazing.

No, wait. Correction.

Seeing him happy was the best thing ever.

There was no what-have-I-done moment of regret from him about finally coming out to his boss. Or even telling Sergeant De Silva.

That he'd felt the need to tell him that I was *taken* probably shouldn't have given me such a thrill. But it did.

And the truth was, for my duration in Hartbridge, I *was* taken.

I was taken with Colson.

I was also taken by him.

I was his. For as long as I stayed in Hartbridge. Which I tried not to think about.

Because there was an end date. My time here was running

out. I was shortlisted for another temporary teaching stint in Spokane not long after Hartbridge.

It wasn't confirmed yet, and I needed to make contact to see . . . But I just didn't want to.

I didn't want to confirm that my time here was over. Or my time with Colson. I didn't want it to end.

Colson booped me on the nose. "What are you frowning for? I don't like that look."

"What look?"

"You being sad. What's wrong?" His mouth pulled down. "Did I do something? I can go and see Rosie at the store, maybe she can order you some English baked beans."

That made me laugh. "It's not the baked beans."

His eyes flickered with a realisation. "Are you homesick? For England?"

I shook my head. "No."

"Then what is it?"

I sighed. "I was just thinking . . . about how my time here is running out." His face changed. Like I'd slapped him or something.

His jaw ticked and his eyes hardened and softened at the same time. And with a gentle hand around my neck, he pulled me against him. "Can we not talk about it?" He swallowed. "Please?"

I sighed against him and relented a nod. "Sorry, I . . . I didn't mean to be a downer."

He held me a little tighter. "Do I want to know how long you have left?"

"Probably not," I whispered. "I leave at the start of the new year."

His breath caught but he held me against him, and for the longest time, we stood there in his kitchen. Just holding each other. Too scared to look at him, for fear of what I might see.

Too scared to admit what I was feeling, and sure as hell too scared to say it out loud.

"Why the long face?" Gunter asked me.

It was the first time I'd ever been to his house. Hamish decided I needed to go with him. Well, after meeting Hamish at the diner for coffee, he'd decided I needed to spend the afternoon with him running some errands.

Despite my mood, or because of it, I couldn't guess.

"He won't say," Hamish said. "But I can guess it has something to do with a certain sexy deputy."

I sighed. "I don't want to put it out there in the universe," I admitted. "If I speak of it, it's real, right?"

We were in his kitchen, standing by the sink, overlooking the backyard to a line of trees. Clay was out there with his truck and a chainsaw. We all stood there and watched him for a moment, being all strong and manly, cutting up a log and throwing firewood as if it weighed nothing.

"The view is terrible," Hamish murmured with a smirk. "I could watch it all day."

Gunter laughed. "Hm. Terrible." The man had hearts in his eyes as he said it. The complete adoration he had for Clay was very clear on his face.

It made my heart hurt even more. I shook my head and tried to change the subject. I looked around at his expensive art, his fancy furniture, and his gorgeous Christmas tree. "Your house is very beautiful, Gunter. I mean, Clay is too. Of course."

"Thank you." He smiled, but it was laced with concern. He watched me for a moment. "You don't want to leave Hartbridge."

Hamish nodded. "Bingo."

I groaned. "But I don't really have a choice. My contract here is almost over, and I have to work. Not just for the money but for my visa. I think I have my next job lined up in Spokane, which I don't want, because my god, Colson is so perfect, in every single way." I put my hand through my hair. "Whyyyyy did I have to meet him? Why did he have to be so perfect?" I put my hand to my heart. "And why does it hurt to think about saying goodbye?"

Hamish put his hand over mine, still pressed to my chest. "My poor sweet boy. You got tag-teamed by Cupid and Santa. It's what happens here."

Gunter snorted. "I hate to agree with him, but . . ."

I laughed out a sigh and let my head fall back. "Bollocks. Just . . . bollocks."

Hamish sighed and was serious then. "Braithe, you need to ask yourself some serious questions."

"I know." I swallowed. "That's the problem. Because I'm pretty sure I already know the answers."

"You want to stay?"

I nodded.

"For you? Or for him?"

I shrugged. "Both. I think. For me. I love it here."

"And him? You love him too?"

I made a face and sagged. "I don't know. Is it too soon? Is it ridiculous? Because it feels right, but the rational part of my brain is telling me it's far too soon to feel like this." I pulled my hair and groaned. "And even if it's not, I'm leaving, so what does it matter? It doesn't matter. Nothing matters. It's all for nothing, and all I've done is gone and made two people miserable. He's finally told his boss that he's gay. He's half out of the closet because of me, because he realised if he wants to be happy at some point, he needs to live his truth. If he wants to live with someone and wake up next to them and cook them breakfast and suck their dick in the shower, then he needs to be true to himself."

"He came out?" Gunter asked.

"He made you breakfast, then sucked your dick in the shower?" Hamish asked at the same time.

I buried my face in my hands. "I am in way over my head."

"You love him," Gunter said softly. "It's not too soon. There are no time limits. If the heart knows, it knows."

I put my hand to my forehead. "I don't know if I love him, but the thought of leaving him makes me feel a bit ill. And when Sergeant De Silva asked Colson about me, he was like, *back off, he's mine*, and I have to tell you, that did something to me."

Hamish tilted his head. "Sergeant who?"

I shook my head quickly. "No one, nothing."

So he looked at Gunter. "Do you know a Sergeant De Silva?"

Gunter shook his head. "No. Is he a policeman?"

Clay pulled his boots off in the mudroom. "No, he's a—"

"He's not relevant to this story!" I said loudly.

Gunter and Hamish were now staring at Clay. Clay, thankfully, clued in and walked to the fridge, smiling. He pulled out a jug of water. He smelled of sweat and sawdust, and honestly, I could see the appeal.

"I think he might be relevant to this story," Hamish said.

"I think you're missing the point I was trying to make."

Hamish and I looked at Gunter to see which side he was on, but he was too busy staring at Clay with love-struck googly eyes.

Hamish nudged me. "See? Cupid got him good."

I sighed just as my phone beeped. It was a message from Colson.

Is the invitation to the dinner party still open?

I smiled as I replied.

Sure is.

I think I'd like to go.

I think I'd like to take you.

I ignored the swoop of my belly and how my heart beat a little faster, and when I looked up, Hamish, Gunter, and Clay were all watching me.

"He's coming to the Christmas dinner party."

Hamish grinned and grabbed my arm. "Excellent. Good for him."

He understood it wasn't *just* a dinner for Colson. It was another coming out.

But then Hamish's eyes met mine and his smile was replaced by determination. "Okay, real talk, Braithe. We need to figure out a way for you to stay in Hartbridge."

I WAS at work early on Monday morning, buzzing for the busy week ahead. I'd barely slept, with Hamish's words playing on a loop in my head and late-night texts with Colson while he was at work. And I was trying not to think about leaving or staying; my brain and my heart were warring with each other.

I knew I probably should have called my parents, but the thought of perhaps hearing them—and missing them—wasn't the best idea for either my brain or my heart. I sent them an email update instead, telling them that I was fine and everything was great.

And if all that wasn't bad enough, the universe sent me another message.

I walked into the staff lounge at recess to find we had a

visitor. Emily Poole, the teacher I was subbing for, came in with her brand-new baby whom everyone was *oohing* and *aahing* over, and all I could do was plaster a smile on my face and pretend.

Pretend I was happy that she'd be replacing me soon enough.

As I'd replaced her, I guess.

Why is it so hard?

It wasn't Emily's fault. By all accounts, she seemed perfectly lovely. She was maybe late thirties and had been teaching forever, she loved all her students, and they loved her just as much.

When class resumed, she brought her baby into the kindergarten room. All the students were happy to see her, and they all thought the baby was cute. It was a good distraction after running around on the playground and a great way for them to settle down, knowing they had to be quiet for a sleeping baby.

"You fit in so well," Emily said. "The kids respond well to you." I had them continue with the letter tracing we'd been doing earlier.

"They're great kids," I said. "It's a great school."

She nodded, then glanced up at the new artwork on the walls and the Christmas decorations we'd made. "Such a fun time of year."

"It really is," I agreed. "We began practising for our Christmas play. You must come on the day and watch them. I'm sure they'd love for you to be here."

She smiled, a little emotional. "I wouldn't miss it." Her baby began to stir and fuss, so she said her goodbyes and our class continued like any other day.

At lunch, I saw I had a text message from Colson.

Do I need to bring anything to this dinner party?

He'd sent it a little while ago when he was probably at the store. It was his day off, after all, and he usually went shopping and did his meal prep for the week. He'd be back home now, for sure.

No need to bring anything. I'm picking up pizzas on the way. Unless you wanted some beers or soda?

His reply came through a few seconds later.

Okay, on it.

I smiled as I pocketed my phone and got involved in discussions about the Christmas play day and what other classes were doing. It was going to be a fun day for the kids, and I loved the excitement for it, all the while a part of me dreading it because I knew I was leaving.

Why did my brain keep circling back to this?

I didn't know whether to blame Hamish for putting the stupid idea in my head or blame myself for being resigned to leaving.

I GOT to Colson's around five thirty. It was already dark, so I parked my car on the street across the road. I smiled at the Christmas lights flickering through the front window and my heart was thumping against my ribs as I knocked.

He opened the door, his smile lighting up his whole face when he saw me. "Evening," he said, stepping aside.

"Good evening, C2," I replied, walking in.

He closed the front door and I stopped for a brief kiss. He smelled so good. "Are you okay? You look tired? Kids running you around crazy all day?"

I laughed. "No, I'm fine. I didn't sleep too well last night, that's all." Because I didn't want him to worry, I added, "And the kids run me around crazy every day. Do you know what it's like to practise for a class play? It's like having eighteen puppies all running in different directions."

He chuckled. "I can't even imagine."

I got another subtle waft of something sweet and soft. Whatever it was smelled expensive. "Are you wearing cologne?"

He baulked, his cheeks going red. "I . . . I didn't know what to do. Is it too much? Should I take a quick shower?"

Oh, this sweet, sweet man. He was nervous.

"It's perfect. Smells great, actually."

He groaned and gestured down to his jeans and sweater. "Do I look okay?"

I rubbed his arm. "You look great."

He didn't look convinced.

Then I noticed the bottles lined up on the kitchen counter. "Uh, hosting a party?"

He grimaced. "I, uh, I didn't know what to bring." There were some different sodas, a few different wines, and two six-packs of beer. "I don't drink too often," he went on. "And I'd be happy with soda, but maybe they'd think that was lame. Then I thought maybe I should take something as a gift? Like a bottle of wine, but I wasn't sure on red or white, so I got both. Or even a six-pack. I don't know. Do you know what they drink?"

I took his hand and waited for him to look at me. "Colson, it's fine. I promise you they will like you no matter what. A bottle of wine as a gift is a lovely idea. I'm sure someone will take a beer if you brought them along. But you don't need to worry. Just be yourself."

He let out a slow breath. "Am I overreacting?"

I shook my head. "No. You're allowed to be nervous and overwhelmed. It's fine. These guys are all down-to-earth, regular guys."

"They know I'm . . ."

I smiled. "They know you're what? The sexy deputy? Yes. They know that. Do they know you're nailing me? Well, yes, they know that too. But they don't assume anything. They just want you to know you're welcome and that you're safe with them, that's all."

His shoulders relaxed and he let out a breath. "Okay."

"If you want to leave at any time, you just say the word and we'll go."

His eyes met mine and he nodded. "You're good at this."

"I've had years of practice."

His smile faltered into a nose scrunch. "So they do know I'm—what did you call it—nailing you?"

I laughed. "Well, yes. I might have told Hamish about the good and thorough nailing I've been getting."

He sighed and rolled his eyes, his cheeks deep red. "Oh great."

I leaned up on my toes and kissed him. "Don't be embarrassed. You should be proud. You're worthy of accolades."

He dropped his forehead to my shoulder. "Awesome."

I gave him a hug and rubbed his back. "Are you ready to go then? We need to pick up the pizzas on the way. I rang through and ordered them."

He looked at me then, let out a sigh, and eventually nodded. "I'm ready. But perhaps we could hold off on the nailing comments while I'm there."

I laughed. "Deal." Then I thought about it. "Well, from me, yes. But I can make no promises about what comes out of Hamish's mouth."

Chapter Fourteen

COLSON

I was a ball of nerves pulling up to Ren and Hamish's house. There were other cars there already. Cass Campion's truck from the B&B I recognised, and Gunter Zuniga's car, and of course Ren and Hamish's truck. I could only assume that also meant Jayden and Clay were here too, just like Braithe had said they would be.

Recognising every car in town came with the territory of being a deputy, and it was a relief knowing who to expect. Not that there couldn't be other people here, but I knew some of the faces to expect upon entering the house.

It was reassuring.

I carried the drinks and Braithe carried the pizzas, and we walked up the front steps. There was laughter and what sounded like Bing Crosby music, and there was a warm glow from the windows and a Christmas wreath on the front door.

It all made me smile, and for some reason tamped down the nerves.

It made me feel . . . invited.

"Are you ready?" Braithe asked.

I gave a nod. "Yeah."

He knocked on the door. "Oh, I'll get it," a voice called. Pretty sure it was Hamish. He was Australian, anyway. It could have been Jayden . . . The door swung inwards, and sure enough, Hamish stood there wearing a Christmas sweater and a grin. "Come in, come in."

He closed the door behind us, and not knowing what else to do, I offered him both bottles of wine. "For you," I said. "As thanks, I, uh . . ."

His smile softened and he nudged Braithe. "You were right. He's the sweetest."

Oh, dear god.

Ren swooped in and relieved me of the six-pack. "At least let them come through the door before you horrify them," he said to Hamish, leading me into the family room.

Their house was gorgeous. All wood and homey, with a fire and a huge Christmas tree, expertly decorated. There was an open kitchen and living room, and at the centre of the room was a table fully decked out in Christmas decorations.

Cass was taking something out of the oven, Jayden was describing something to Gunter with his hands, and Clay walked right up to me.

"Good to see you again," he said, offering me his hand to shake.

"Likewise."

I was introduced formally to Gunter and Jayden, and then Cass. I knew them by name, as I knew most people in Hartbridge. And Ren, of course, though everyone in town knew Ren.

"Deputy," Jayden said with a nod. I'd spoken to him a hundred times at the diner but never been introduced. Not really.

"Call me Colson," I said, feeling all eyes on me. I tried to let out a steady breath. "It's, uh, thanks for the invite."

Ren put a beer in my hand and Clay began talking about the job on Cottonwood Road, which reminded Ren of something one of his customers had told him, and Cass mentioned the Christmas Light Festival, and before I knew it, we'd been there an hour.

There was no awkwardness, no silences. Just conversation about the town, the people we knew. We talked about hockey, we laughed a lot, and we sat down at a table full of all kinds of food.

Braithe sat next to me, his hand on my thigh or around my shoulder. He gave my shoulder a squeeze when he got up and my initial response was to freeze.

A reaction only he noticed, I'm sure.

But no one else noticed. No one else cared. Jayden was too busy telling a funny story, and I realised that I didn't have to hide here.

What had Braithe said before?

I was safe with these guys.

I hadn't thought much of his words at the time, but they struck me now. And the way Braithe smiled at me from the kitchen, holding up a bottle of pop to ask if I'd like one, and how I'd nodded to him.

I was safe here.

Though I did notice Hamish watching us with a small smile.

Okay, so maybe he noticed.

But to everyone else, this was normal. This was their normal. Good food and good conversation.

I didn't know what I'd expected. Maybe conversations about gay things? I really had no clue. I'd never been to a dinner party exclusive for queer men, and movies and TV shows were a far cry from reality.

But this was just . . . normal.

And so very perfect.

Ren had his arm around Hamish most of the night, and every time Jayden laughed, he'd lean into Cass. Gunter looked at Clay like he hung the moon, and Clay doted on him.

And Braithe?

When he wasn't laughing or swapping barbs with the Australians about cricket and rugby, he was watching me. His hand on my thigh or giving my fingers a quick squeeze, as if he knew exactly what I needed.

A gentle reassurance. A private gesture, a comfort that I was doing great. "Okay, I have a question," Braithe asked. "What do you call a popsicle stick? Like the stick in an ice lolly."

Ren tilted his head. "An ice lolly?"

I chuckled. "That's what *I* said."

"You mean a Paddle Pop stick?" Hamish asked.

Braithe stared at him. "What on earth is a Paddle Pop, and why does it have a stick?"

"It's an ice cream. On a stick."

"An ice block," Jayden added.

"An ice block?" Gunter and Cass said at the same time.

Clay squinted at him. "Are you making an igloo?"

"No," Jayden said with a laugh. "Not a block of ice, but an ice block . . . Oh, this whole conversation is bad."

"An ice lolly is what they're called in England," Braithe added.

"A lolly to me is candy to these guys," Hamish said, pointing his thumb to the Americans. "Except not all lollies are. Like I would call jelly beans a lolly, or candy for these guys, but a chocolate bar is not candy. It's a chocolate bar."

"Agreed," Braithe said.

"Wrong," I said.

Ren snorted and gave Hamish a nudge. "Tell them what you call cotton candy."

He shrank with a sigh. "Fairy floss."

Braithe laughed. "You mean candy floss."

Everyone squinted at him, me included. "Candy floss?" I asked. "Really?"

"Don't even mention pudding," Jayden said, looking right at Braithe. "It's still a thing all these years later."

Gunter was still staring at Hamish. "You call cotton candy fairy floss?"

Braithe laughed. "Should we even mention the word biscuit here?"

"Oh, please don't," Jayden added, with a look that said *that* was an exhausting conversation he'd had many times.

Braithe snorted and I laughed.

"Look," Braithe began. "If I just call it a popsicle stick, everyone will know what I'm talking about."

"Why are you even talking about popsicle sticks?"

"A Christmas craft in my classroom," he explained. "We made little Christmas trees where you stack squares of sticks, large to small, to make a pyramid. Paint them green and stick little pompoms on for baubles. And we made ornaments by sticking cellophane paper to squares with a pipe cleaner so they can hang on a tree."

"That's so cute," Jayden said.

"Making Christmas crafts was my favourite time of year at school," Ren said.

Hamish laughed. "I thought making out with half the football team was your favourite time of year."

Ren and Cass both put their hands up. "Hey. We agreed to never bring that up," Cass said, and everyone laughed, Hamish and Jayden especially.

There was definitely a story there.

But there was so much love at this table. It was so easy. So easy to just be myself. For the first time ever, I was in a social setting where I didn't have to pretend.

When Braithe, Cass, and Ren cleared the table, Hamish, Jayden, and Gunter played some kind of tic-tac-toe game with funny pieces, and Clay offered me a port wine at the fire.

I took the small glass. "Thanks."

"How've you been?" he asked quietly.

I almost laughed. "Uh, good. I guess. It's been a crazy week, that's for sure."

He sipped his drink. "You know the saying 'it gets easier' sounds kinda cheesy, but it's true." He studied the fire. "When I first came out, I was scared as hell. I worried about what people might think. In the town, that is. I worried it'd affect the business."

I nodded because I got that. I understood completely.

"Most people were great. Actually, most people were shocked and didn't believe me." He snorted. "I mean, look at me."

He was a six-foot lumberjack, complete with a plaid shirt and beard.

"There'll always be people who don't like it, or agree with it," he continued. "The thing is, they don't have to. If they got a problem with it, that's exactly what it is: their problem. Not mine."

I nodded again. I appreciated him saying that. "Thanks." I let out a puff of air. "I told Ronny. He was great. He . . . he was fine with it, and that means a lot. Since I've been here, he's been like a father to me."

Clay smiled at that. "He's a good guy. He and my old man go way back."

I wasn't sure how to ask this . . . "Was . . . was having such a history here in Hartbridge a good or bad thing for you?" I shrugged. "Coming out, I mean. I'm still kinda new, and I don't have any family . . . Ronny mentioned Ren's dad and the history . . . I dunno. It kinda feels like I'm standing in the spotlight by myself, which is terrifying."

He smiled at the fire. "I get what you're saying. Ren had his dad's support," he murmured. "And my dad's great."

"He is. Everyone loves Cliff."

Clay's eyes met mine and he smiled sadly. "Having family support is, well, it's everything to me. My dad and I are close, and I couldn't even imagine what I would've done if he didn't like me falling in love with a guy. But Gunter has no one. Jayden has no family here. And I'll tell you something, Colson." He met my eyes. "You're not alone here. You got family." He gave a pointed nod around the room, and I followed his line of sight. To the three in the kitchen washing dishes, to the three on the sofa laughing about the eggplant and peach game pieces.

"It might be a different kinda family than you were hoping for," Clay said gently. "But it's a family all the same."

I had to blink back tears and I ignored the way my nose burned. I turned back to the fire and sipped my drink. "Thanks."

Clay sighed. "And when I say they're family, I mean it in the sense that you don't get to pick them. They just take you in, and they'll annoy you and drive you crazy, but you wouldn't swap them for anything."

I let out a teary laugh. "Sounds like a family."

I didn't know if Clay signalled for Braithe to come over, but he was suddenly beside me. He slid his arm around my lower back and rested his cheek on my shoulder, looking up at me. "You okay?"

I let out a breathy laugh. "Yeah. I'm fine."

"You wanna go?"

I nodded. "Yeah. Is that okay?"

He gave me a soft smile. "Of course it is." Then he turned and spoke to the room. "Okay, guys, we have to get going. I have class early tomorrow."

He thanked everyone for the food and the lovely evening, and I shook hands with Clay. "Thanks, for before."

"Anytime. I'll drop by sometime. We'll have a beer."

I couldn't help but smile. "I'd like that."

Ren and Cass both shook my hand. "So glad you could make it," Ren said. "Next time we're having a get-together, I'll let you know."

"Sounds good."

Sounded great, actually.

"Coffee in the diner is our usual go-to," Gunter said. "With the promise of coffee and cake, it takes no convincing. You're welcome to join us anytime."

I nodded. "Thank you."

Hamish linked his arm through mine and led me to the front door. "Okay, so here's the thing," he began.

"Hamish, let go of him," Braithe said behind us. "Colson, don't believe a word he says."

Hamish laughed. "I was just going to say we'd see him at the light festival."

"You absolutely were not," Braithe said with a smile. He slipped his hand into mine and pulled me outside onto the front porch. The air was cold, the night dark, and a few flurries of snow feathered to the ground.

"Oh look," Hamish said. "It's snowing!"

Everyone came to the front to see, and Braithe and I waved from the car. Looking up at them all standing there, with the Christmas lights in the window, felt kinda surreal.

So utterly bizarre that I could have this. That this could be my reality. It didn't feel real.

Braithe drove, of course, and soon we were on the road heading back into town. "You sure you're okay?"

I nodded. "I am. I just . . ." And again with the tears. "I don't know why I'm upset. Happy tears, I think." I let out a breath and shook my head, more at myself for being so foolish. "And also not-happy tears, I think. I don't even know."

"Oh, Colson," he said, reaching over and taking my hand. "It's okay. Whatever you're feeling is okay."

"I just . . . it feels surreal. Like a dream," I tried to explain. "It was so perfect and so normal and everything I thought I'd never get to have."

He nodded, his eyes full of concern.

"And it makes me sad and angry that I've been deprived of this for so long. Because I didn't allow myself . . . I wouldn't allow myself to have that. God, I feel so stupid." I scrubbed a tear from my cheek, mad at myself for not being in control of my emotions. "Those guys are great, and Clay said some stuff about family that hit home, and . . ."

I didn't realise we'd pulled up to my place. Braithe cut the engine and got out, waiting for me to do the same. But the original plan had been that he'd drop me home, then he'd go back to his place.

I got out. "Wh-what are you doing?"

"I'm not leaving you alone tonight," he said. "Come on. Yes, the snow is pretty but it's cold."

Right.

I went up the steps and opened the front door, holding it for him. While he took his boots and coat off, I stoked the fire and tried to get my thoughts in order.

When I turned around, Braithe had my quilt over him on the couch. He held the end open for me. "Come into my little cocoon."

I pulled off my coat and tossed it on the other couch, then joined him under the quilt. It was warm and cosy and perfect.

"You wanna talk about it?" He asked. "It's okay to feel conflicted."

That was exactly how I felt.

Conflicted.

"Those guys are all great. They're good people," I said. "And it was just so . . . normal. I know I keep saying that, but it's the only word to describe it. I didn't know what to expect. I didn't know what we'd talk about or anything. I've never been to a dinner party just for queer people."

"Did you think we'd watch *Drag Race* or *Queer Eye* or something?" He smiled at me and threaded his fingers with mine.

I snorted, finally smiling. "Honestly, I wasn't sure. I've never . . . I've never been in a place that's just queer men, gay men. I, uh . . . I didn't know."

His face softened and he leaned into me. "I'm sorry. I didn't mean to make a joke of it."

"No, it's fine. I didn't know what to expect. But it was all just so . . . normal." There was that word again. "I hate that word. But *normal* conversations like I'd have with anyone anywhere."

"Were you disappointed?"

"No! The opposite. It was the best part. It was so perfect. These guys are just like everyone else. Because we are just like everyone else."

He nodded now, smiling at me.

"And then I got mad at myself because I'd denied myself such a simple thing. For so long, I told myself I could never have that. I could never . . ." I shook my head, tired of fighting the tears. I let them fall instead. "My parents told me I'd never have that. That I'd be alone forever and I'd deserve it, and I believed them. I excluded myself from . . . that part of me. From who I am. And then tonight, it was just so perfect and nice. It was so fucking nice. I'm mad at myself for not letting me have some kind of happiness."

Braithe was curled up against me, playing with the hair at the back of my collar. He looked sad, but he listened, his big blue eyes studying my face.

"You don't have to deny yourself anything anymore," he murmured.

"I don't want to. And it might be scary as hell, and chances are I could have some friends who won't be my friends anymore."

His whole face was a mask of sadness.

"You wanna know what Clay said?" I asked.

He nodded.

"That now I had a different kind of family." Fresh tears rolled down my face and I scrubbed them away. "That all those guys are now my family, and we might not get to choose them, but they're family all the same."

Braithe nodded, teary-eyed. "Found family, Colson. The people who choose to love and support you."

I let out a sigh and dropped my head back on the sofa. "God. What a night."

"I'm proud of you," he said. "You've come a long way in a short time. Don't feel pressured or that you need to rush anything. Take a minute to breathe and see how far you've come."

Keeping my head on the backrest of the sofa, I looked at him. "I couldn't have done this without you."

"Yes, you would have," he murmured. "Maybe not right now, but someday."

I rubbed his back. "You're kinda great, you know that?"

He grinned, then sliding his leg over mine, he straddled

me, the comforter around his shoulders. My hands found his hips and he shuffled in as close as the couch allowed. He pressed his forehead to mine. "I am kinda great. Wanna know what else I am?"

"What's that?"

"I'm kinda horny." He rolled his hips, trying to find friction. "Should we go to bed, or do you want to do me right here?"

I groaned out a laugh. "You have an early start tomorrow."

He lifted my chin so he could kiss me. "Then hurry up and take me to bed, Deputy."

"Is that an order?"

"Yes."

Keeping him pinned to my hips, I stood up and carried him easily. He laughed and threw his arms around my neck to hold on as I walked down the hall to my bed, and so god help me, this perfect night just got a whole lot more perfect.

Chapter Fifteen

BRAITHE

THE WEEK at school passed in a blur. We followed the lesson plans, of course, but we also spent all our craft time making more Christmas decorations. We used crepe paper and cotton wool balls to make Santas, and painted reindeer and used tiny twigs for antlers, and we practised our nativity play after lunch every day, and I finished off the backdrop in the afternoons after class.

Mrs Parson cooked dinner for me on Wednesday and Thursday nights, and she totally kicked my arse at *Jeopardy* again.

I texted Colson every night while he was at work. Not that I expected speedy responses, but I wanted him to know I was thinking of him. That he wasn't alone.

I grinned like a fool every time my phone beeped with a message. I kept telling myself it was foolish and I was setting myself up for inevitable heartbreak when it came time for me to leave. But the undeniable truth was, he made me happy.

Whether he was out or not, it didn't matter to me. The man he was in the public eye wasn't my concern. The man he was when he was alone with me was. And that man, the gentle, caring, warm man was. It didn't hurt any that he was incredibly attentive in bed, that his hands could play me like a harp, plucking strings I didn't even know I had.

But it wasn't just him. I fell in love with this town a little bit more each day. The picturesque town, the people.

I didn't miss home one bit. I missed my family, sure. But not enough to pack my bags and go home.

But maybe I was conflicted enough to risk having a conversation with Principal Nancy O'Connor.

On Friday afternoon, she stuck her head into my classroom. "Oh, you're still here," she said. "I wondered if you'd left the lights on."

I put the paintbrush down. "Just finishing up now."

She came in to take a better look at the backdrop for the play. "It looks great." Then she tilted her head a little, and it made me laugh.

"The stable is a bit wonky."

She smiled. "It's fine. Perfect, even. Practice for the play coming along nicely?"

"Oh, yes. The students are very excited. We have more animals and palm trees than is probably standard, but I wanted every child to have a part."

Her smile softened. "Lovely idea."

Okay, so here went nothing.

"While I have you, can I ask you something?" I tried not to grimace, but my nerves got the better of me. "It's more of a blanket-statement, putting-my-hat-in-the-ring type of thing."

She nodded as if she knew exactly what I was about to say.

"I know Emily Poole is due to come back after New Year's and that's wonderful. The kids were all very excited to see her when she called in the other day."

"Yes," she hedged cautiously. "And?"

"Well, should her circumstances change or if she requires a

longer period of leave, I'd love to be considered for an extension."

She smiled then, her suspicions clearly correct.

"I just love it here," I added. "The town, the people, the kids. This school. You've fostered a truly caring environment here, and it's one of the best schools I've ever taught at."

She gave a nod. She was a smart woman, and I assumed she had a knack for seeing through people. I hoped she saw that my intentions were good.

"Anyway," I added, "I just wanted you to know in case you needed a substitute, although I am supposed to be leaving, I would change my plans to stay longer. If you need. That's all. I'm not implying I should replace anyone. I'm just offering. Should you need . . ." I grimaced again, shoving my hands into my pockets so I'd stop waving them around. "I don't mean to sound as if I'm imposing or treading on anyone's toes. Sorry, I just . . . wanted you to be aware."

Her smile widened, probably at my rambling. "Thank you," she said. "There've been no requests for leave, extended or otherwise, at this time, but I'll keep you in mind."

I almost sagged with relief, feeling better just having asked. "Thank you." I cleaned the brushes and grabbed my coat and beanie, following Nancy out. It was Friday afternoon, getting dark already as winter curled its icy fingers around us. I'd made plans to catch up with Hamish at the diner, so I headed straight there.

I pulled my beanie down and popped up my scarf to warm my neck. Brrr, it was cold. I should have brought my gloves today . . .

I pushed on the diner door and almost bumped into a family as they were leaving. "Mr Branson!" a little voice said.

"Oh, Lucy," I said. She was in my class, and she was as cute as a button. I recognised Lucy's mom. She'd been one of the parents who'd made a point of dropping in to meet the new teacher. I couldn't remember her name. Beth? Becky?

"Bridgette," she said, tucking Lucy into her side. "Nice to see you again."

"Yes, how lovely," I replied. I focused more on Lucy because I didn't want to give Bridgette the wrong idea. "Did Lucy tell you she's a sheep in the Christmas play? We've been practising very hard, haven't we?"

Lucy gave me a grin, her front tooth missing, and she nodded. "It's fun!"

I held up my paint-covered hands. "It sure is."

"What are you getting?" Lucy asked. "I had a chocolate cupcake. With sprinkles."

I patted her head. "You know what? That sounds perfect. With a big hot chocolate with marshmallows."

Lucy thought this was funny, and I smiled at Bridgette. "I hope to see you at the school play."

Bridgette gave a breathy laugh as she nodded and took Lucy's hand and led her to the door. "We sure will. Enjoy your weekend. Bye now."

I waved at Lucy, and only once they were gone did I turn around to find Hamish and Gunter grinning at me.

I all but fell into the booth beside Hamish with a tired sigh. He laughed. "Do all the mothers flirt with you like that?"

"Yes. It's better now. It was bad in the beginning."

"Poor things," Hamish said. "Do they know they're wasting their time?"

I rolled my eyes. "I need chocolate. Who wants what?" I ordered enough for the three of us, along with a container of the lunch special to take home later. Mrs Parson would be at her daughter's again and I was too tired to make anything myself, or even to call past the shop.

"You look tired," Gunter noted.

I sighed. "I might have told Principal O'Connor today that I'd be interested in a longer position if there should be any leave requests put in."

Hamish gasped and grabbed my arm. "And?"

I'd have thought the look on my face said enough. "She said no."

Hamish deflated, and Gunter frowned. "I'm sorry."

"Me too," I replied.

"But you asked," Hamish added. "And that's good. It certainly can't hurt. At least she knows now."

I nodded and gave him a smile, trying to harvest some of his optimism. "Fingers crossed." I couldn't help feeling a little sad though. "I am disappointed. I mean, I'm not surprised. But still. Like I finally admitted it, put it out into the universe, and got told no."

"Have you told Colson?" Gunter asked.

I met his gaze and shook my head. "I don't want to disappoint him. It's probably for the best if he assumes I'm leaving, right? If I give him false hope, it will be so much harder for him." Then I shrugged. "Goodness, listen to me. Talking as if he'll be utterly devastated. He might not even be thinking long term. I mean, he shouldn't be. It was never on the table, and those parameters haven't changed at all. I was always leaving. And that's still true."

Hamish frowned and pushed the chocolate cake toward me. "You need this."

"I'm going to need a new wardrobe at this rate," I said as I stabbed the cake with my fork. "All we ever do is eat."

Hamish gave me a nudge and murmured, "You need to work it off in other ways. You know, for cardio health purposes."

I laughed just as I shovelled in a huge piece of cake, exactly as the bell chimed above the door and a cold blast of air came in. I didn't turn around, but I noticed Gunter's eyes light up and he gave me a tap with his foot under the table.

I turned to see Colson, standing there smiling at us, looking mighty fine in his uniform.

And there I was, laughing with a mouth full of chocolate cake, now trying not to choke.

"Ah, Deputy Price," Hamish said. "Nice to see you."

He took his hat off and walked over, his eyes and his smile on me. "Afternoon."

I washed down the chocolate cake with a sip of my hot chocolate. "Afternoon," I managed, not flustered at all.

Gunter chuckled. "Cold out there?"

"Yeah, it's got some bite," he replied, his eyes landing on me again. "You okay there?"

"Oh yes, quite fine, thank you," I said, patting down my sweater. "I should know better than to eat while Hamish is talking."

He grinned, but then Carl hollered from behind the counter. "Ah, Deputy Price. Here's your order." He lifted a large bag of containers. "Tell Charity I said to wish her a happy birthday."

"Will do."

While he paid at the counter, I took out my phone and sent him a quick text.

Okay if I'm at your house when you finish work tonight?

A second later, his phone beeped. He took it out and read the message. Carl handed him his receipt, and Colson pocketed his phone. But he looked at me, smiled right at me, dipped his hat with a nod, and walked out.

I felt like a giddy schoolboy. I very nearly swooned, and I didn't care that Hamish and Gunter were both watching me.

But then Hamish's smile faltered a little and he turned his

coffee cup in his hand. "You know before when you said you didn't know if he'd be upset when you leave?"

My good mood deflated, because . . .

Gunter nodded. "Oh yeah. He will be."

Hamish's eyes met mine. "And he won't be the only one."

I USED the spare key at the back of Colson's house to let myself in just after nine. I fixed his fire, switched on all the Christmas lights, and made myself a cup of tea. I noted there were only three teabags left, and I made a mental list to run to the store tomorrow and grab some more.

Then, upon thinking twice about it, I went and checked in his room.

There were two left.

Thank god.

I'd be asking him to use both tonight because I wanted him to absolutely rail me.

I couldn't get what Hamish and Gunter had said to me out of my head.

That Colson would be devastated when I left. I knew he would be, and I didn't want to think about it. I'd be devastated too.

Gutted.

Made worse by the fact I'd asked Nancy, putting my cards on the table, and lost.

I needed him tonight. I needed him to take me to bed and have me any way he wanted. I needed him to wreck me. I needed to be worked over, thoroughly.

Just after ten, my phone lit up with Colson's number on the screen. I feared he was calling to tell me he'd be late.

"Hello?"

"Hey," he replied, his voice deep and slow. "You still awake?"

"Very much so. I'm on your couch in front of the fire with a book."

He made a sound. Not a sigh, not a grunt; something in between. "Sounds perfect."

"Everything okay?"

"Oh yeah, I'm just out in the cruiser. Thought I'd give you a call."

I hummed. "Will you be home after midnight?"

"Should be."

"Good. I'll be ready."

"Ready for what?"

"The condom–teabag tally now stands at two remaining, each. We're not sleeping tonight until the condoms win."

There was a beat of silence. "Christ, Braithe."

I chuckled, warmth pooling in my belly. "As I said, I'll be ready. Don't be late."

I clicked off the call and smiled.

And at ten minutes before midnight, I'd not long been out of the shower and had spent a good while prepping myself, when I heard Colson's cruiser pull up.

He was early, and by the sound of him running inside and bursting through the front door, he sounded in a hurry. I came out to meet him, concerned. "Is everything okay?"

He collected me in his arms and lifted me onto his hips. "Stop talking," he said, kissing me as he walked us into his bedroom.

I laughed, trying to get his jacket off his shoulders. He dumped me on the bed and followed me up the mattress, pulling my thigh up as he claimed my mouth with his.

He was rock-hard and desperate. "You don't play fair," he

mumbled, trying to get his belt undone, still kissing me. "And fuck, you're so warm."

I laughed. "Just got out of the shower. I even lubed myself up. When I said I'd be ready—"

He knelt back, flipped me over onto my front, and pulled my sleep pants down to reveal my arse. By the time I'd untangled my legs, he'd ripped the foil wrapper open, rolled the condom on, and squirted more lube down my crack.

I barely got to lift my hips when he positioned himself and pushed into me. In one long thrust, he was inside me. Breaching me, filling me. It was almost too much, and I cried out at the intrusion.

He pressed his weight on my back, holding me down, holding me still, his breath hot in my ear. "Fuck," he grunted.

I'd needed him to take me to bed and have me any way he wanted. I'd needed him to wreck me, like I'd needed to be worked over, thoroughly. And that's exactly what he did.

He was still fully dressed. He still had his boots and belt on, but he drove up into me, thrusting and grunting, gripping one arm under my shoulder, his other hand at the top of my head, holding me. He kissed my shoulder, moaning whispers of sweet nothings.

Any pain or discomfort was replaced with pleasure and ecstasy. Being so desired, so wanted. So perfect. I never wanted this to end.

"Yes, just like this," I murmured. "Don't stop."

"Not gonna last like this," he moaned. "Fuck, you feel so good. Too good." Then he bucked up hard and deep, pushing me to the edge of bliss.

"Oh god," I cried. "Yes, yes. Colson, please."

And he didn't stop, relentlessly driving into me until I unravelled underneath him, and he cried out as he came, shuddering and shaking as his orgasm took hold.

He collapsed on top of me, panting hard and gasping for breath.

All I could do was laugh. "You okay?"

He made a pained sound. "God, Braithe, I'm so sorry. Are you okay?" He pulled out slowly, making me whimper. He rolled me over and cupped my face. "Are you okay? I was too rough. I was—"

"You were perfect," I said, still riding a blissful high. "That was exactly what I needed. What I hoped you'd do to me."

He searched my eyes. "What?"

I laughed again and wiped the smear of come from my belly. "And we still have one condom to go tonight." He looked a little uncertain, so I lifted my head and kissed him, smiling, dreamy. "We're not letting the teabags win."

His gaze softened as he smiled. "If you're sure you're okay . . ." I kissed him again. "I'm so much better than okay. But how about we have a shower and maybe some hot chocolate by the fire. I don't have to get up early tomorrow, and I plan to be so thoroughly worked over that I sleep in late."

IT WAS A CRUEL IRONY, really, that with every passing day, I loved Hartbridge more and more, and every day that passed was a day closer to me having to leave.

It was a good thing that school was busy. And it was also a lot of fun and incredibly rewarding. Getting to see the kids learn and grow was always my favourite part of teaching. And practising their play, getting to see snippets of their little personalities, it was the highlight for me.

"You had a good day," Colson said. He might have snuck in to see me when he was doing his rounds on Wednesday night. It was late, well after nine, and he'd parked his cruiser down the road a short way and tiptoed down Mrs Parson's driveway to my place.

"I did," I replied, sliding my arms around him. "Even better now." He sighed as he kissed me.

"Damn," he mumbled. "Seeing you all warm and snug in your PJs like this just makes me wanna call in sick to work and stay right here."

I hummed with satisfaction as I planted a soft kiss on his lips. I liked knowing he wanted me as much as I wanted him. "I wouldn't mind."

He groaned and put me at arm's length. "Didn't you say you had something to ask me?"

I whined, missing his arms around me. "Well, yes. I just wanted to remind you that our school play is this Friday and the students have been working really hard on it, and I'd love for you to drop by. If you can. Totally as an honorary guest of the class, given how much they loved having you visit."

He smirked. "For the kids, huh?"

I nodded. "Totally."

"And not for the cute teacher?"

I gave him a smiley pout. "For the children."

He chuckled and pulled me back into his arms. "You shouldn't pout like that," he murmured. "Plays right into my weaknesses."

I chuckled victoriously. "Ten o'clock. There's a lunch afterwards. Half the town will be there."

He smiled and ran his hand down over my arse. "Then I should come in uniform. Make it official."

I happily wiggled against him, smiling, until the movement registered something else pressing firmly against me. "Mm. Speaking of coming in uniform," I murmured, then I sank to my knees right where we stood and unzipped his fly.

Chapter Sixteen

COLSON

I KNOCKED on Ronny's door and waited for him to glance up from his paperwork. "Got a second?"

"Sure thing," he said, dropping his pen onto the papers he was reading. I saw him notice that I'd left his door open so this wasn't a personal chat. "What's up?"

I sat in the chair opposite him. "I just wanted to run something by you."

"Okay?"

"I've been invited to the school again for the Christmas play-concert-day thing. Not really in an official capacity, but I thought I should wear my uniform anyway. Just wondered if that was okay." Not that I thought he'd have a problem with it, but it only felt right to ask.

"Not in an official capacity . . . ?" he repeated, clearly wanting more of an explanation.

I'd wanted to avoid mentioning him but there was no avoiding it. "The teacher of the kindergarten students asked me. He thought the kids might like me to watch their play after they'd made me the Christmas tree and all."

I gave a glance over my shoulder at my desk, where the tree still sat. It sounded like a flimsy excuse, even to me.

"Ah," Ronny said with a nod. "The young Englishman who stopped by to hand deliver it."

Ronny was far too astute to not connect the dots, as he saw right through me, and I felt my face flame.

"Um. Yes. He just thought the children might like it if I came back."

He sat there studying me for a good few seconds before he fought a smile and lost. "Well, that's mighty nice of him to ask, don't you think?" His moustache twitched. "I mean, it'd be rude for you not to go."

I felt stupid and giddy, as if I'd just asked my own father and not my boss. "Thank you." I stood up. "I'll, uh, I'll accept the invitation."

Ronny was still smiling. "So . . . uh . . ."

Oh, dear god.

"He's a nice young fellow," Ronny said. "Word around town is that he's a decent guy, anyway. Kids love him anyway. I even heard that he's made some good friends . . ."

I didn't like where this had gone, and dread seeped into my belly. "Friends?"

"Oh yes, you know," he said, brushing off my concern. "That he's been spotted at the diner with Hamish and the other Australian . . ."

"Jayden," I filled in for him.

And in that split second, I got it. This was a small town. People talked. The rumour mill worked overtime. But the crux of this whole thing was glaringly obvious because it was this very reason that stopped me from coming out.

"So everyone assumes he's gay, right?" I asked quietly. I hadn't meant for it to sound so bitter, but I wasn't sorry. "Is that deductive reasoning or just stereotyping?"

He sighed. "Colson—"

"It's that right there, that assumption that stops me from including those guys in my circle of friends. Or why I have to get Braithe to drive me to Ren's place for a harmless Christmas dinner so people don't see my cruiser parked at their place. Why I can't even grab coffee at the diner with them."

Ronny sighed, his shoulders deflated. "I didn't mean that."

"No one ever does. No one means anything by it, but they still notice all the same." I ran my hand through my hair and tried to calm down. He wasn't the one I wanted to aim this anger at. I shook my head, now mad at myself for letting my emotions get the best of me. "Sorry. Sorry for the outburst, Sheriff. If you don't mind, there are some papers that need to be served out past Hemlock Junction."

I turned and, collecting the paperwork off my desk, grabbed my coat and hat and walked out.

The drive would do me good.

Clearing my mind would do me good.

Because I'd been so immersed in the bubble that Braithe afforded me, that safety net of privacy and discretion, that I'd thought maybe fully coming out was possible.

And then with one throwaway comment from Ronny— that the town was talking about Braithe hanging out with the gay guys and therefore that could only mean one thing—my bubble burst.

Reality was cold, stark, and incredibly heavy.

Not even the passing scenery blanketed in fresh snow lifted my mood. Normally I found a trace of joy in that, but not today.

Goddammit.

I'd been so consumed by Braithe that I forgot what my reality was.

Everything was so perfect with him. The texts, him staying at my house, sleeping in my bed, me sneaking into his place.

But it was all on the down-low.

No public, no drama.

No risk.

And I'd let myself dream that it could be my reality.

When the actual reality was that this town talked behind people's backs. Rumours that began with *Oh, did you hear about . . .* or *You know who I saw the other day . . .* and *You'll never guess who I saw talking to . . .*

Was I ready for that?

Because if I was seen in public with Braithe, or with any of the other guys, that's what the town would do to me.

Not to mention what they'd say about Braithe or what the parents of the school might think.

God.

What a mess.

Maybe I shouldn't go to the school play. Maybe I should tell him it wouldn't be a good idea.

Because the truth was, Braithe was leaving in what, two weeks? Less than that? Two weeks . . .

That reality hit me so damn hard I had to pull off the road —like a punch to the gut, to the heart—and try and catch my breath.

I sat there with my hands on the steering wheel, surrounded by snow-white trees and silence, and tried to remember what the hell I'd been thinking. Why did I ever think this was doable?

The radio crackled to life, scaring the life out of me. "Base to C2, come in. Over."

I picked up the receiver. "C2 here. Over."

"Just got a call from Betsy Hammond on Cedar Bark Road. She said there's some cattle through the fence and on the road. Her boys are rounding them up, but you might wanna go by and check it out. Over."

"Will do. Just on my way to Hemlock. Will swing past on my way back in. Over."

The distraction was just what I needed.

Work. Work was what I needed. The one constant thing in my life. I hung the receiver in the cradle and pulled back onto the road. I served the papers, nothing devastating, thank god, and by the time the Hammonds had their cattle back in and the fence fixed and I got back to the office, it was well after dark.

Ronny was gone, and I was glad.

I'd owe him an apology tomorrow, but I didn't have it in me tonight.

All evening, I stuck to myself, sat at my desk, and filled in the never-ending supply of paperwork. My phone had beeped with some messages from Braithe, but I wasn't up for replying tonight.

Sometime around ten, Charity put a cup of coffee on my desk. "You okay?"

"Oh, sure," I said. With a quick glance around the room, I saw that Bouchard was gone.

"He's off patrolling," she said, clearly reading my surprise.

I'd completely lost track of time. "Oh, right. Of course."

She studied me for a second. "Is everything okay, Colson?" I met her gaze, not sure what she knew, what she'd heard on the Hartbridge grapevine, or what my face gave away.

"It's only that I noticed you were upset the other day and you've been distracted and quiet," she added quickly. "I don't mean to pry."

"I, uh, yeah, sure." I felt a little ill. "I'm fine."

She studied me, clearly knowing I was not fine at all.

"Would your troubles have anything to do with a certain

someone who gave you this?" She touched the Christmas tree made of popsicle sticks.

Yep. I felt more than a little ill. Like I was about to be sick. I opened my mouth and pushed my hand against my stomach, trying to tamp down the urge to vomit. "Jesus Christ," I mumbled. "What did you . . . who said . . . ?"

She grabbed my shoulder and squeezed, making me look at her. Not a menacing grip but a reassuring one. "Colson, it's okay, hun. I didn't hear anything. No one said anything." She raised her eyebrows, her gaze serious. "Okay? No one said a word. You're okay. You feel okay? You look a little pale."

I let out a few short, sharp breaths, trying not to freak out. "It's just . . . it's nothing." Except it was, and if she hadn't heard it from anyone, then I'd just given myself away. God, I was a fool. "How did you . . . if no one told you?"

She gave me a sad smile. "That day you were in there talking to Ronny about something serious, you looked the same as you do now. Like you could just about puke. Then in walked that cute little Englishman, and honey, my gosh, you looked at him with hearts in your eyes. Like Bugs Bunny when his eyes pop hearts right out of his head." She frowned. "Now you look like a rabbit caught in a spotlight."

I shook my head, not sure what to say. I didn't have it in me to lie to her. I swallowed back tears. "I came out to my friends and family when I was eighteen. And it cost me everything."

"Oh, honey," she breathed, her eyes full of sorrow. "I'm so sorry."

"I had nothing and no one. I was homeless. I . . ." I inhaled sharply, resisting the urge to let the tears win. "I told myself never again. I could just have a career and keep a lid on my personal life. I was happy on my own."

She frowned, her shoulders sagging. "Until you met someone."

I nodded. "I thought maybe I . . ." I shrugged. "I didn't know what I thought."

"That you deserved to be happy?"

I looked at her then. "Stupid, huh?"

"Why is it? Why is it stupid?"

"Because in this town I can't even be seen talking to him without people assuming. I can't have a cup of coffee with him at the diner, or with Ren or Clay, because everyone assumes whatever they want. 'Oh, he was talking to that gay man so he must be gay too,'" I mimicked. "It's bullshit, and it's not fair. I can't lose everything again. I just . . . I can't."

She let out a shaky breath and her genuine sadness surprised me. "You listen to me," she said quietly. "You won't lose anything. You've got real friends here."

"I thought I had real friends before. My family . . ."

"Is that why you never celebrated the holidays before?"

I nodded.

She took a second to think about that, then nodded as if she'd come to some conclusion on her own. "Well, you've got a family now."

I looked at her. "Where?"

"Here!" she gestured to the empty office. "The whole team here."

"You think someone won't take issue with it?" I looked at the empty desks, picturing the officers who sat at them. "Ray and Buck? I mean, they're nice guys but they're old school."

She pursed her lips. "I think they might surprise you. But at the end of the day, it's none of their business. If they don't like it, who cares? It's their problem, not yours. And I'd dare one of them to say something."

I appreciated her optimism. "Yeah, I don't know." I shook

my head, so unsure. My mind was a mess. "Thank you for being okay with it."

She gave my shoulder a bit of a shake. "Of course, honey. And don't you worry about this town talking. They'll talk about you for a hot minute and then they'll be onto the next thing. And then it'll all be over. Like ripping off a Band-Aid."

Easy for her to say.

We both sat there for a second, the office far too quiet. "You told Ronny?" she asked.

I nodded. "Yeah. And he was great."

"He is great."

"But then today he said something that . . ." I shook my head again. "It was just a throwaway comment, but it stung, and it proved to me that while people can say they have no problem with it, they still see being gay as different." I let out a deep sigh and groaned. "I'll need to apologise to him tomorrow."

She gave me a smile and squeezed my shoulder again. "You'll be okay, you'll see. It's the holidays. If Christmas isn't about acceptance and new beginnings, then what's it even for?"

I relented a grateful smile. "Thanks."

She was quiet for a moment, then glanced at my phone. "So, that's the reason you're ignoring the way your phone's been beeping all night?" She winced. "Not ignoring that cute Englishman, I hope."

I snorted out a laugh, then ran my hands over my face. "I thought it was for the best. Given I'd convinced myself to step back and put a stop to it. Not really in the right frame of mind."

"Then maybe you could tell him that," she said. "Ask for time."

God, I didn't know whether to laugh or cry. "Time is the one thing we don't have. He's leaving after the new year."

Her face looked as miserable as mine. "Oh."

"So it's all for nothing, isn't it," I admitted quietly.

She shook her head. "No, Colson. It's for you. And you're worth it."

Of course, my phone beeped with another message and I didn't even need to see the screen to know who it was from. It made my heart ache.

Charity gave my shoulder another shake. "Reply to him." She went back to her desk. "Or better yet, call him. Go into Ronny's office for some privacy."

I let out the mother of all sighs and turned my phone over.

There were a lot of messages.

I have to finish some of the outfits for the play at the school on Saturday if you wanted to join me again. 10am if you're interested.

I asked Hamish but he's busy at the store.

I'm sure you already know but Mrs Parson said we're in for a dumping of snow. Not a blizzard, thankfully.

Oh, I also ordered you a small Christmas gift. I was too excited not to tell you. I saw it and thought of you.

I don't expect anything in return, if that's why you think I told you . . .

Sorry, you must be busy at work. I hope that means you're okay. You can call past my place any time you need. I won't mind. <winky face>

Good night, Colson. Be safe.

His last message was just a minute ago, so taking Charity's suggestion, I hit Call and walked into Ronny's office.

He answered on the first ring. "Hey, you."

His concern burned behind my sternum, and it was clear

to me right then that I was in way over my head already. "Hey," I replied.

"Everything okay?"

"Uh, not really," I said with a long, drawn-out sigh. "I haven't exactly had a good day."

"Oh my goodness," he murmured. "Was it something at work?"

"No, not really. Just me being all up in my head again. Freaking out and wondering if I'm making a huge mistake."

"Oh, Colson. I'm coming over to your place," he said. It sounded as if he was getting out of bed.

"No, Braithe, stop," I said. "It's okay. It's late already and you have an early start tomorrow."

"But if you need to talk to someone," he began. "I don't mind."

"No, it's fine. I just had a long talk with Charity, and I feel better." No clearer about what I was supposed to do, but I did feel better. "But maybe you could stay tomorrow night? If that's okay?"

"Of course I can. Are you sure?"

"Yeah, I'm sure." The truth was I'd be terrible company tonight and I needed to figure stuff out on my own. "Tomorrow night sounds good though."

"I can be at your place when you get home," he offered. "I'll make sure your fire's going. It's supposed to snow a bit tomorrow."

I sighed. "I feel better already. Even just talking with you on the phone helps."

"I'm glad. You can call me anytime." He was quiet for a beat. "So you talked to Charity too?"

I let out a bit of a laugh. "She, uh, she kinda guessed. But she asked me if I was okay. She asked if it had anything to do with a certain someone who delivered the little Christmas tree on my desk."

Another beat of silence. "She what?"

"She said, apparently, I looked at you like a cartoon character with hearts in his eyes. Bugs Bunny, to be exact."

Braithe snorted. "Oh."

"And I've been having a rough time lately, having a few closed-door conversations with Ronny. She said no one told her anything, she just put the pieces together. She's the comms manager here," I explained. "It's her job to read into situations."

"And she was okay?"

"Yeah. She was great." My nose burned with tears again. I was getting sick of being such a basket case lately.

"Colson, are you sure you're okay?"

I nodded, though he couldn't see. "Yeah. I am." I did feel better now. "Thank you."

He hummed. "I'm proud of you."

His words hit me harder than I'd been expecting and again with unshed tears. "Oh. Uh . . ."

He chuckled. "I take it that's something you don't hear too often."

"Uh, no. Only from you."

He sighed. I'm sure he wanted to grumble about my horrible family, but he decided not to. "Well, I am proud of you."

"Thank you."

"I should let you go," he said softly. "I'm sorry for the barrage of text messages. I assumed you were busy so I just kept talking to you and thought you'd reply when you could. I liked that you called though. Your voice is so lovely."

The glow that burned behind my sternum burned a little warmer.

"Hearing your voice really helped me, Braithe." I stopped short of saying I'd not realised how much I'd needed to hear him. Or needed him in general. "Get some sleep. I'll see you tomorrow night."

"Okay."

"Oh," I tacked on. "And I ordered you a little something for Christmas too. Just so you don't think I only did because you told me you got me something. I ordered it last week, so technically I did it first. And yes, I'd love to help you on Saturday. I make no promises about the quality of my crafting skills. Dexterity and finesse aren't my forte. I'm more of a heavy-lifting kind of guy."

He chuckled. "I think you don't know how dextrous you can be, Colson," he murmured. "Because my body knows exactly the levels of finesse you—"

"Okay, okay," I said with a laugh. "Don't go there because tomorrow night is forever away."

He hummed out a laugh. "Good night, C2."

I smiled, my heart swelling. "Sweet dreams."

I clicked off the call and, after a deep breath, went back out. Charity took one look at me and smiled.

THE NEXT MORNING, I was moving some firewood from the shed into the house when I saw a familiar cruiser pull into my drive.

Ronny?

What was he doing here?

Maybe he was coming to see me before I got to work. Maybe he thought my apology should be delivered before I was on the clock. That'd be fair, I reasoned. I clapped the wood debris from my gloves and pulled them off, heading out to meet him as he was getting out of the vehicle.

When the passenger door opened, Charity got out too.

I stopped where I stood. Rooted in fear, and a cold and familiar dread seeped into my belly. I had to fight against my fight-or-flight response.

And the urge not to lose my breakfast.

Ronny came up to me and clapped his huge hand on my arm. "Got a coffee maker, son?" he asked. "How about a cup of joe?"

Ronny headed for the door to my mudroom and Charity gave me a smile. A reassuring smile, encouragement in her eyes. "It's all good, I promise."

Chapter Seventeen

BRAITHE

I LET myself into Colson's place around nine o'clock. Mrs Parson's prediction of a decent dumping of snow had proved correct, and not only was there now half a foot of snow blanketing the whole town, the temperature had nosedived along with it.

It was bitterly cold.

I stoked up Colson's fire and made a steaming cup of tea. I'd also brought along a new box of ten teabags but smiled knowing there was a replenished stash of condoms in my bag too.

I curled up on his couch with a blanket and my book, smiling at the gentle glow of Christmas lights. And at little Conifer Aniston, who looked as if she'd sprouted new foliage.

I must have dozed off because I woke to a gentle hand on my shoulder. "Braithe," Colson murmured. "Wake up, sweetheart. Let's get you to bed."

I sat up and my book fell to the floor. Colson picked it up and set it on the coffee table while I tried to get my bearings. "Sorry. I tried to stay awake."

He put his hand to my cheek. "You looked so peaceful. I

didn't want to wake you." His eyes studied mine as his thumb stroked my jaw. "And beautiful."

My smile became a yawn. "Oh, sorry." Wait. "Did you call me sweetheart?"

He laughed and helped me to my feet. "Come on. To bed with you."

I tried to protest and he led me down the hall. "I want to talk to you," I tried. "To see how you are. Are you okay?"

He pulled the covers back and sat me on the bed. "I'm real good," he said, tilting my face up for a kiss. "I'll tell you all about it tomorrow. I was outside most of the night so I need a shower. Why don't you lie down? I'll just be a minute."

"Outside?" I asked. "But it's so cold."

He chuckled. "Routine traffic work. No big deal." He pulled the blankets up and kissed me again. "You're so cute, and I like you in my bed, more than what's probably good for me."

"Don't be long in the shower," I mumbled. "And I'll make it good for you." And as much as I wanted that to be true, as soon as I closed my eyes, my hectic week at work had well and truly caught up to me and sleep claimed me.

In my defence, his bed was super comfy and warm, and it smelled of him. And when I woke up early in the morning, I was the little spoon to his big spoon, his arms were wrapped around me.

I'd never been more comfortable. I'd never slept that well. Warm and safe and . . .

I pressed my arse against him, feeling him in all the right places and wiggling for good measure. He stirred and his hold on me instinctively tightened. Then he froze, and I knew his senses had woken him, and I chuckled.

"Good morning," I said, pushing my arse back again.

His hand found my hip and he flexed his hips, his now also-awake dick hard. "Mm. Good morning indeed."

"So, orgasm before breakfast, or after?" I asked. "Or before *and* after?"

He chuckled sleepily into the back of my neck, but his hand gripped my hip and he rubbed himself against me. "Are you letting me choose?"

I groaned out a laugh, aching for more. "Both, it is," I whispered.

"START FROM THE BEGINNING," I said, my breakfast all but forgotten. "Ronny and Charity came here to ambush you?"

Colson laughed. "I thought it was an ambush. And I guess it kinda was. But in a good way."

"What happened?"

"Well, after my little chat with Charity and coming out to her, I guess, she called Ronny and told him we all needed to have a little chat." He sighed and put his fork down. "I thought the worst," he admitted. "Because you know, a dog that's been kicked before will always flinch, right?"

I reached over and took his hand. God, that made my chest hurt. "Oh, Colson."

He gave me a sad smile. "Charity's a real nice woman. She's kinda like the mom of the station. She's a no-nonsense type and she means business, but she's real sweet. Anyway, she told Ronny we needed to set a few things straight." He winced. "No pun intended."

I smiled, glad he could make a joke of it. "And it went okay?"

He nodded. "Better than okay, I guess. I owed Ronny an

apology for the way I'd spoken to him the day before, which I did feel bad about. But he said he should apologise to me instead. He hadn't meant anything by what he said, and I knew that. He's a good man. But Charity thought if I wasn't feeling welcome, then I might consider leaving, and they didn't want to lose me."

"What did Ronny say to you to warrant an apology?"

He sighed then. "Just a silly throwaway comment about seeing you talking with Hamish and the guys at the diner, and it was harmless, but it pissed me off because while he says he has no problem with me being gay, he still notices these things. And people assume someone might be gay just because of who they're seen with, so that tells me he still sees us as not the norm. Anyway, I told him those assumptions were the reason why I felt I had to hide, or why I can't have coffee with you in the diner, or why you had to drive to a harmless Christmas dinner party because god forbid someone in this town sees my car parked at Ren's house."

He shook his head and sighed. "Anyway, I spoke with less respect than he deserved, so I did need to apologise to him."

I gave his hand a squeeze. "But what you said wasn't wrong."

"No, it wasn't. And he acknowledged that and said he'd try to do better." I got a little teary-eyed. "Colson."

His eyes were glassy too. "I know! I couldn't believe it. And Charity said maybe the whole department needed to do better, because thinking anyone might not feel entirely welcome wasn't good. She was real sorry to hear about my family kicking me out, and she said I had a family here now. The department, and the sheriff's office." He gave a teary smile. "It felt real good to hear that."

I couldn't help it. I needed to be closer to him. So I

scooted his chair out a little and planted myself on his lap so I could hug him. "I'm so happy for you."

He hugged me back, tight, and didn't let go for a long time. "I wouldn't have done this without you," he whispered. "I'll never be able to thank you enough."

I kissed him softly. "You just did."

"ARE you sure you won't get into trouble? Am I allowed to be there?" I grinned at Colson. He was so cute.

"Of course you are. I have permission to be here, and you're helping me. Plus, you're the town deputy. It's not like I'm bringing a criminal to help me."

I pulled into the school parking lot, seeing other cars were there too. Oh boy. "Uh, okay, damn."

He looked at me. "You know, that's the first time I've ever heard you cuss."

"Damn? Can that even be considered a cuss word?"

"I had some Sunday school teachers who would vehemently agree, yes."

I snorted. "Sorry. I'm well-practised in the art of not swearing. Being a teacher of small and impressionable children, I can't afford to be dropping F-bombs without thinking."

He smiled. "That's fair."

I cut the engine and Colson glanced at the other cars. "Hey, if you want me to drive you home, I totally will," I offered. "I didn't know anyone else would be here. I'm sorry."

He shot me a glance, then looked back at the cars, then at the school entrance. He fidgeted his hands in his lap so I reached over and gave his hand a squeeze.

"Don't apologise," he said quietly. "You know what?" He

gave me a smile that was more grimace than he'd probably intended. But then he straightened up and raised his chin. "I want to go in. I don't care what anyone else might think. Let them assume whatever they will. It's a . . . It's about time. Gotta rip off the Band-Aid sometime, right?"

I grinned at him. "Okay. Just remember, we can leave at any time. And we're doing nothing wrong."

He nodded, bolstered.

"You ready?"

"Yep." He was smiling now, even keen to get it over with. We got out of the car, and walking in, I did notice Raeleen's car so I fully expected her to assume what was going on. She was clearly one to gossip, but like Colson said, he had to do this sometime . . .

We walked in through the doors, and I could hear chatter coming from the staffroom and children laughing from down the hall. One or some of the teachers here had brought their kids along, and I was grateful for the casual approach.

"Gimme one sec," I said. I poked my head into the teachers' lounge. "Hi," I said brightly. "Just gonna be in my classroom."

"Props for the school play?" Raeleen asked.

I nodded with a smile. "Yep."

"Same," Sandra added. She was the grade three teacher. "Don't mind my two kids. If they bother you, don't be afraid to send them packing."

I laughed. "I'm sure they'll be no bother."

I left them to their coffees and grabbed Colson's arm, leading him to my classroom. Once inside, I flipped on the lights and let out a sigh. "Okay, so Raeleen is here. And she's lovely and well-meaning . . ."

"She's the one who assumed you were gay because you had coffee with Hamish?"

I nodded. "Yeah. I just thought you should know. That if she knows you're here with me, she'll jump to the same conclusion."

He gave me a half smile. "It's okay." He looked around the room and clapped his hands. "*So*, what needs to be done?"

I came out of the craft room holding a storage tub almost bigger than me. Colson jumped to help. "It's okay. It's not heavy."

I took the lid off and pulled out the first headband. It was a strip of cardboard, two inches wide, stapled so the ends joined, making a circle. I showed him the writing on the inside. "Bailey, bull," I said. "It's sized to fit Bailey's head, and he's being a bull. So we need to add ears and a crepe paper fringe. Oh, and tape over the staples so it doesn't scratch his head."

Colson grinned at me. "This is pretty cool." He took out another cardboard ring. "Mackenzie, palm tree."

"Nativity scenes have limited roles to play," I explained. "And I wanted to give every child a part. We have all kinds of animals and palm trees." I lifted out some cardboard fronds with crepe paper hanging from them. "See? And the sheep are always fun, with cotton wool."

"I love that you include them all," he murmured. "It's sweet."

Our eyes met and my heart skipped a beat. A rush of butterflies skittered along my nerves, and for a split second, my lungs stopped working.

Oh boy.

He must have had a similar reaction because he started, looking away as he clapped his hands together. "Okay," he said. "Where are the cotton balls? May as well get started on all the sheep first."

He started gluing cotton wool balls on, getting more stuck

to his fingers than the headband, and I did my best not to laugh at him.

Or think about how utterly perfect he was.

How perfect this was, he and I doing this together.

I stapled on some donkey ears and crepe paper fringes, and then some bull horns.

"Uh, what is this?" Colson asked, pulling out a rather large, bright yellow triangle.

"Oh, that goes on Ebony's headband. She's the star the three wise men follow to the stable."

He laughed just as the classroom door opened. And sure enough, Raeleen came in. And stopped. "Oh," she said, looking between me and Colson. "I didn't know you had company. I was just . . . I was just going to ask if I could get you to help me carry the board . . ." She gestured to the door, then smiled at Colson. "Deputy Price."

Then her eyes went to me as she waited for me to speak. To explain, no doubt. "Raeleen," he replied, putting the star down. "Nice to see you again."

"We can help you carry something," I said. I didn't need to explain myself and I certainly wasn't going to give her any juicy details. "A board, you said?"

"Oh, yes," she smiled back at the door. "If it's no trouble. I didn't mean to interrupt . . ."

"Interrupt gluing on crepe paper?" I said with a laugh. She smiled and looked between me and Colson again and was clearly just itching to ask. "So . . ."

"So, where's the board you need some help with?" I asked. I wasn't playing this game. "I'm a bit short on time this morning."

"Oh, of course," she said, leading the way out.

I caught Colson's gaze as we followed her and stopped short of rolling my eyes. He surprised me by smiling.

It was an old classroom chalkboard on wheels, and it had a painted backdrop for her class play tacked to it. The frame was a little rickety, and honestly, it did need two people, mostly to hold it steady while the other one steered.

Colson did the heavy lifting, as if it weighed absolutely nothing. I wasn't surprised, considering I knew all too well the body his clothes hid.

"Oh, thank you so much," Raeleen said with a smile. "I really appreciate the help."

"Anytime," Colson replied, pleasant as always. He wiped his hands on the arse of his jeans and looked at me to direct the conversation.

"Right, yes," I said. "We should get back to it. We have a whole stable of animal headbands to finish."

Colson gave a bit of a wave and went back to my classroom.

"Yes, of course," she agreed, looking at where Colson had disappeared to, then to me. "I, uh, I didn't know he . . ."

"And you still don't know." I smiled at her, an edge to the cheer in my voice. "I'll see you on Monday morning, bright and early!"

She stopped, her smile faltering. "Oh, yes, of course. See you then."

I left her in the hallway and went back into my room. Colson was holding a headband, staring at it.

"You okay?" I asked quietly.

He surprised me again by smiling. "You know, I think I am."

I glanced back at the door. "She already assumes . . ."

"I know." He shrugged. "And I'm sure by dinner time tonight the whole of Hartbridge will know. So maybe she's doing me a favour?"

Oh, okay. Wow. I hadn't expected that reaction.

I picked up a horse headband. "Are you sure you're okay?"

His eyes met mine and he smiled with a small nod. "You know," he hedged, "maybe we should hurry to finish up here and grab lunch at the diner." He shrugged one shoulder. "Together."

My smile was slowly spreading. "Are you . . . are you sure?"

He let out a long breath, clearly a little nervous but determined. "Yeah." He showed me the headband. "Uh, a mouse? Was there a mouse in the nativity scene?"

I laughed. "Of course. Every stable has a mouse." Reaching into the tub, I fished out a small cardboard cone with elastic attached. "Here's the nose."

Just then, the door opened again. This time it was the principal, Nancy O'Conner. Great.

"Hello," I said.

She stared straight at Colson, and I wondered for one split terrifying moment how this would go. "Oh, Deputy Price," she said. "Raeleen just said you were here."

Of course she did.

"Oh, yes," Colson said with a wince. "If my being here—"

"Is perfect timing," she said. "We need help pulling the stacked chairs from the back of the storage room. With the play this week and all. Michael Miller, Judy's husband, is here. Would you be a dear and help him?"

She led him out and he glanced over his shoulder at me before he disappeared out the door. I couldn't help but laugh.

He was gone for about twenty minutes, and I got most of the headbands done, all separated to dry. I hit the lights on the way out and went in search of him.

I followed the sound of voices and headed toward the hall, finding Nancy directing various others. Judy Miller, the grade six teacher, was up a ladder stapling Christmas tinsel above the stage, Raeleen was bringing a table over from the far corner while Colson was carrying in a stack of chairs with a tall man to align it with several other stacks of chairs. I presumed the man to be Judy's husband, Michael.

No sooner had they put that stack down than they left to get more, this time with Nancy following them, offloading more instructions as she walked.

Figuring I wasn't leaving right now, I went over to Raeleen and helped her with the table. "Here, let me help you."

"Oh, thank you."

It wasn't heavy. Just awkward to carry on your own. "Is this the last of them?"

"Yes, I think so," she said. We placed it along the side wall with the row of other tables. "Look, what I said before," she whispered, "I didn't mean to upset you. I didn't presume anything—"

Well, she kinda had. But I knew she wasn't a terrible person. She just liked to gossip. But I also wasn't one to hold grudges.

"It's okay," I said. "I know you didn't mean any harm. It's just . . ." I chose my words carefully. "We shouldn't assume anything about anyone, that's all."

She nodded and a dimple appeared in her cheek when she pursed her lips together before she smiled at me. "He's such a nice guy," she said quietly. "Always been quiet, but never without a smile. No one ever says a bad word about him. Ever."

I gave her a nod. "Let's hope it stays that way." She cocked her head, and I could see the rumour mill cogs beginning to crank in her eyes. But then the doors opened and Colson appeared, backside first as he held the low end of the stack of chairs, Michael at the tall end. It was all the distraction I needed.

They put the chairs down and Colson dusted his hands on

his jeans, and he smiled when he saw me. "That's the last of the chairs," he said. "If you're done?"

The look in his eyes said he was ready to leave.

"I'm good to go," I replied.

He turned to Michael and extended his hand. "Good to see you again."

"You too," he replied, shaking his hand.

We said our goodbyes, Nancy thanking him again. "Thank you, Deputy," she said. "You saved my back."

"No problem," he replied. "If you ever need a hand, just let me know. If I'm not working, I'll be more than happy to drop by."

She beamed up at him. "You're worth more money. I'll tell Ronny that too."

Colson laughed. "All part of the service."

We didn't speak until we were in the car. "Was everything okay back there?" I asked.

"Oh sure," he answered. "I just saw that storage room and I knew I'd be there till dark if I didn't tell them I had to work today." He flattened his palm to his stomach. "And I'm starving."

"Still up for lunch at the diner?" I asked. "Or did you want me to take you home? I don't mind either way, whichever you'd prefer."

He smiled at me. "Diner."

I wasn't sure why I was surprised. I guess I expected the gravity of it all would bear down on him, but no. He really was okay.

"Good, because I'm starving too."

Walking into the diner, I was grateful for the booth at the back by the kitchen door. People usually avoided it because of the foot traffic and noise, but it suited us perfectly today.

Having some privacy while still being in public was perfect.

Jayden was at the grill, and he glanced up and did a quick double take when he saw Colson, but he smiled at me before going back to his order. He was busy; it was Saturday lunchtime, after all.

I sat facing the room, which kind of afforded Colson a bit more anonymity, and it let me forewarn him should someone recognise him or decide to come over.

"You okay?" I asked again. He seemed fine, but that could change in an instant, and I knew him being here in public with a gay man was a big step for him.

He nodded nervously. "You know, I think I am."

I took a menu and pretended to read it over. "Is . . . is this your first date in public with a man?"

A smile broke out, changing his whole face, and gosh, he was so handsome . . . "It is. If this is a date." He cleared his throat. "Is that what this is?"

"I think it might be, yes."

He grinned at me, laughing with a shake of his head. "Crazy, huh?"

I knocked my knee to his. "I'm proud of you."

He blushed a little, deciding to pick up a menu. "What are you thinking looks good?"

"Well, you." I shrugged. "It's actually distracting, if I'm being honest. I look at you and lose my train of thought."

He laughed again. "I meant what looks good on the menu."

Oh.

"Oh." I wasn't embarrassed at all. Much. "Well, I'm not sure . . . because I looked at you and got distracted and lost my train of thought."

Christa came to the table and filled two cups of coffee.

"Now, Braithe. Before you order, the cook wanted me to tell you he has a surprise for you. Just give him one sec, he wants to bring it over."

"Oh?" I was startled, but a quick glance over at Jayden and I saw him smiling as he was plating something up.

He came out carrying one plate with a . . . Oh my days. He put it in front of me. "I've been toying with the Christmas menu, and given you're new to town, I thought I'd try something British."

It was a single Yorkshire pudding.

I put my hand to my heart. "Jayden . . ."

He grinned. "I thought I'd top it with roast turkey and cranberry chutney on a small bed of mashed potato. Kind of like a savoury tart, but not."

I looked from the plate up to him, surprised by how emotional it made me. "You made this for me?"

"Well, I like to try new recipes for Christmas dinners. Here, and at the B&B. I'd never made Yorkshire puddings before, but I think they turned out okay."

Colson squinted at the plate. "A savoury pudding?"

I couldn't help but laugh, but Jayden explained. "Not a pudding as you'd know it. It's a pastry, as a side to the main meal."

Colson looked visibly relieved. "Oh, thank god."

Christa, picking up a plate from the next table, stepped back into the conversation. "That's exactly what I said."

I laughed and cut the Yorkshire pudding right down the middle and slid the plate between Colson and me. "Try it. These are a very English thing, and a very English *Christmas* thing. Jayden, I'm truly touched that you made these."

"Don't thank me yet. You haven't tried it."

I picked up my half, bit into it, and closed my eyes, immediately transported to another time and place. "Oh my," I said.

"Jayden, it tastes like I'm sitting at my grandmother's table for Christmas lunch." I had to blink back some unexpected tears. "It's my childhood and very fond memories."

Jayden looked like I'd told him he'd won the lotto. "Really? Oh, that's the best compliment I think I've ever got." He beamed, glancing back to the kitchen. "I've gotta get back to work, but thank you."

"Gosh, no. Thank you!" I said.

He gave Colson a quick clap on the shoulder. "Good to see you here." Then he went back into the kitchen.

Colson was still looking at the plate, very unsure. It made me chuckle. "Try it. It's so good."

He grimaced a little, but he did take a bite. "It's not what I was expecting, but it's not bad."

I'd almost finished my half. "It reminds me of home."

His eyes flinched and his lip pulled down. "Do you . . . do you miss home?" It wasn't the first time he'd asked me that, as if he was scared that one day I'd tell him I was going back for good.

"Yes, and no. It will always be home, and I miss my family, of course. But I have no plans to go back yet."

Yet.

It hung in the air between us.

"Can I ask you something?"

Oh dear.

"Of course."

"How long until you do go back? To England?"

"About eighteen months."

He frowned, nodding.

There was always an end date. Not for me leaving Hartbridge, but for me leaving the United States.

The sadness on his face just killed me.

"I asked Nancy if she could extend my work here in Hartbridge," I admitted quietly. I needed him to know that I'd tried to stay. I didn't want to leave in two weeks.

Less than two weeks now . . .

His eyes shot to mine, hopeful. "And?"

I shook my head.

I didn't need to say it out loud.

He deflated. "Oh."

I sighed. "And I need to work, so . . ."

He nodded but wouldn't look at me. I reached over and squeezed his hand, just for a second. "Hey," I tried. "No sads today. Today's a good day. A big day for you." I looked around the diner, then leaned in closer so I could whisper. "Your first real date, remember? And you were starving before." I slid the menu in front of him and tapped my watch. "And you start work in just over an hour, so we need to order."

He'd clearly lost his appetite, and truth be told, I had too. I finished off my half of the Yorkshire pudding and ordered a hearty soup for my lunch. Colson ordered the brisket and he managed to eat most of it, but he pushed his plate to the side and declared he was done.

No one really paid us any attention. I saw a few people look our way but nothing out of the ordinary. Bailey and his mom came in for a takeaway order and he gave me a little wave. Of course, I smiled and waved back.

Man, I was really going to miss this town.

I was going to miss one man in particular.

It hurt to think about.

And I didn't want to ruin what remaining time I had left with him. I braved a smile I didn't really feel and tried to be the supportive friend he needed.

"We better get you home so you can get ready for work," I said.

He gave me a smile, and as we were leaving, a few people gave him a nod. "Deputy," they each said.

"Afternoon," he replied in turn.

They then looked at me, registering that yes, we were here together. I got a nod too, some said hello, but as we walked out there were a few glances and silence.

The cold air outside was a welcome reprieve, and again, we didn't speak until we were in the car.

I kept my eyes on him, waiting for his cue. "Well, that wasn't so bad," he said, though he looked uncomfortable. He let out a quick puff of air. "I guess it's done now. The entire town will be talking about me, and by tomorrow, everyone will know."

I wanted to hug him. "They'll know you had lunch with me," I tried. "Everything else is speculation."

He nodded, even though we both knew that speculation in a small town was as good as gospel, and being seen with a man who was outwardly gay was all it took for people to assume the same of him.

He seemed to gather himself and gave me a tight smile. "It's a good thing though, right? I mean, it's done. I haven't announced anything, exactly. But . . ." He made a face. "Maybe it's time I did."

"Did what?"

"Made an announcement." He let out a laugh that sounded a little strained as he ran a hand through his hair. "I need to tell people at work. If they're gonna hear it from someone—and Lord knows they will—I'd rather they hear it from me."

Holy cow.

"Uh, are you sure you're ready for that?" I was bordering on worried. "Colson, that's a lot."

His smile was more genuine, his eyes locked on mine, and

he gave a nod. "I think I am. Ready, as I'll ever be. And if people don't like it," he shrugged. "Then so be it. I'm done hiding the real me."

I could have cried. "Oh, Colson." I reached over and squeezed his hand. "You must call me and let me know how it goes. I can be at your place in like a minute if you need. Even though I'm sure it'll all be fine."

He let out a puff of air and wiped his palms on his thighs, nodding out the windshield. "Yeah. Me too. But, uh, thanks."

I drove to his place and pulled up out the front. "Remember, you have support from the people who matter. Ronny and Charity, and you know all of the guys will have your back. Ren and Hamish and Clay, and those guys, I mean. And I'm sure your police friends will be the same. But you have people here who support you no matter what. And I'm just a phone call away, okay?"

He gave a nod, clearly nervous, trying to gear himself up for what he was about to do. "Okay. Thank you." He looked at me then. "I mean that. I couldn't do this without you."

I wanted to kiss him so bad, but it wasn't the place for that. "You would have found the right time," I said gently. "But I'm glad I'm here to help."

He looked at my lips as if he wanted to kiss me too but stopped himself with a shake of his head. He got out and went inside and I drove back to my place, hoping like hell he'd be okay.

Chapter Eighteen

COLSON

I walked into the station on a mission. I was also so damn nervous I didn't know if my lunch was about to make a reappearance, but I was determined.

It was a Saturday, just before two o'clock. The station was busy enough. We were about to have a shift rotation, so the crossover meant there was more here than if I'd been half an hour earlier or later. Most of the guys were at their desks getting ready for the shift change. Ronny was even in his office.

If there was a perfect time to do this, it was now.

I gave a quick rap on his door and went in. "Hey, uh, if you don't mind, I think I'd like to make an announcement," I said. The reappearance of my lunch was still undecided.

"Oh," he said with surprise. "Sure thing. If it's what I think you're about to announce, that is."

"Uh, yeah. I think it is."

He got to his feet, a slow smile under his moustache. "Okay, then." I nodded and let out a slow breath. My lunch was now in favour of resurfacing, but I breathed through it. "Okay, then."

Holy hell. I was doing this.

Remember, you have support from the people who matter.

I clung to those words that Braithe had said as I walked out of Ronny's office and stood near the row of hat and coat hooks so everyone could see me. "Uh, guys," I said, nowhere near loud enough. Typical that my voice decided to bail on me.

"Attention, please!" Ronny hollered, and everyone in the open office dropped what they were doing and turned to face him. "Deputy Price has something to say."

Then all eyes were on me.

Not now, lunch. Not now.

"Right, yes. Uh, thank you," I said to Ronny. I licked my lips, my mouth bone dry. "I have something to say. Given the way the rumour mill works in this town, chances are you're about to hear some things about me, and I'd rather you hear it from me."

They all stared. No one spoke. Pretty sure no one breathed. Somewhere a phone rang, but I noticed Charity then, smiling at me with a nod, and it gave me the confidence to continue.

"I am . . . I'm gay." I let out a quick, heavy sigh. More of a gasp, but those words were finally out. "I have been forever, will be forever. It's not something I can change, and I wouldn't if I could. I spent a lot of years wishing I wasn't, trying not to be." I shrugged. "But I am. And I needed you all to hear it from me."

I was feeling a little lightheaded and had to breathe through the urge to keep my lunch where it was.

"To be completely honest with you," I added, "my being gay doesn't change anything. I know some of you guys won't agree with that and you might not like it, and that's fine. It already cost me my entire family so if I can get through that when I was just eighteen, I can get through it again now."

So there it was.

Done.

I didn't dare look at anyone's faces. I couldn't have focused if I'd wanted to. I turned to look at Ronny like he was a support pillar. He gave me a proud smile.

"Ain't no one here gonna have a problem," he said, loud enough to make a point. Then he gave a nod. "Well done," he said, softer this time.

I felt like an unbearable weight was off my shoulders and I turned just in time for Charity to collect me in a hug. She gave a tight squeeze and let me go, saying nothing. Not needing to. It was written all over her face.

"Thank you," I whispered.

Then Bouchard stood up and raised his hand. "Uh, while we're announcing stuff," he said with a smile. "I'm straight."

I stared at him. I think it was his way of telling me it was no big deal. I mean, he was smiling at me . . .

Then Police Sergeant Cody Blackwood stood up and did the same. "Yep. Straight."

Then Probation Officer Katie Barr raised her hand. "Same. As much as I sometimes wish it were otherwise, I am, unfortunately, attracted to men."

Everyone laughed, and I really wasn't sure what to make of this whole exchange. But they were all kinda smiling, and out of all of them, I knew Bouchard best. He'd been nice to me for years, so I took it as a joke. "Yeah, thanks, guys. I think."

Then Aaron Stamford stood up. He'd been a detective in Bozeman before he came here a few years back. Maybe thirty-five years old, and I'd had all of ten conversations with him in the last year, but he seemed nice. "Well, if I had to pick, I'd say I'm straight. But I did four years of crazy shit in college, and I got zero regrets if you know what I'm sayin'," he said with a sly grin. "Oh, and between me and my wife, I got two celebrity free passes, and one of 'em is Bruno Mars, so take that for what it is."

Some of the officers cracked up laughing, and I stared at him. "Uh, I'm thinking you might not be as straight as you think," I said quietly.

He shrugged, seemingly unfazed. He literally did not care. Zanetti was rubbing his temples like this entire conversation hurt, though I was pretty sure he was smiling.

"Who's the other one?" Bouchard asked. "You said you got two celebrity free passes. Bruno Mars and who?"

Aaron's grin widened. "The blonde dragon momma from *Game of Thrones*." Everyone kind of nodded, even Charity and Katie, and Zanetti. Hell, even I could appreciate that choice.

But then conversation around the room morphed into that TV show and everything I'd said was water under the bridge.

Just like that.

I did notice a few of the other officers didn't say much, didn't smile, and certainly didn't stick around long after. Their shifts were over so that was no great surprise, but it was just the feeling I got. It wasn't like I knew them that well. And I was sure there'd be things said later, both to my face and behind my back, but I didn't care.

It was done. And as a whole, it went exceptionally well. And there was only one person I wanted to tell.

Just before six, after I'd cleared the urgent things off my desk, I grabbed my coat and my keys. "Be back in ten," I called out. Bouchard gave a nod and Charity, who was on a call, gave me a wave.

I drove straight to Braithe's.

I pulled up directly out the front of Mrs Parson's house—no hiding anymore—and only thought to call him to see if he was home as I began walking down the driveway to the small apartment out back.

He answered on the first ring. "Oh, I've been worried. How did it go?"

"Come outside," I said, just as I rounded the back of Mrs Parson's.

His front door opened and he appeared, concerned, wary.

Until he saw me and I grinned at him.

He sagged, still with his phone to his ear, and he laughed as he stepped outside. I collected him in a hug, lifted him off his feet, and walked him back inside. Where it was warm and where I could hold him, my face against his neck.

"I was so worried," he whispered. "So it went well?"

I pulled back, still smiling. I wasn't sure I'd stopped yet. "It did! I mean, for now. Everyone was great. A few of the officers joked around and announced being straight. One guy announced he was mostly straight, but he'd basically done all kinds of shit in college and his celebrity free pass is Bruno Mars." I shrugged and shook my head, still trying to get my head around that whole conversation. "But I said coming out at eighteen cost me my family and how I was the same person they'd always known, so I hoped everyone would be okay with it. Then Ronny said everyone kinda had to be okay with it whether they liked it or not, so . . ." I realised I was babbling and on the verge of crying. I let out a shaky breath. "God, what a day."

He put his hand to my cheek and searched my eyes. "How do you feel?"

"So good. Like I can breathe. Like I've finally put down a heavy weight. I didn't even realise how heavy it was, I didn't fully understand the strain of carrying it until I didn't have to carry it anymore."

Smiling, he kissed me softly. "I'm so proud of you."

I laughed. "I couldn't have done it without you. I wouldn't have. I'd have convinced myself it was okay to be miserable if I kept my walls up. And I'd be alone forever and that was okay. Because being alone by choice is easier than being alone because of someone else's decision." I put my hand to my forehead. "I don't even know if I'm making sense."

He stood up on his tiptoes and slid his arms around my neck, bringing me in for a hug. "It makes perfect sense."

"I had to come and see you," I mumbled.

"Thank you," he whispered.

And neither of us pulled away for the longest minute. It was just a hug for a hug's sake. Soul-mending contact, a connection to another human being.

And after I'd been alone for far too long, there weren't the words to explain just how soul-mending it was.

Like he was stitching me back together, one breath at a time.

I wished I could have stood there holding him all night. I wished I didn't have to go back to work. I wished . . .

"I know this is a lot to ask," I said, pulling back and diving into his blue, blue eyes. "But tomorrow's Sunday and you don't have to work, so I was hoping—"

"That I'd sleep at your place tonight?"

I let out an embarrassed laugh, looking down at the space between us. "I just . . . I'd really like to not sleep alone tonight. I can come back here if you'd prefer." I shrugged. "Not that I have to hide my cruiser anymore, but I don't want people to think I'm visiting Mrs Parson."

He laughed, his smile breathtaking. "I'd love to spend the

night at your place." He kissed me softly. "I just have some laundry to finish up, which is a terribly exciting way to spend my Saturday night. But I can be there in about an hour or two. Is that okay?"

"Perfect. I don't finish until after midnight."

"Then I'll be in your bed, sound asleep." He winked. "Feel free to wake me."

I laughed, took his face in my hands, and kissed him. "Sounds perfect." I swear, having the normalcy of someone at home when I finished work, in my bed, was something I never dreamed I'd get to have. *Perfect* didn't begin to describe it.

"I better go," I said, having to make myself open the door. "I'll see you soon."

"You will." He smiled so sweetly, even a little shy. It sent my heart into a frenzy.

I barely got one foot outside when a voice startled me. "Deputy Colson," Mrs Parson said.

I froze, a deer in headlights. Uhhh. My first instinct was to lie, to make up a reason for me being caught with a man. So ingrained, so instinctual.

No longer necessary, I realised.

Braithe was more accustomed than me. He poked his head out, giving her a wave. "Hello, Mrs Parson."

She smirked at him. "Everything okay, dear?"

"Oh yes, never better," he replied.

"Say, Deputy," she hedged, sizing me up. "The reason for your visit wouldn't be the same reason I saw you leaving here, walking down the driveway the other night, around one o'clock in the morning, is it?"

Uh.

Uhhh.

"Um."

She laughed. "Your obligation to civic duty does go

beyond, doesn't it? Braithe's lucky to have himself such a dedicated officer looking out for his best . . . interests."

Oh dear god.

Braithe laughed. "Oh Mrs Parson, you're making him blush."

Yeah. I wasn't sure I was up for jokes about booty calls with a man. Not yet, anyway.

"I, uh, I have to get back to work," I said, tipping my hat to Mrs Parson.

"Okay, dear," she said. "Be safe tonight."

I gave Braithe an embarrassed nod and began down the driveway.

"Braithe," I heard her say. "Have you had dinner? I should brew us some tea."

"Tea would be lovely," he replied.

I smiled as I kept walking. Pretty much smiled the rest of the night. I knew it wouldn't always be like this. I knew and expected some close-minded person to take great offence and to let me know all about it. But I promised myself that I'd remember this feeling. This happiness, this absolute high.

The feeling of finally being me.

I FINISHED work after midnight and smiled when I walked through my front door to find the fire just a few hours old instead of almost out. The Christmas lights were the only lights on, my bedroom door cracked ajar. I dumped my boots at the door, my coat on the couch, and I poked my head into my darkened room.

Braithe was asleep on my side of the bed, his hands curled up under his chin, his lips slightly parted.

So freaking beautiful.

It tugged at a thread inside my chest, threatening to unravel me.

I took a quick steaming-hot shower and climbed into bed with him, on not-my side of the bed. I'd no sooner put my head on the pillow than he rolled over and snuggled into me, his head on my chest, his arm over my stomach.

"You're home," he mumbled.

I sighed and gave him a squeeze, pressing a kiss to his forehead. This felt like home to me. "Yeah. I am."

"I MEANT TO STAY AWAKE," he said, handing me a cup of coffee. "I'm so sorry." It wasn't even eight o'clock on a Sunday morning. He wore long winter pyjamas and socks, his hair was a mess, and he was leaning against my kitchen counter holding his cup of tea, looking more perfect than I had the words to describe.

"It's fine," I replied. "Coming home to find you in my bed made up for it."

"I wanted to stay up and chat, ask you how it all went. Did anyone say anything to you after I saw you?"

I shook my head. "No. It was all very normal. But I suspect there'll be someone who says something, sooner or later."

"Or not," he offered. "We can hope, anyway." He studied me for a second as he sipped his tea. "Have you stopped smiling yet?"

I laughed. "I don't think so. And then there's you, standing in my kitchen in your pyjamas with your bedhead. I mean, what's not to smile about?"

His smile turned shy and he tapped his socked toe to mine. "Mrs Parson thinks you're cute when you blush. She told me."

Oh god, I'd forgotten about that. "Did she really see me leaving that night?"

He nodded with a laugh. "Yep."

"Oh, good Lord. Please tell me she didn't hear anything." He laughed louder.

"I don't think so. Maybe she's too polite to say." I grimaced, but he shook his head. "She's a lot cooler than you think. She's not bothered about that. In fact, she wanted to know if you treated me well and with *consideration*."

I stared at him. "She did not."

He burst out laughing. "She absolutely did. Consideration. I think that was her way to ask if you were a considerate lover. You know, if you were a gentle top. But she's old school."

I felt my entire face burn from my scalp down my neck. "I am not ready for those conversations."

He put his tea down and slid his arms around me. "Then I'd suggest you avoid Hamish because he has no filter."

I chuckled, still not believing that this was somehow my life now.

I put my coffee down and sighed, relishing every second he was in my arms. "Do I want to know what you told Mrs Parson?"

He laughed but stayed right where he was, even snuggled his forehead into my neck a little more. "I told her a gentleman never kisses and tells. Which she loved, by the way. But then I told her if I was inclined to defend your reputation, I would say yes. You treat me well and with *much* consideration."

"Oh, sweet heavens."

He pulled back then, smiling up at me. "Would you rather I tell her exactly what you did to me the night she saw you leaving?"

I had flashbacks of me taking him in a not-so-considerate

way while still wearing my uniform, and I blanched. "Absolutely not."

He laughed again, putting his head back to that spot against my neck and humming as he wriggled in all the right places. "Some of my best memories," he murmured. "Want to do me again like that?"

I laughed, thinking he was joking, hoping he was because it was embarrassing . . . He looked up at me, clearly not joking at all. The evidence was hardening against me as he rubbed his hips to mine. "Deputy," he said. "I believe that was an order."

I took his hand and led him back to the bedroom. "Yes, sir."

Chapter Nineteen

BRAITHE

I was so proud of Colson.

If I was being honest, I was also scared for him.

I was also petrified that some jerk would say something awful to him and he'd relive his parents' rejection all over again. I feared the town might shun him, being an officer of the law and in a position of power, and that there'd be ramifications.

I'd called Hamish on Sunday night and told him that Colson had come out at work, and although it had gone well, he might want to tell Ren, and Jayden at the diner, that there may be some whispers around town.

To perhaps keep one ear to the grapevine so we could give Colson a heads up, should he need it.

"Is he okay?" Hamish asked.

"He's fine," I answered.

"Hmm."

"I just worry for him," I elaborated with a sigh. "He had a terrible experience last time and if people are jerks to him, I'm not sure how he'll handle it."

"Did someone at work say something to him?"

"No, he said it went well. But he's at work right now and will be until after midnight. I worry about him, that's all. I know he's the deputy and can come across as stoic sometimes, but he's not like that. He's very soft-hearted, and he was so hurt by his horrible family."

Hamish was quiet for a second. "How are those no-strings-attached strings feeling about now?"

I sighed, and normally I'd have joked and told him to shut up, but I wasn't feeling it tonight. "Yeah."

"Oh, Braithe."

"And the school principal hasn't said anything?"

"No."

He made a sad sound, and I could picture him pouting.

"Anyway," I said, trying to brighten the mood. "I have a busy week at work so I might not get to see you, but are you still coming to the school play on Friday?"

"Of course."

"Great. I'll see you then."

"I'll tell Ren to keep an ear out for any rumours."

"Thank you."

I clicked off the call and went about making myself some dinner. I tidied up, read the email update from my folks and replied with the same from me. I scrolled my socials for a bit, checking all the goings on back at home—certain I hadn't missed a single thing—and tried to read my book. Trying anything I could to distract myself, but after nine, I sent Colson a text.

Hope your night's okay? Everyone treating you well?

He replied about twenty minutes later.

Mostly fine.

Hmm. Mostly fine. That didn't sound good.

What do you mean mostly?

Just a few of the other guys were a bit standoffish when I got here. But they're not on my shift so it's okay.

I wasn't sure what to say to that, and after I tried to reply and deleted everything I started, my phone rang.

Colson's name was on-screen, and when I answered, he laughed. "Your little text bubble kept disappearing," he said.

"I didn't know what to say."

"I'm okay, Braithe," he said gently. "I promise."

"Did they say anything to you?"

"No. It was just two of the older officers. I wouldn't exactly call them friends of mine, and I've never worked with them because they do the morning shift. But before, they'd at least smile at me at shift change. Today there was none of that." He sighed. "You know, maybe I just imagined it. Maybe I'm looking for signs that aren't there. It just felt . . . deliberate, ya know?"

The thing was, I did know.

I knew exactly.

"Yeah, I get it."

"But Bouchard and Charity are fine. Nothing's different. Bouchard even asked me to help him pick between two different gift ideas for his sister. I don't know if he assumed I'd have some magic gay shopping expertise, but I was exactly zero help. Charity told him which one."

I chuckled, happy to hear he sounded as okay as he said he was.

"And I saw Ray today," he said. "He's the sergeant I'd sometimes go fishing and hunting with. He wasn't here for my big announcement, but he clearly got told. He had to rush out for a job not long after I got in, so he was in go-mode, but he clapped my shoulder on the way out." He was quiet a second. "Dunno if I'll get any more invites to go fishing, but it felt like an acknowledgement that he knew and that he was okay."

"I hope so," I offered. "It sounds like it. But hey," I said. "If not, I'm sure you can wrangle Clay and Ren into a fishing trip. Maybe Cass, but he's busy a lot, and Jayden works two jobs basically . . . Gunter might go. He's such a nice guy."

"What about Hamish?"

I snorted. "Fishing? Uh, just gonna put a real quick no on that."

He chuckled and it ended with a sigh. "I'm off work tomorrow," he said. "I can have dinner at your place. If you want. I don't mean to invite myself. If you'd rather—"

"Six o'clock. Don't be late."

"Should I bring pizza?"

"Yes, you should."

"Okay," he said softly. "I should go. Considering I'm at work and all."

I laughed. "Yes, you should. But thank you for calling. I was worried." He was quiet and I wondered if he was smiling like I was.

"Night, Braithe."

"Night, Colson."

SCHOOL WAS super busy and the kids were so excited about the approaching concert day. We practised our parts in between curriculum and playtime. With just four days to go, it was reciting lines, places to stand, and costume checks.

They were all so stinking cute.

We were also in the countdown to the Christmas Light Festival and Christmas Day.

I tried really hard not to dampen their countdown excitement with my own.

My countdown until my last day.

Until I left the kids; until I left Hartbridge.

Until I left Colson.

Yeah, I tried really hard not to think about that.

But as the week progressed, nothing happened. Colson came around for dinner at my place on Monday night, and I went to his on Tuesday night.

He was happy.

He said people at the store had treated him the same, more or less, saying hello and moving on. A few smiled, a few didn't. Nothing unusual there.

But there was an edge of caution in his eyes and maybe I imagined it. Maybe I was looking for something that wasn't there.

But he was happier.

He said he'd never felt so free.

So I took him at his word and just gave him extra hugs and kisses.

By the time Friday came around, I was exhausted but oh-so excited.

It was the Christmas concert day.

The school was abuzz, the kids close to bursting with excitement. The hall was jam-packed with as many seats as possible and there were food stalls and game stands under the covered play area outside.

The wind was cold and there was a good foot of snow on the ground, but the sun was out and it made for a beautiful day.

Everyone had arrived early to ensure everything was perfect.

And it was.

Before the plays began, it was a good time for parents to visit their kids' classrooms and see any projects they'd been working on. The parents that came past my classroom loved to see all the Christmas art on the walls, and I wished I could have chatted with them all for longer.

Without bragging, the kids liked me, and their parents did too. Not just the moms like before, but the dads and the grandparents as well. And even the occasional aunt and uncle who dropped by.

The energy I'd tried to bring to the classroom—the smiles and positive attitude, the friendly environment, which fostered manners and being thoughtful of others—was always well received.

They could think what they liked about me as a person—and I'm sure they did—but they couldn't deny I was a damn good teacher.

I was helping Bailey find his Christmas ornament to show his mom when someone else walked in. In full uniform and trying not to smile too big. "Good morning," Colson said, looking right at me.

My heart thumped erratically. "Morning," I said, trying to maintain some level of decorum and resist the urge to climb him like a tree.

"Deputy!" Bailey yelled, running over to him.

Colson grinned, then took his hat off and put it on Bailey's head. I would have to tell him later that sharing hats with school kids is probably not a great idea.

"Morning," Bailey's mom said to him, though she looked between us for a beat and I was sure she clocked that there was something unsaid between us.

"Just thought I'd drop by," Colson added, "to see if there were any little deputies in here like last time."

Bailey, still wearing the hat, put his hand up. "Me! Is the fire truck here again?"

Colson laughed. "Not that I know of."

Lucy came in with her dad and she wanted to show him all

her artwork too, and her desk and who she sat next to, and while I was talking to them, Colson gave me a smile and a wave from the door before he disappeared. He had his hat back on at least, and Bailey's mom was gone, so thankfully she didn't see the way he blushed and ducked his head as he left.

It was a look and a smile that made my belly swoop.

But then Brayden and his family came in and then Grace and her grandparents, and before I knew it, it was time to assemble the troops to get dressed into costumes, and I did have the help from Olivia's mom and Ricky's mom to get it all done.

Getting eighteen excited kids into their costumes while trying to keep them calm enough so there was the least amount of tears—overexcited and nervous kids usually ended with one or two tears—was no small feat. But when I asked them to stand in their lines of two, they did. When I asked them to stop yelling, they did. When I asked Bailey the bull to stop trying to use his cardboard horns to gouge Tahli the palm tree, he did.

Nancy came into the classroom to see if we needed any last-minute help and she was impressed by the order in which she found us. And by how cute they all looked, no doubt.

"Are we ready, class?" she asked.

They all chorused, "Yes!"

"Okay, class," I said at the head of the line. "Remember what I said. What are we going to have today?"

"Fun!" they all yelled.

I grinned, almost as excited as them. Though the nerves were kicking in, and as I led the class to the back of the hall stage, my stomach was a ball of knots.

I put my hands up to get the kids' attention. "Okay," I whispered loudly. "We need quiet as we walk out on stage. Does everyone remember their places?"

We'd practised on the stage twice during the week, but I knew once they saw the hall full of faces, all the practising we'd done would go out the window.

They'd be scanning the crowd looking for familiar faces, and that was expected. The one thing not to expect from kindergarteners was perfection.

Anything short of a disaster would be a win.

Principal Nancy O'Connor took the stage and introduced us. "Our next production is brought to you by a lot of hard work, a lot of patience, and a fair amount of crepe paper and paint," she said. "Mr Branson has only had the kindergarten class for four weeks, and what a wonderful job he's done, as I'm sure you're all about to see."

She looked to the wing of the stage, to me, and that was our cue.

Oh boy.

"Okay, class," I whispered loudly. I walked them out onto the stage so they could take their places.

Even I was surprised by the crowd in the hall, as I'm sure the kids were too. And there was a hum around the crowd, some laughter and excitement, as all my little students took their places.

The palm trees raised their arms and waved their crepe paper fronds, the cows mooed, the bulls stomped their feet, the sheep bleated, and the horses neighed.

It was a chorus of well-practised but ill-timed noise, and then Patrick the donkey walked in front of an Avalyn/Mary holding a doll baby, and a Ricky/Joseph. Then Ebony the North Star twirled across the stage—who was not supposed to twirl—followed by three wise men, which was fine until Bailey the bull tried to gouge one with his cardboard horns, and the goat bleated unexpectantly and earned himself a shove from Lucy the sheep. Grace the mouse was a hit, though the palm trees seemed to be embroiled in a waving contest, one of the wise men forgot his lines or the ability to speak, struck with stage fright as he stared blankly at the crowd, and Mary dropped the baby.

But they got through it, to minimal laughter from the crowd and rousing applause at the end.

I could have cried.

I almost did.

I was so proud of them.

And, if I was honest, I was a little proud of myself too. But mostly proud of them. I took to the stage and managed an awkward bow with the class as we'd practised, and I saw Colson at the back of the hall, standing alongside Hamish, Ren, Jayden, and Cass.

Pretty sure they all clapped the loudest. Colson's grin was breathtaking, even from a distance.

After rounding all the students up and telling them they were great, then taking some of the props back to the classroom, I was officially done for the day. And that meant I was free to check out the food stalls and find people to talk to.

Namely a certain deputy.

When I snuck back into the hall, the sixth graders were wrapping their play, and I found Jayden and Cass watching their boy Wyatt on stage, alongside Hamish and Ren, who were still at the back of the hall.

And Colson, of course. Standing with the queer group for the whole town to see.

Like he'd been scared to do up until now.

I made my way over to them as quietly as I could while the play was still going on and got to Hamish first. "Hey."

He grabbed my arm. "Oh my god, your kids were so funny," he whispered. "Best thing I've ever seen."

I grinned. "Thanks."

He pointed to the side of the stage. "We saw you in the wings being the stage production manager."

"More like the emergency diversion manager," I whispered back.

The audience broke out into applause and the last play of the day was done. Nancy took to the stage to thank all the visitors, and to remind everyone to stay for the food and games, and of course to have a safe and merry Christmas.

And then the hall was loud and crowded, and Colson came by to stand next to me. "Awesome play," he said. "Very cute."

"Thank you. I'm so glad you could come."

"I will have to get going soon," he said, checking his watch.

People were filing out of the hall, meaning they had to exit right by us. Almost everyone said hello to Ren or Colson, and some parents commended me on a job well done.

Cass and Jayden were still talking with his kids and another couple, the woman I guessed was Cass's ex, the mom to his kids. It was so sweet that they all got along so well.

"Shall we go out," Ren said.

"Yes," Hamish said. "We can't stay long. We have to get back to the store."

"Thank you both so much for coming," I said as we walked out to the undercover area that was now full of kids and families buying food, Christmas crafts, and playing games like ring-toss and cornhole.

Everyone wore coats, beanies, and scarves, but they also wore happy smiles, and the sounds of kids laughing was always a joy to my ears.

Ren clapped Colson on the arm. "Good to see you here," he said, and Hamish gave me a fond smile before they left.

"How was your day?" I asked Colson when we were finally

alone. I mean, there were a hundred or more people around us but no one too close.

He grinned at me. "This has been a lot of fun," he said. "And yeah, I'm sure people are trying not to look at me, but it's okay. It's good, actually. I'm ready for this." Then he made a face. "I think."

I couldn't help but laugh because I was almost certain he hadn't stopped smiling all week. But after a quick glance around, I could see he was right. There were a few sidelong looks.

They'd clearly heard the rumours that the town's deputy was gay, and here he was talking to me: the small, effeminate Englishman who'd been seen by half the town having coffee with the other gay men in town.

There really weren't many dots to join, and they'd been well and truly joined.

"Are you done for the day?" he asked.

"No, I'll be around all afternoon, packing away chairs and tidying up. I'll try and make the rounds to see some parents."

"Excuse me, Mr Branson," Olivia said with big eyes. She reached up to the horse headband she was still wearing. "Can we keep these? Mom said I had to ask."

"Yes, you absolutely can," I said brightly. Hers had long strands of crepe paper at the back for a tail or a mane, or something, and she clearly loved to wear it.

"Mom, he said yes," she yelled as she ran back to her family. Her mom gave me a smile and a nod, and I waved.

I noticed then that Emily Poole was here with her new baby in a pram, the man at her side I presumed to be her husband. People *ooh*ed and *aah*ed over the baby and I tried not to let it bother me that I'd be handing my class back to her in a week . . .

"Okay, Mr Branson," Colson murmured. "I'll let you go do your thing. Text me later."

"I will. Thanks again," I said, giving him a smile. "I'm really glad you were here."

He gave me a tip of his hat and a smile that unleashed butterflies in my belly, then he turned and ran into someone he knew and shook his hand. I turned back to Olivia's family, switching back into teacher mode, walking over to introduce myself.

It was a fun afternoon, and by the time we had the hall packed up and our classrooms cleaned, it was well after three and the remaining teachers and a few parents collapsed into our seats in the staffroom for a coffee.

It'd been a big day, a great day, but we were beat.

I sipped my coffee, not even mad that it wasn't tea. "So," Raeleen said as she sat next to me.

I knew what was coming.

"It was nice of Deputy Price to show up."

Aaaand there it was.

"It was." I aimed for pleasant but short.

She waited for me to elaborate.

I didn't.

"And I might have heard a whisper," she added.

She might have started the whisper.

"That he's g—"

"That he's a good man who loves this town?" I asked. "Because I heard that too."

Her smile skewed. "Well, yes."

All she wanted was gossip. About Colson, about the rumours around town that he'd come out as gay, and about how he'd now been seen twice with me.

Anything I said to her would be broadcast almost the second it left my mouth, and I wasn't going to let that happen.

If she could tell I wasn't in the mood for it, or perhaps she knew damn well it wasn't appropriate to talk about other people and what they did or didn't do in their bedrooms. But either way, she dropped it.

I hadn't noticed Emily come into the staff room, pushing her pram, but there she was. I couldn't begrudge her at all. These were her colleagues, her friends, long before they were mine. And they would be again long after I left.

Raeleen left me, thankfully, to fuss over the baby, and Emily came and sat down beside me.

"Raeleen's a little partial to gossip," she murmured, just for me to hear.

"Ah, yes," I said with a laugh. "I've come to realise."

"I don't think she's malicious," she furthered. "But yeah . . ." I nodded. I got the same feeling. But yeah . . .

"The play today was wonderful," she said. "Such a joy to watch."

I smiled at her. "They all worked very hard."

"They've adapted to you so well," she said, then she sighed with a smile, and I realised then how tired she looked. I knew all new parents were sleep deprived, but she looked beat. She watched as the others fussed and fawned over her baby with a fond smile.

"Are you okay?" I asked quietly.

"Oh, yes, thank you," she said, looking at me then. She was smiling and I didn't know her at all, but she seemed a little sad. No, perhaps not sad. More pensive. "Just trying to get used to the idea of coming back to work."

Oh man.

I didn't want to say anything that may influence her, and I certainly wouldn't be adding on more guilt than she clearly already felt.

"It can't be an easy decision," I said. "And one I don't envy you having to make. But," I hedged gently, "if you need a little more time, I can stick around."

She grew a little teary then, and I feared I'd overstepped.

But hope fluttered in my belly, and it was a dangerous feeling.

"No pressure," I added, patting her arm. "Whatever you need." She nodded quickly but took a deep breath in and shook off whatever she was feeling. Her baby began to fuss, so with a smile at me, she got up, and upon leaving, most people saw it as their excuse to follow.

It was getting late, after all.

"Have a great Christmas," everyone chorused. "See you all back here on Thursday."

For my last two days of work . . .

I found myself cleaning up the staff room alone with Nancy. I washed the sink down. "A successful day," I said.

"It was," she agreed, making sure the window was locked. "Got any plans for Christmas?"

"Christmas lunch, yes," I admitted. Colson had to work at night, even though it was normally his day off, and I hadn't really planned anything on my own for the evening. "I'll probably FaceTime my folks back home. Spending Christmas night in front of a fire with a good book isn't exactly terrible."

Waiting for someone to get home . . .

"No crazy party then? No gallons of eggnog and arguments with relatives?"

I snorted. "If you mean crazy party with a pot of tea, then yes. Maybe I'll even live dangerously and have two pots of tea while I finish my book."

She laughed, but her smile turned sad. "Oh, Braithe. I'll be sorry to see you go."

I sighed, all merriment gone. "Me too."

She tried to brighten as we walked out. "Will I see you at the light festival?"

"Oh yes. I've heard it's a great night."

"It is. Main Street looks magical, with lots of families, Santa photos, train rides for the little ones, and hot food stalls."

"I'm really looking forward to it."

"See you then," she said, locking the doors to the school building.

I got in my car, ready to get home and decompress for a few hours. After pulling on some comfy clothes and making a fresh pot of tea, I opened my laptop.

Something got me thinking . . .

And I began reading the fine print of my working visa when I got an email from my placement agency regarding my next employment position at McKinley Elementary in Spokane.

Mr Braithe Branson, we are pleased to offer you . . .

Chapter Twenty

COLSON

I GOT BACK to my place at almost one o'clock in the morning, knowing Braithe would be there.

I gotta tell ya, it was a nice feeling.

Even seeing his shoes at the door made my heart sing.

The lights were off and the fire was a few hours old so I could deduce he'd gone to bed a while ago. I poked my head into my room and saw his sleeping frame on my side of the bed again.

I leaned against the door jamb and let out a sigh, wishing like crazy it was a permanent thing.

I stoked the fire and took a hot shower, and when I went back into my room, he had his eyes closed so I tried being extra quiet. But then he lifted the corner of the covers.

"In here," he mumbled. "With me."

How could I ever say no to that?

I slid in under the covers and as soon as I had my arms around him, he snuggled in tight, holding me close, his face buried in my neck. And not really in a cute way, but in a just-had-a-bad-dream way.

I kissed the side of his head. "Everything okay?"

"Mm," he said, holding me even tighter.

And he stayed like that all night. Every time I moved or tried to roll over, he was stuck to me like glue.

Not that I minded. In fact, it was my new favourite way to sleep. But when I woke up, his side of the bed was empty. I heard him mumbling from the living room and I checked my phone. It wasn't quite seven, and while I'd have liked another hour or two of sleep, I didn't want to miss a minute with him. I rolled out of bed, pulled on my robe, and found him sitting in front of the fire, poking it and mumbling under his breath. The view out the window looked very white and cold.

"Are you cold?" I asked.

He startled a little. "Oh, you should stay in bed," he said. Then he noticed my robe. "Why haven't I seen that before? Actually, more to the point, why haven't I worn it before?"

I snorted, still half asleep. "You okay? Is the fire in trouble? Or do people in England often chastise fires? Is it a cultural-difference thing?"

"I wasn't chastising the fire," he said. "I was chastising the log. Which is different."

I chuckled as I walked into the kitchen. "I can only imagine it must have deserved it." I took two mugs out of the cupboard. "Want tea or coffee?"

He followed me into the kitchen and wedged himself in between me and the worktop, undoing my robe, and slipping his arms around me. I laughed and wrapped my robe around him the best I could.

"You okay? If you're cold, I have plenty of hoodies and coats."

"I'm okay now," he mumbled into my neck.

He didn't sound okay. He wasn't acting like he was. "You sure? You were cuddly when I got home last night too."

"Is that a complaint?"

I gave him a squeeze. "Absolutely not."

He sighed. "How was work?"

"Kinda busy. I didn't get home till almost one."

"Hm. I was tired, sorry."

"It's fine," I murmured. "Gotta say, I like coming home and seeing your shoes at the door. It's like my new favourite thing. Well, until I see you in my bed. Then that's my new favourite thing, every time."

I felt him smile against my neck, and with a deep breath, he pulled back. His eyes, normally blue and bright, were troubled.

I slid my hand to his jaw and thumbed his cheek. "Tell me what's wrong."

He frowned. "If I tell you, then it will make it real and I . . ." He looked down, his chin wobbling. "I don't want it to be real."

My stomach dropped and my heart suddenly felt heavy. "Is it about you leaving?"

He nodded.

So I pulled him back against me and held him a little too tight. "Then don't tell me. Don't make it real."

He nodded and made a sound that was half laugh, half cry. "Oh, Colson."

I squeezed him and held him as tight as I could, and we stood there in my kitchen for the longest time, just holding each other, neither one of us brave enough to say the words out loud.

He'd always said he was leaving. From the very beginning, he'd been upfront about it and said whatever happened between us could be no strings attached . . .

Only now I was so tangled up in the strings of him I didn't think I'd ever get free. Part of me—or all of me—would be attached to him in some way forever.

I didn't want him leaving to be real.

I needed every second he was here to count. "Can I ask you something? And you can feel free to say no, I'll totally understand."

He pulled back and looked up into my eyes and waited.

"I know you've agreed with Mrs Parson to rent her place for the duration of your stay, and I'm not sure what payment agreement you've made, and that's none of my business . . ." I winced. This was coming out all wrong. "But maybe you could stay here instead. Just until . . ." I couldn't even bring myself to say it. "For as long as you need. I don't know how much time I have left with you, and I don't want to miss a minute. We already work different shifts and have different days off, so I feel robbed as it is. But if you stayed here . . ." I sighed and put my forehead to his. "Then I wouldn't miss a moment."

He closed his eyes, a soft smile pulled at his lips, and when he opened his eyes again, his endless blue gaze met mine. "Are you sure?"

I laughed because, oh my god, he was actually going to do it. "Yes. One hundred per cent, yes. Stay here. With me. In my bed. I'll make you tea, and you can keep your shoes by my door so I smile when I get home. We can keep the Christmas lights on all the time if you want, and I'll try and make some of those savoury pudding things that Jayden made that you said reminded you of home, and—"

He leaned up on his toes and kissed me softly, his eyelashes wet. "I would like that very much. Except maybe not the Yorkshire puddings. They're not easy to make and—"

"I will learn."

His grin widened. "Are you absolutely sure? Because Mrs Parson won't mind. It's all paid up, so it makes no difference how long I stay. I think she's away at her daughter's for

Christmas anyway. I'm sure she'll just be happy that I'm not alone for the holidays." His chin wobbled. "I would like very much to leave my shoes at your door."

I pulled him in for a long, tight hug. "Let's make some coffee and breakfast, then we can go grab your things."

He nodded into my neck. "Tea and breakfast."

I laughed and kissed the side of his head. "Of course. Anything for you."

"Do you have baked beans? For a full English breakfast, maybe . . ."

I froze. Baked beans for breakfast? "Okay, anything for you, but not that."

He laughed, and when he pulled back, he was now smiling. A little teary, but the genuine smile was a win. "Then just tea and toast will be fine."

"Tea and toast I can do!"

Tea, toast, and a steamy, crowded shower later, we drove to Braithe's place. As we walked down the driveway, Mrs Parson was gathering some firewood from her shed.

"Here, let me get that for you," I said, quickly rushing to take her bucket.

"Oh, thank you," she said. "I wondered if I'd see you today, Braithe." I might have been throwing some wood pieces into a bucket, but I managed to catch the wink she gave him.

"Yes, well, about that," he said. "I needed to tell you that I'm moving out. I only have a week left, and I'd rather spend that time with . . . uh, somewhere else." He put his hand up. "And before you ask, I don't expect a refund of any kind. I just wanted to give you the courtesy of knowing I won't be here for dinner during the week, and you're free to rent out the annexe over Christmas, should someone need it."

She looked at him, then at me holding her wood bucket, and back at him. She smiled. "Oh, well, this is a wonderful development. Is he still treating you with *consideration*? He's not coercing you in any way, is he?"

The strangled noise I made surprised even me, and Braithe laughed. "Uh, no. No coercion. There are considerable benefits, however."

I almost dropped the bucket. "Braithe!"

Mrs Parson laughed, delighted, but then she sighed, her eyes softening at him. "Promise me you'll stop by for dinner one night before you leave."

He nodded. "I would love that."

"One week, you said?" she asked.

He gave a solemn nod.

Damn.

One week.

"I, uh, I've been offered to start at McKinley Elementary in Spokane, the first Monday of the new year."

Oh.

That's what he didn't want to tell me. The reason he was clingy and sad. The truth that would make it real.

Braithe's eyes met mine and I couldn't look away. My heart felt close to breaking, shattering.

Mrs Parson took the bucket from me. "I'll let you two pack up," she said softly. "Come see me when you're done."

"Spokane," I whispered. "A week."

He gave a nod, his face a mask of sadness.

"Spokane's not that far," I tried. Though with the different schedules, the different days we had off, I wasn't sure how it worked.

Clearly Braithe thought the same. "I'm sorry. I wish . . . I wish . . ." Unable to bear the sadness in his eyes or the way his lip trembled, I went to him and with my hand around the back of his neck, I pulled him against me. "I wish too."

He nodded but then he pulled back and shook off his

mood. "Right, then. No more wasting time. Let's get me packed up. It will take all of ten minutes because everything I own basically fits into a suitcase." He let out a sharp breath. "And then you can take me home and make me feel better."

I gave his arm a squeeze. "Anything."

"Except beans on toast, right?"

"Correct. Except that. Because I googled it, and it's a definite no from me." He was smiling again, and unlocking his door, he swung it inward.

"I'll make it for you one day and you'll love it."

He was right about it not taking long. Twenty minutes later, he went in to speak to Mrs Parson alone while I carried Spruce Willis to Braithe's car.

He joined me a short while later, pulling his beanie down. "Phew, it's turned cold today."

"Is Mrs Parson okay?" I asked.

"Yes, she's happy for me. She was serious about the dinner offer and she did ask if you'd be joining me, but I explained that you worked nights."

That made me happier than it should have. "I still can't believe people in this town are okay with it," I admitted. "Me being gay, I mean. Well, they're mostly okay. No one has said anything to me, but I did get a few strange looks at the school yesterday."

"So let them look," I said. "They'll get over it. With Christmas around the corner, I'm sure there'll be another town scandal for people to talk about. Then it'll all be old news and you'll be free to . . ." He stopped and made a face, leaving me to wonder what he was about to say.

Free to date someone else? Free to find someone else? "Free to be yourself," he finished. It was absolutely not what he was going to say. But he started the engine and shot me a smile. "Let's get my three things unpacked at your place, then you can get me out of these wet clothes and warm me up."

"Wet clothes?"

He smiled. "Yes, I think some snow touched the hem of my jeans."

I snorted. "Then yes, we need to get you out of them stat."

SETTING some room aside in my closet and dresser for Braithe gave me a thrill I wasn't prepared for.

I kept telling myself it was only temporary, to enjoy it for what it was.

I was out now, free of the closet I'd barricaded myself in for years.

So it was ironic how making space in my actual closet had me smiling. As did seeing his box of teabags in the pantry, and his electric kettle on my kitchen counter, and his shoes in a neat row at my door.

I hadn't stopped smiling yet.

I didn't want to go to work. I didn't want to leave him. Even after we'd spent hours in bed . . .

He'd reasoned that bringing his own boxes of teabags and condoms had weighted the teabag to condom ratio and we needed to even the playing field.

It was a contest I had no intention of losing. Not if it meant having him sprawled out in my bed, thoroughly had and snoozing with a smile on his face.

And I didn't want to leave him when I was dressed for work and at the door and he was wearing my fluffy robe with his hair a blond mop of disarray. And he'd leaned up on his tiptoes to kiss me softly.

"I'll be here when you get back," he murmured, his eyes a

dreamy blue. "And when you come to bed and when you wake up. You'll be sick of me."

I laughed and lifted his chin for a soft kiss. "Not possible." I had to drag myself away and make myself go to work. But I arrived smiling, happier than I could ever remember being.

The same people said hello; the same few people refused to look at me.

It was more obvious now. It had happened every day since my announcement, and there was no excuse for being too busy or having to rush out the door like there was on the first day.

I'd barely gotten a nod of acknowledgement from Buck or Johnson in the breakroom, and they'd turned their backs on me in the open office.

So yeah, their ignoring me was obvious and deliberate.

But I wasn't letting it get to me.

It was their problem, not mine, I reminded myself. If they chose to confront me or heckle or antagonise me, then I'd make it my problem. But until then, I was happy to pretend they didn't exist.

This was what Braithe meant when he'd said if any of my friends or colleagues didn't like it, then they weren't real friends.

And I was okay with that.

Ronny called me into his office for a rundown of today's duties and to get ready for the light festival tomorrow night. It involved road closures and detours, ensuring all boxes were ticked on insurance and whatnot.

It made for a busy two days ahead.

"And I heard you were at the school for the Christmas concert," he said.

He knew I was going, so . . . "It was a great event. Lots of families, and the kids had a ball." But I was guessing he knew that already and it wasn't why he brought it up. "And when you say you heard, do you mean that in a bad way? Because I was in uniform, which I had your permission for. I thought it'd be good to represent us in the community."

He smiled and gave a nod. "It wasn't bad," he replied softly. "Just people were noticing, that's all. After your announcement here and then you being there with your friends . . ."

"You mean my gay friends?"

He sighed. "You know I have no issue with it. I'm mindful now about how the words we use can make a difference since you pointed it out to me, and I'm learning. But the folks around town might need a little time to learn as well." He put his hand up in a stop fashion. "I'm not making excuses. I'm just saying they're not up to speed on what's acceptable. But they will learn." He shrugged. "Eventually. And I made a point of saying as much."

I gave him a smile. "Thank you. And I know people will talk." I glanced back at the desks on the other side of the glass wall. "And I know not everyone out there is a fan. But I'm okay with it."

Ronny's moustache flattened as his lips thinned into a line. "Mm, don't you worry about them. Just do your job as you've always done, and if any of them say anything to you, you let me know."

I nodded, so grateful he was on my side. "I will, thank you."

He leaned back in his chair and let out a sigh. "Now, about that apple pie I owe you."

I snorted. "You don't have to worry about it."

"Too late. Geraldine's already made it. I'll drop it off tomorrow morning."

I felt a rush of warmth, something that felt a lot like pride and gratitude. "Perfect."

"Now," he said. "Given circumstances might have changed, have you got any plans for Christmas Day dinner? You're more than welcome to stop by my place before you start work, grab a plate. We always have too much food and there'll already be twenty people in my dining room; one more won't make a lick of difference."

That pang of missing my family, the ache I'd felt every holiday season, seemed to fill with something else. A new sense of family. That Ronny would now include me in his, it really meant a lot.

"I'm grateful, sir," I said. "And any other time I'd jump at the chance. But I have plans for Christmas dinner this year . . ." My cheeks flamed and, of course, he didn't miss it.

"Oh?"

"Y-yes. Uh, Braithe Branson is staying with me for the rest of his stay in Hartbridge. It's not permanent." I swallowed hard, the word *unfortunately* getting stuck in my throat. "But he wants us to eat together before I start work. Some traditional English meal. I'm not sure, to be honest."

His smile was slow to spread wide. "Well, that sounds real nice."

I let out a rush of air, fighting a grin. "It does. It'll be my first Christmas in a long time that I've had any reason to celebrate. And he has no family here, so yeah, it'll be nice."

"He's, uh, he's not staying in town?"

I shook my head. "He's been offered another teaching position in Spokane in the new year."

Ronny frowned. "That's a shame."

"It is," I managed to say.

His phone rang, and with a nod, I left him to it. I went

back to my desk and took out the paperwork from my inbox and made myself busy.

I WOKE up with sunlight barely cracking through the curtains and Braithe still asleep next to me. I couldn't help but lie there and watch him. Peaceful, beautiful. Mine.

For one more week.

I wished my mind could take photographs or videos that I could replay when he was gone. Videos that didn't fade like memories do.

I never wanted to forget this.

Because I knew my memories of him would begin to fade and the finer details of his face would disappear in time. That tiny, faded scar on his cheek, the cupid's bow of his mouth. The curve of his cheekbone, the fan of his eyelashes.

They would merge and blur eventually until only a vague likeness of pale skin, blond hair, and blue eyes remained.

Like the memories of my family had faded.

And that was a memory lane I didn't want to walk down. Not today, not these holidays. Not ever.

I snuck my phone off the bedside, and switching it to silent, I took some photos of Braithe asleep and facing me. Then a short video, only for his eyes to crack open.

"What are you doing?"

Startled, I almost dropped my phone. "Shit. Sorry. I was just . . ."

"Taking photos of me?"

I sighed. "I don't want to forget," I whispered. "This moment, of you being asleep in my bed. You're just the most beautiful man I've ever seen, and I don't want to forget what you look like."

He smiled and reached out to take my hand. "Okay, so you went from creepy to sweet in one sentence."

I chuckled, despite my heavy heart. "I don't remember the finer details of my parents' faces. I remember what they look like, of course, but you know when you haven't seen someone in years and you only have a general likeness in your mind." I sighed at the ceiling. "Sorry. I don't know why I woke up thinking about them."

"Because it's Christmas Eve," Braithe said, leaning up on his elbow as he put his hand on my chest. "Do you want to try and reach out to them?"

I shook my head. "No. I tried that after a year, and again the year after that, and the response was the same, probably worse the second time. They won't change and I've made my peace with that. It's their loss, right?"

He nodded. "It absolutely is. Here, give me your phone," he said, wiggling into the crook of my arm. He put his head on my chest and we took some selfies of us in bed, smiling, making funny faces, laughing as he tickled me, me kissing the side of his head.

No more sadness. No more melancholy. Just happiness and kisses, and warm hugs, and tea.

So much tea.

BRAITHE HAD BEEN to the store yesterday and bought what he needed to make us Christmas dinner. He wanted to prep it all today, before the light festival tonight, so all he had to do tomorrow was pop it in the oven.

He had me help, of course.

We peeled potatoes and carrots, and he simmered some cranberry mix to have with the brown gravy. He'd managed to find a boneless turkey to roast. He'd said it wasn't ideal given what was left two days before Christmas.

But it all sounded perfect to me.

"I didn't want to leave it until today," he said, stirring the sauce on the stovetop. "There was hardly anything left as it was. Though I didn't get anything in the way of dessert. I wasn't sure what you'd like, and I tried googling *traditional American Christmas desserts*, but it was all so varied so I thought I'd just ask and go back today."

I came up behind him at the stove, slid my arms around him, and kissed the back of his neck. "I forgot to tell you," I murmured. "Ronny's wife was making me an apple pie as a thank you for working Christmas Day."

And right on cue, Ronny's cruiser pulled up out front. "Ah, speak of the devil." Ronny came up the front steps holding a white cake box.

I opened the front door for him with a grin and stood aside. "Ronny, please come in."

"Morning," he said, stepping inside and he handed me the box. "One apple pie, as promised."

"Please tell Geraldine I said thank you." I walked toward the kitchen and Braithe came walking out, wiping his hands on a tea towel.

"Sheriff Harper," he said. "Lovely to see you again."

Ronny tipped his hat. "Same, same. Colson here was telling me you'd be staying with him for a week or so."

Braithe gave me a smile. "Yes. He was gracious to offer."

"Glad to hear it," he said. Then clapped his hands in the way that he did before he announced his departure. "Well, I better get back to it. They'll be closing off Main Street within the hour."

I gave him a nod. "Then I better get myself ready for work." He tipped his hat to Braithe again as he left, and when

I closed the door behind him, I turned back to Braithe and laughed. "I'll never get used to it," I said.

He grinned right back at me. "What? Having your boss drop off a pie when the guy you're clearly shagging is in your house? And he's like, 'You boys take care now,'" he said, imitating Ronny's gruff voice.

I laughed. "Yes!"

He came over to me, leaned up, and gave me a soft kiss. "He's sweet. But you better get your fine arse to work. I don't want him to think I'm a bad influence on you."

"You're coming down tonight though, right?" I asked. "With Hamish and the others?"

"To the famous Hartbridge Light Festival? I wouldn't miss it for the world."

IT WAS ALWAYS busy blocking off Main Street, setting up detours and traffic diversion signs, and ensuring everyone setting up had their permits. Not that anyone didn't ever not have their permits, and we knew every single person there. But still. Protocols and procedures.

I helped unload hay bales, set up barricades, signs, and I even shovelled some snow off the sidewalks. It was busy but fun, and the sense of community was always my favourite part.

Did Chad McClaremont not stop for a chat like he'd done a hundred times over the years? Did he barely give me a nod before he kept on his way?

Yep.

And did Louanne Miller give me a distasteful up and down, when just last week she'd said a cheery hello to me in the Home Mart?

Yep.

Okay, so two more townsfolk I could cross off my I-thought-were-my-friends list.

Don't let it bother you, Colson. Don't let them get to you. Being busy helped.

Seeing Ren at his store helped. Helping Jayden pull out the hot food cart helped me forget about the people who didn't like me now that they knew I was gay.

The kind smiles and friendly nods other people gave me helped.

For the most part, the people of Hartbridge were the best you could ever meet.

And as daylight faded and the crowds poured in, it became more apparent. Most people were great, like nothing had changed.

Some people weren't. Some folks pretended they didn't see me, pretended not to hear my "Good evening" or "Merry Christmas."

I couldn't deny it. It stung.

As much as I tried to tell myself it didn't matter, it kinda did.

People who I'd thought would be okay . . . people who I'd thought better of.

Seeing Braithe with Hamish was like a sigh of relief. He wore his dark jeans and white coat, grey beanie, and scarf. And the smile that lit his face when he saw me . . .

I'd remember that forever.

"Have you ever seen anything so beautiful?" he asked me, gesturing to the streetlights, the Christmas lights.

I nodded, looking right at him. "I was just thinking the same thing."

Hamish laughed. "Hm-mm. Except he was talking about the lights."

Braithe nudged him but his smile landed on me. I

couldn't tell if his cheeks were pink from embarrassment or the cold. "So, the Santa photos look like fun. Hamish said it's Clay's dad in the Santa suit. Maybe we could sneak a photo later?"

I looked over to the Winter Wonderland area, to where Cliff Henderson sat in the big Santa chair with a kid on his knee having their photo taken. Clay and Gunter were standing by, grinning from ear-to-ear, but the line to get a photo was long.

"Well, I'm technically working, so maybe not," I replied. "But later, if there's no line, and if I'm not busy . . ."

Braithe's grin was dazzling under the pretty lights. "Okay, I'll come find you."

"Hello, Mr Branson," some little boys yelled as they ran past. Kids from his class, no doubt.

"Hi," he yelled back. "Bailey, slow down!" He shook his head and sighed just as a man and woman followed after them.

"If you know how to get him to slow down, by all means," the woman said. I thought it was Melinda Brown from Oak Street. "He's been a charging bull since the play yesterday. Next year we might make him a sloth instead."

Braithe laughed. "Sounds like a good idea."

"Have a good night," she said, smiling as they kept going.

My radio crackled to life. "Base to C2."

I held the receiver. "This is C2. Over."

"Reports of some kids down by the river," Charity said over the radio. "Might wanna check it out. Bouchard's on his way."

"Roger that. Over." I gave Braithe a nod. "Duty calls."

"Go get 'em, C2," he said.

I resisted rolling my eyes, but I headed down toward the bridge and sure enough, some teenagers were climbing down the embankment. Trying to steal a cigarette or a first kiss, I didn't know. I didn't ask. I just hunted them back up to safer ground.

"Kids being kids," Bouchard said as I met him up on the top of the embankment.

"Yep." I dusted my hands off. "Harmless."

"Until one of 'em ends up in the water."

"True."

I looked back at the river. It was moving pretty well, icy and dark. The fact the fire truck was parked on the grassy area near the huge lit Christmas tree was both good and bad. It meant kids were running around, but the extra spotlights from the truck certainly helped.

"Been down to Vern's," Bouchard said.

Vern's was the bar on the edge of town. "Oh? Trouble?"

He rolled his eyes. "Just two guys who had too much to drink and started fighting. Brothers-in-law, apparently. Gonna make for an interesting Christmas dinner."

I chuckled. "We'll probably get called out tomorrow."

He snorted and shook his head. "Don't jinx us."

We spotted Ronny and the mayor and made our way over. "Merry Christmas," I said.

"Merry Christmas," they replied.

Geraldine put her hand on my arm. "Please tell me Ronald delivered that apple pie and didn't eat it himself," she said. "Because he's supposed to be watching his cholesterol."

I laughed. "He did, yes. Thank you so much. It'll be the crown on my Christmas dinner tomorrow. Very much looking forward to it." I gestured to Bouchard. "I'll even bring some to work tomorrow for Bouchard."

"I won't say no," he replied.

Geraldine looked pleased as punch.

Of course, Chad McClaremont chose that particular time

to walk past and say his hellos to everyone but me. It was blatant enough that Bouchard and Ronny noticed.

"Don't let 'em get to ya," Ronny mumbled, and Bouchard gave me a clap on the arm.

I tried to smile. "It's all good."

But the night went on and was not too uneventful. Someone moved a barricade, a car had a dead battery, and kids running amok and having the time of their lives non-stop made for a busy night.

By the time I caught up with Braithe again, the train ride crew were packing up, the line was all but gone at the Santa photo stand, and Jayden's food cart looked to be almost sold out.

"Ooh, can we sneak a photo?" Braithe asked.

"Do you think Santa will mind?" I asked.

Clay laughed. "You gotta sit on his lap."

And I don't know what made me look . . . but some kids running down near the big Christmas tree caught my eye. It was Bailey and his friend who had ran past us earlier. Don't think he'd stopped running all night.

And he kept running, and I kept watching.

"What is it?" Braithe asked beside me.

"He's too close to the edge," I mumbled, my heart beginning to kick.

And then Bailey disappeared, right over the side, and his little friend stopped. He turned around to look for someone, a grown-up, probably. He pointed and yelled . . .

I was already running.

Chapter Twenty-One

BRAITHE

COLSON KNEW something was wrong before it even happened. He was staring down at the river, past the huge Christmas tree, and then he was running before any screaming could be heard.

He sprinted.

Faster than anyone there.

He raced down past the tree and when he got to the embankment, he went straight over.

"Oh my god," I mumbled, fear rooting me to the spot until reality kicked in and I began running too.

Colson, no.

Other people were noticing now, all turned and watching, running to the river.

My heart was in my throat, my legs shaking.

Colson . . .

By the time I got to the embankment, other people were there, and there was yelling and the river was so dark.

But then men who stood at the edge grabbed little arms and Bailey was being hoisted up. He was pale, dripping wet, and was very quickly carried to safety, and the fire department was there with thermal blankets, and he looked okay. His mother was crying and hugging him and Bailey was fine, but Colson.

Where the hell was Colson?

Bouchard was halfway down the embankment and Ronny was at the top. Together, they pulled Colson up.

He was a wet and muddied mess, his hands were shaking, and he was looking for Bailey. "Is he okay?"

"He'll be fine," Ronny said, clearly worried about Colson.

"We need another blanket here!" one of the men yelled. A fireman raced another blanket over and they wrapped Colson up. His teeth were chattering.

"He needs to get home," Ronny said. "Out of these wet clothes."

"I'll take him," Bouchard said. "I'll go get the patrol car and bring it down." He was already running up the street.

Colson's eyes landed on me, and I very nearly buckled right there. I wasn't sure I'd breathed at all. Then Ronny grabbed me and we were bundled into a police car. "Get him home. I'll be right behind you."

Colson was shaking and I was trying not to cry.

"Are you okay?" I asked.

"C-c-cold," he said, his teeth still chattering, but he was smiling.

"Which one's yours?" Bouchard asked. "I knew you were on Juniper Lane." I hadn't even realised where we were. I looked out the windscreen and saw my car parked out the front of Colson's house. "Behind the gold Toyota there."

We bundled Colson up the porch steps and I fumbled with the key before I managed to push our way in. I sat him on the floor in front of the fire and began taking his boots off while Bouchard put more wood on the fire. I'd stoked it up before I'd left, but that was a few hours ago now.

I got one wet boot off, then his other, trying to pull his wet socks off. He was shaking and his skin was so cold.

"We need to get your trousers off," I said. "Can you stand up?" Then Bouchard was behind him and lifted him to his feet. He was stronger than he looked. I got Colson's belt off and undid his trousers, getting them off as fast as I could. His coat and shirts were next. Thankfully his phone was in his coat, not his trousers.

Bouchard came back holding towels and the covers from Colson's bed. "I just grabbed what I could find," he said apologetically.

"Thank you." I dried Colson off the best I could, then wrapped him up. I raced to grab some trackpants and a hoodie, and with Bouchard's help, we got him into warm, dry clothes as fast as we could, wrapped him back up in the bedcovers, and sat him by the fire.

Ronny came through the front door, followed by Hamish and Ren and two other men I'd never seen before. They weren't in uniform, but I assumed they were officers, though I really didn't know.

"How is he?" Ronny asked. His voice was so loud and gruff that it startled me.

"He's okay," I said. "His feet are warming up."

Ronny was in front of Colson then. "Good, good. How're ya feeling, son?"

Colson nodded. "'M okay. How's th-the kid?"

"He's gonna be fine," Ronny said. "The fire department had it all under control." Ronny pulled up Colson's hood and patted his head. "Keep your knees up to your chest and take deep breaths." Then he looked up at me. "He needs a warm drink. Milk with sugar, if you have it."

I nodded and went into the kitchen to make that, and Hamish came with me. "You okay?" he whispered.

I put a spoonful of sugar in a mug of milk and put it into the microwave. "I will one hundred per cent fall apart later, but I'm okay. Just worried right now."

Hamish rubbed my back. "He'll be okay."

I nodded quickly, needing to *not* fall apart right now.

"You coulda made the Olympic team with that sprint," one of the police guys said to Colson.

"We saw you runnin' from the top of the street," the other one added. "Like the freaking Flash, you were."

"I-I saw him go over," Colson said. "The kid. I was w-watching them run, and since I hunted those older kids from the riverbank earlier in the night, I kept my eye on them."

Taking the warm milk, I knelt before Colson and handed him the mug. His hands shook, but he smiled at me. I rubbed the top of his socked feet, trying to procure some more warmth.

"You feeling better?" I asked.

He smiled and nodded before he sipped his drink. "Thank you."

Ronny helped Colson up onto the sofa. "Okay, not too close to the fire now," he said, then he peered into his eyes. "Pupils look okay. How's your head? Feeling dizzy?"

Colson managed a smile. "I'm okay. Much better now."

"Want me to call the doctor?"

He shook his head. "Nah. I'll be okay."

I picked up Colson's wet clothes off the floor, including his belt. It was heavier than I remembered when I'd taken it off him, then I realised why. "Oh my god, a gun."

I held it out like it was a dead rodent for Ronny to take. Colson smiled and so did the other two guys, and Bouchard too.

"Sorry," I said. "Englishman, here. We don't do guns."

"I'll take care of it," Ronny said, looking at Colson for some kind of approval. "I'll put it in the safe at work."

Colson nodded. "Thanks." Then he shrugged. "It went into the water."

Ronny gave a nod because apparently that meant something.

I fished a set of keys from the wet pockets and gave them to Ronny as well. "I assume Colson's cruiser's parked somewhere down Main Street," I said. "Though the keys are wet too."

Ronny smiled at me. "We'll take care of it."

"Thanks, Ronny," Colson said. "For everything."

"You sure you're okay, son?"

"Yeah," Colson said. "Although I'd like an update on the kid when you hear something. Just to know if he's okay."

"Sure thing," Ronny said. "You know that kid you saved is Chad McClaremont's nephew."

"Bailey Brown," I said, filling in the details for anyone who needed it. "He's in my kindergarten class. I spoke to his mom earlier tonight."

Ronny nodded. "Melinda is Chad's sister. Reckon he might be a little more respectful next time he sees you." He clapped Colson on the shoulder as he stood up. "Right, then. I'll leave him in your care," he said to me. "If he starts to drop, meaning slurred speech or shaking, you call 911, okay? Then you call me."

I nodded dutifully. "Of course."

Bouchard gave me a nod. "Call the station if you need anything, okay?"

I didn't know whether to laugh or cry. "I will."

Before they could file out the door, Clay and Gunter came through it. They looked worried, eyes fixed on Colson. "We just heard," Clay said.

Ronny shook his hand. "Look after him, all of you," he said to the room, and with a nod, they all left.

Gunter shut the door and they came around the sofa, along with Hamish and Ren. "You know," Ren said. "I hear the river's good for swimming this time of year."

Colson cracked a smile. "Not really, no."

"Zero stars, do not recommend," I said, sitting beside Colson and finding his hand under the blankets.

He finished his warm milk and Hamish took the cup. "Can I get you anything else?" Hamish asked.

Colson shook his head. "I'm a little embarrassed, to be honest. With everyone fussing over me."

I squeezed his hand. "Get used to it."

His eyes met mine. "Scared you, huh?"

"Ah, you could say that," I replied. "I watched you run and jump straight off the edge." I swallowed back my tears because I didn't want to lose it in front of these guys.

"I'm sorry," he said with a smiley frown. "I didn't mean to scare you." I pulled his hand and lifted his arm so I could get in under the blanket with him. I snuggled in close, not caring that they were watching.

For body heat purposes, of course.

"You're quite the talk of the town," Gunter said. "In a good way. Heard the word hero a few times and how you saved that boy's life."

Colson let out a sigh. "It'll be a nice change from this week."

I sat up so I could look at him. "What did Ronny mean when he said that man might show a bit more respect this week?"

Colson gave me a sad smile. "He was just a bit of a dick to me earlier. Clearly not a fan of gay Colson. Straight Colson was fine though."

"Then you went and saved his nephew's life," Ren said.

"I didn't even think," Colson said. "I just saw him go over the edge and I ran. I was down there earlier in the night, telling those teenagers not to be stupid. So I kept half an eye on the river all night." He shrugged. "Lucky I did."

I settled back against Colson, my head on his shoulder. "Are you warm enough now?"

"Yeah. I can't believe you stripped me in front of Bouchard. Dunno how I'm supposed to look him in the eye tomorrow."

I snorted. "Tell him it was his Christmas gift and he should say thank you."

"Uh, Braithe," Hamish said flatly. "Is that your Christmas tree?"

I looked at the two potted trees. "Yes. That's Spruce Willis, and this one's Conifer Aniston."

They all burst out laughing, Clay laughed the loudest, and I sat up. "Are you all mocking our Christmas trees?"

Hamish shook his head. "No. I just . . . didn't realise your tree was *here*."

"Oh." I made a face. "Well, I might be staying here. Until I have to leave. I moved out of Mrs Parson's."

Hamish gasped loudly. "And you were going to tell me this when? I spent hours with you tonight and you didn't think this was important information?"

I laughed and leaned back against Colson. "It's just until I leave."

Hamish sighed again. "Are you still talking about that leaving nonsense?" He gestured to me and Colson. "Because it doesn't look like either of you two want that."

I groaned. "Maybe tonight's not the night for that conversation," I said. "I think Colson's been through enough."

"Tonight's the perfect night for that conversation," Hamish replied.

"Hame," Ren chastised him gently, shaking his head.

Hamish, in true Hamish form, wasn't deterred. He smiled at us. "Colson, Braithe does not want to leave. He might be trying to put on a brave face so you don't feel cornered or pressured, or whatever unreasonable British reasoning he has in his head. But he does not want to leave, because the strings he was determined to keep unattached are *very well* attached. And I'm pretty sure you don't want him to leave either." He didn't give either of us time to speak. "So now that I've opened the channel for this conversation, we'll leave you alone so you can talk and sort this mess out." He hooked his arm through Ren's. "I'm glad you're feeling okay, Colson," Hamish added. "It was a very brave thing to do and we're all very proud of you."

Colson shrank back a little and I squeezed his hand under the blankets to let him know it was okay.

Gunter stood and waited for Clay to do the same. "Don't get up. We'll see ourselves out," Gunter said. Then he checked his watch. "And Merry Christmas."

I glanced at the clock to find it was 12.03.

It was Christmas Day.

"Ooh, Merry Christmas," Hamish said. Then he winked at me. "Hope Santa's kind. And, though I'm sure you're both aware, maintaining body heat is best done through skin-to-skin contact."

"Okay, that's enough," Ren said, dragging Hamish to the door. "Glad you're okay, Colson."

"See you tomorrow afternoon?" Gunter asked me.

I nodded. "Sure thing. Have a good Christmas morning."

"We will," Clay said. "You too."

"Thanks for coming by," Colson said. "All of you. It means a lot."

"Any time," Ren replied, and they pulled the door shut behind them, leaving Colson and me alone in a very silent house.

His eyes met mine. "Are you sure you're okay? How are your feet?"

He wiggled his socked toes so I could see. "Toasty. Now." Then he sighed. "Thank you. For getting me home and warm again. That water was freezing. Colder than ice. And I didn't even think. I just went in, and he was fully in the water, head under." He shuddered at the memory. "Lucky I only went in to my waist, I guess."

"You saved his life." I tried to smile for him, but he needed to know. "You scared the hell out of me though. I thought . . . I thought the worst."

"I'm sorry," he murmured, kissing me softly. "I didn't mean to scare anyone. I was surprised, actually, that everyone came back to check on me."

Oh, Colson.

I smiled, though it was honestly sad that he was so shocked. "People care about you, Colson. You have real friends here. I think Ronny was genuinely worried. He's very fond of you. Like a son, perhaps."

"He's like a dad to me," he admitted. "Not that I'd tell him that. It'd make it weird."

I chuckled and ended with a sigh, searching his eyes. We needed to talk about what Hamish had said and, despite the night we'd had, this conversation was long overdue. "I'm sorry if Hamish made you uncomfortable. He has no filter."

His eyes met mine, searching. "I don't want you to leave."

"I don't want to leave either." I shrugged. "I think what we have is kind of wonderful. And you know those guys joked about this town and how Santa and Cupid team up to tag team queer people, and so god help me, I think they might be right."

He chuckled at that, clearly confused. "I . . . I don't know where to start with any of that."

I let my head fall back to his shoulder and we watched the fire for a few moments.

At least knowing he was as torn about my leaving as I was made me feel better. I just didn't know what it meant for us.

"What do we do?" I asked, hoping he had some answers.

"I don't know," he whispered.

The silence that followed hung heavy. The firelight and gentle Christmas lights were lulling me to sleep, coupled with the exhausting day and the adrenaline drop, now that everything was okay, I was suddenly sleepy.

"Ready for bed?" I asked.

He nodded, so I got up, helping him to his feet. "Now, you have to tell me if you start to feel poorly or if you notice any changes. Sheriff's orders, and I don't want to get on Ronny's bad side." I kept the bedcovers tucked in around him and walked him to bed, sitting him down. "You get in. I'll go and make sure everything's locked and turned off."

A few seconds later, I joined him. Fully naked. I snuggled in and he was quick to wrap me up in his arms. I held him just as tight.

"What Hamish said about exchanging body heat is true," I said. "But there'll be no exchanging of body fluids until tomorrow, and only if you're feeling okay."

"I feel fine now," he tried.

"Not tonight," I murmured. His body had been through enough for one night. "But if you wake me up in the morning for a thorough shagging, I won't mind. You know, being Christmas and all."

He chuckled and gave me a squeeze, kissing the side of my head. "Merry Christmas, Braithe."

I kissed his chest. "Merry Christmas, Colson."

As it turned out, he woke me up by being the big spoon and wiggling his very eager erection against my arse.

"Mm, good morning," I mumbled.

"I've been waiting forever for you to wake up," he replied.

"Clearly you're feeling fine," I said with a laugh, writhing against him.

His hand on my hip held me where he wanted me, and the hard heat of his cock felt so damn good. I reached behind me and tried to pull his trackpants down, desperate to feel his skin against mine.

He groaned and pushed me onto my stomach, quickly rolling on top of me, pressing his weight on my back.

"You sleeping naked is a dangerous thing," he murmured, kissing the back of my neck.

I spread my legs wide and tried to raise my arse. "I'm going to sleep naked next to you every night."

He groaned, and after he manoeuvred his trackpants, suddenly his erection was against the crack of my arse. Hot, hard, and very bare.

Skin on skin.

So good.

I rolled my hips again, trying to get him to move, trying to position him where I needed him.

"Colson," I said, sounding pitifully desperate.

He sat up on his haunches, reached over, and took the lube and a condom.

Hell, yes.

And he applied both, then began by thumbing the lube into me.

It wasn't what I wanted.

"Just do it," I urged him. "I need you inside me." He made a strangled noise and he leaned forward, pressing against my hole. So close . . .

"Braithe." His voice was a plead. A prayer.

"Please," I whispered, trying to back onto him. "Colson." And he pushed in, slow, breaching and far too big. I almost regretted begging . . . until he sank in all the way, groaning as he reached his hilt.

It was a lot, and almost too much, but also so very good. The bite of pain soon gave way to pleasure as he began to move.

His weight on me, his cock inside me, his fingers digging into my sides, scraping and trying to find purchase, trying to hold me.

He was made for this.

For taking me like this. For giving me what I needed, exactly how my body craved it. For taking me to heights I'd never been.

So slow. So deep. Every thrust sounded like it tortured him. Different to how he'd fucked me before.

Because this wasn't just fucking.

This was feelings and longing, desperate and daunting.

He pulled out and flipped me over, and without a word, he folded my legs up to my chest and buried himself inside me again. His gaze glued to mine.

There was no hiding.

Everything lay bare between us.

Everything we felt but couldn't say was exchanged.

Feelings. Fears.

What I saw in his eyes should have frightened me, but it only made it better.

Stronger.

Bolstered.

And when he drove up into me one final time, his restraint finally crumbling, he cried out as he came. I held him, his face in my neck and his body trembling.

And I knew one thing for certain.

I wasn't leaving.

Chapter Twenty-Two
COLSON

Sweet mother of god.

Merry Christmas, indeed.

Sex with Braithe was always amazing, but this . . . this was something else.

Like we'd poured ourselves into the act of it. Like we gave in and let ourselves freefall.

I was never coming out of it.

What I felt for him, what he brought out in me.

I was forever changed, and I was in love.

I was in love with Braithe Branson.

Head over heels, like nothing I'd ever experienced.

I guess going into an almost-frozen river would bring some truths to the surface. And finally facing the fact that he was supposed to be leaving?

I didn't know exactly what the future held, but I knew we'd work it out.

We had to.

Whatever it takes.

It also took a good few minutes for my brain to come back online and for me to realise he hadn't come yet. So I shuffled down his body, took his dick into my mouth, and used my fingers inside him to beckon another prostate orgasm out of him.

It was a good while before he stopped shuddering, his hands stopped shaking, and the glazed-over smile faded.

"Merry Christmas," I said.

"Mmm." He groaned as he arched his back, still not rid of the aftershocks. "Yes, Christmas."

I laughed. "Want a cup of tea?"

He lifted his arm off the bed and let it fall back to the mattress. "Yes, tea." Then he sat up. "Wait. How are you feeling this morning? After last night?"

I grinned. "Oh, believe me, I feel great."

He smirked, then blinked awake, searching for his phone. "I have to make Christmas lunch."

"I thought you were making dinner?"

His gaze shot to mine, brow furrowed. "But you're working at dinnertime. I was making lunch, Colson. I have the whole thing—"

"Oh, sorry, dinner is..." I wasn't sure I'd ever get used to the different terminology. "We say dinner for the biggest meal of the day."

He squinted at me, then scrubbed his face. "It's too early for this. What time is it?"

"It's not even eight," I said, taking his hand and kissing his knuckles. "How about we do coffee and tea first, and we cook *dinner* together?"

He smiled. "Sounds good."

Sounded perfect to me. "Presents, before breakfast or after?"

A slow smile tugged at his lips. "Tea first."

I laughed. "Deal."

I went out to the kitchen. My phone was on the counter, a

message from Ronny telling me my cruiser was at the station. But seeing my boots drying by the fire, I was reminded of last night. How Braithe had undressed me, cared for me.

Bouchard too.

And then how everyone else had turned up concerned.

I had to admit, it felt kinda nice.

Seeing the Christmas lights still on, the snow outside the window, felt better than nice.

Braithe came out wearing my robe, pressed himself against my back, and slid his arms around my waist. "Whatcha looking at?" he asked.

"Everything," I replied. "The lights, the snow, knowing you're here, and not being alone on Christmas Day for the first time in ten years. How lucky I am."

He held me a little tighter, his face against my back. "You don't have to be alone anymore," he murmured.

I turned in his arms so I could hold him. Did he know what those words meant to me? How hearing someone say that to me made me feel wanted and appreciated?

Loved?

I tried to speak but could only produce tears instead. He pulled back, alarmed. "What's wrong?"

"Nothing," I said quickly. "Just not being alone anymore . . ." I shook my head. "I wouldn't have any of this if it weren't for you. I keep saying that, and I know you don't believe me, but it's true."

He put his hand to my face and wiped a tear with his thumb. "Yes, you would. You'd have realised that you're worth it. I just plucked at something inside you that helped you see it a little sooner."

"Plucked, huh? Those strings you talked about?"

He laughed. "Oh heavens, I regret ever using that term. No strings attached was never going to happen."

I laughed. "There are strings, huh?"

"Many." He smiled up at me. "How's the tea coming along?"

Tea. Right. Yes.

"I didn't get that far," I said, letting him go and finally making it into the kitchen.

"Want some toast?" he asked, reaching for the bread.

"Sure."

Tea, coffee, and toast probably wasn't the most amazing Christmas breakfast ever, but I still couldn't stop smiling.

And as he sipped his tea and bit into his toast with strawberry jam, I could guess he was happy too. In my fluffy robe and his slippers, his legs all tucked up on the couch, and his hair a mess.

I'd never seen anyone look more beautiful.

"You probably shouldn't look at me like that, Deputy," he said. "Or the only lunch we'll be eating will be each other in bed."

Ignoring his remark about how I was looking at him, I laughed. "I wouldn't mind."

He chuckled and took his plate and cup to the sink. "We should do gifts now then I can get the roast and potatoes in the oven. Then we can shower together. How does that sound?"

"Like Merry Christmas to me."

He laughed as he disappeared down the hall, coming back out with an expertly wrapped box, complete with a gold ribbon bow.

"Wait, I'll get yours." I took his gift from where I'd hidden it in the spare room. Compared to his, mine looked more like it'd been wrapped by a toddler.

We sat on the couch and swapped boxes. "You go first," he said. The box he gave me was smaller and lighter, and I was ridiculously excited, torn between wanting to treat it with the respect it deserved and tearing into it like a child.

I pulled at the bow, unravelling it, then slowly slid my finger under the tape. Inside was an ornate box, and inside that were several things. The first was a Christmas ornament. A small Santa wearing a coat of rainbow pride colours, bright and glittery, and utterly perfect.

"It seemed fitting," Braithe said softly. He was watching me, and I couldn't help but get a little teary.

"It's so perfect," I said, laughing at myself for being emotional. "My first Christmas being out."

He reached over and squeezed my hand, then he nodded to what was left in the box. "The next thing is half for me, but it felt weird to wrap something for myself to give to myself."

"For you . . . ?" I mumbled, taking the last gift out.

It was two pairs of socks. One pair of the American flag; one pair of the Union Jack.

When I looked at him to explain what he meant about it being for him as well, he laughed and took them. "I thought we could split them and take one of each. So we both wear one American, one British. Like a mismatched pair, tailored just for us."

"Just like Alex and Prince Henry!"

"Who?"

"Never mind." I laughed. "Oh my god, I love that so much." I shook my head again, not even trying to hide the fact I was so emotional. "It's all so perfect. Thank you."

"Okay, my turn," he said, ripping into the paper. The terrible job I'd done at wrapping it deserved nothing less. "It's kind of heavy," he mumbled as he opened the box. When he saw what it was, he stopped and stared at it. "Oh, Colson," he whispered.

"Do you like it? I wasn't sure . . ."

He pulled the teapot out and laugh-cried. "A Union Jack teapot!" Then he saw what else was there and took it out too. "A red telephone box tea tin. Oh, Colson, it's so lovely."

"And there's English breakfast tea, loose leaf," I said. "I hope you like it because I made the mistake of googling English teabags and somehow ended up on a porn site. So anyway, teabagging is a thing I learned against my will."

He laughed so hard I thought he might drop the teapot. Then he leaned over and kissed my cheek. "Oh, Colson. You are amazing. And I love it all. Thank you so much."

I ignored the way my cheeks burned. "I wanted to get you something you could take with you on your travels," I finished quietly.

His eyes met mine, and he nodded slowly. "I don't think I'll be travelling too far," he whispered. "Or at all, to be honest."

"No?"

His eyes met mine and he shook his head. "If it's okay with you."

I was hit with relief and a rush of emotions, making me both laugh and cry and nod at the same time. "That's so very okay with me. I'd like that very much."

He made a sad face. "Please don't cry. Save the tears. You haven't tasted my cooking yet."

I laughed and blinked the tears away.

"Okay." He held up his teapot. "I think another cup of tea is in order. Would you like to try one?"

I tried not to grimace, but one look at the hope in his big blue eyes and I'd try anything. "Sure."

He laughed as he carried it to the kitchen, and I took my little rainbow ornament and hung it on Conifer Aniston. It weighed down her little branch a bit, but she held strong.

"Perfect," I said.

Everything was perfect.

He was perfect. Dinner was perfect. The apple pie was perfect. The socks were perfect. I came out in my uniform, wearing one US flag sock, one Union Jack sock, and showed him.

"Eee!" He said, his hands to his face. "I love it!"

I gave him the matching pair. "You have to wear them too."

"I will. I'm going around to see the guys. I can't wait to show them."

My boots were almost dry but not quite, so I pulled on my old pair and stood up, my hands looking for what wasn't there. "Feels weird not to have my belt."

"I'm sorry for giving it to Ronny," he said, the corner of his mouth pulling down. "But there was a gun and you weren't in any shape to take it, and I certainly don't—"

I kissed him. "You did the right thing."

He looked up at me, his smile faltering. "Can I ask you something?"

"Sure."

"What am I telling Hamish?" He swallowed hard. "Because he's going to ask about the not-leaving conversation. I don't want to leave, I really don't. And I haven't officially accepted the job in Spokane, so I don't have to go. But I need to work as part of my visa. And for money, of course. And we established that we don't want me to leave, but I don't have a plan or a job. Maybe I can ask at the Home Mart if they need someone to stack shelves—"

I took his face in my hands and pressed my lips to his. "We can work that out. Just you agreeing to stay is enough for now. It's made me the happiest man in Hartbridge. So please don't stress or worry about anything today. It's Christmas. Enjoy your afternoon with the guys. And you're FaceTiming with your family?"

He nodded. "When everyone will be there."

"Then just enjoy it. We can worry about tomorrow *tomorrow*, okay?"

He nodded again but he didn't look convinced.

"Braithe," I said gently. "Do you want to stay?"

He nodded quickly. "Very much."

"Then we'll work it out." I scanned his eyes. "You once told me it'll be different this time because I'm different this time. I'm older and stronger, and I know I'm worth it."

He nodded, his eyes wide and so perfectly blue.

"I wasn't sure," I admitted. "It felt like I was at the foot of Everest. That it was an impossible climb, but you showed me it's just one step at a time. Just one step, baby."

"It is." He smiled and ducked his head, his cheeks pink. "You just called me baby."

I pulled him in for a hug, and oh boy, I almost told him I loved him. It was right on the tip of my tongue. As scary as it was, as too soon as it was.

But then he slid his hand down over my arse, down to the back of my thigh, like he was feeling for something.

"What are you doing?"

He gripped my arse, looked up, and grinned at me. "Just checking to see if these trousers fit you as well as they look like they do. And I'm very pleased to announce they do. It's the sexiest outfit ever."

I faked a snarl at him because he called my uniform an outfit to get this very reaction.

He laughed and it was all I ever wanted—to see him happy.

"Are you ready to go to work?" he asked.

I nodded. "Yeah. But first, I want to say thank you."

"For what? I'm driving you to work. It's like three blocks. If I can't drive my boyfriend to work . . ."

I stared. "Boyfriend?"

He grinned. "You called me baby. It's basically the same thing. And if I'm staying in Hartbridge," he said with a shrug. "Staying with you . . ."

I was so freaking happy I could have burst. "You want to stay here with me?"

"Well, yeah, I thought it was what you—"

I threw my arms around him and squeezed him so hard he squeaked. "Yes, yes, yes," I said. "I wasn't sure if you might want to get your own place once you decided to stay. But to have this every day? Oh my god, Braithe. You have no idea what that means to me. To have you here. To not be alone."

He pulled back, his eyes on mine. "You're not alone anymore."

I had to breathe in deeply and blink back tears.

Braithe smiled up at me. "No crying on Christmas Day," he said. "Unless Ronny yells at me for making you late. Because I would absolutely cry. So can we please go?" Then he looked at the socks I'd given him. "Oh, you're waiting on me. Oh bollocks, Ronny's going to yell at me."

Bollocks.

"Bollocks?" I laughed. "That's the best word ever."

He rushed to the sofa, pulled off his sensible white socks and pulled on our dual national socks instead. Then he grabbed his coat and beanie, his car keys. "Please stop standing there smiling at me, if you're late—"

"I'm not going to be late." I took the container of pie from the counter. "And Ronny would never yell at you. He'd yell at me, not you."

"Not after last night." He pulled on his boots, put his coat on, and shoved his beanie onto his head. "You're the town hero, remember?"

I rolled my eyes. "Hardly." I fixed a wayward strand of his hair. "Take me to work, boyfriend."

He drove me to work and I didn't think anything of the cars in the parking lot. I probably should have noticed there were too many, but I was too happy, too focused on Braithe. I leaned over the console and kissed him. Not that anyone was standing there watching, but I didn't care if anyone inside happened to see. In fact, I kind of hoped they did.

"I'll text you later," he said. "I'll wait up for you." I wanted to tell him he didn't have to, to just go to bed, but damn, if the idea of him waiting up for me didn't make my heart feel two sizes too big for my chest.

"Okay," I whispered.

He pointed to the two cruisers parked by the entrance and then to the office building. "Is Ronny here? I hope he can see that I have you here in good time and that your choosing to sit here and smile at me is on you, not me."

I laughed. "Okay, I'm going." I got out, carrying my container of half the pie, and walked inside like I'd done countless times. Instead of the usual voices, the clicking of keyboards, and scanner radios that greeted me, today a dozen or so people were standing there, apparently waiting for me. Ronny, front and centre, with a huge smile under his moustache, and the Brown family was there with Bailey, the boy I'd pulled from the river.

On Christmas Day?

They were all staring at me, smiling, waiting for someone to say something.

"Here he is," Ronny said, his voice booming. "Hartbridge's newest hero." And then they all began to clap.

Chapter Twenty-Three
BRAITHE

I spent an hour or so at Gunter and Clay's house, along with Clay's dad, Cliff, and his girlfriend Cordelia, and of course, Hamish and Ren.

Jayden and Cass weren't there, being busy at the B&B, and with Cass's kids, of course, but there were plans to catch up with them when they'd had a minute to stop and breathe.

Now that my days in Hartbridge weren't numbered.

Which, of course, made Hamish very happy. "I knew it," he said. "I knew you weren't leaving. It was what I said last night, wasn't it? Can you please tell Ren that I helped? Because he told me I should mind my own business the whole way home."

I laughed. "Sorry, Ren. It helped, yes."

Hamish made an I-told-you-so face at Ren and Ren poked him in the ribs.

"So much for no strings, Braithe," Hamish said with a sly smirk. "Heart strings, huh?"

My cheeks warmed but I nodded. "Yes. Something like that."

"I'm glad you're staying," Ren said to me. "And I'm glad Colson's okay."

"Oh, he's all anyone was talking about last night," Cliff added. "How he went into the water and got that kid."

I couldn't help the rush of pride I felt. "Yes, well," I said. "He is very brave and amazing, but if he could please keep the hero stuff to only when I'm *not* there to see it, that'd be great." I put my hand to my heart. "I'm not built for that kind of excitement."

Hamish patted my knee. "You poor thing. He's okay now though, right?"

"Oh yes, he's fine."

He nudged me. "So, was there any exchanging of gifts?"

I stuck my feet out. "Did you not notice my socks? He's wearing the matching pair."

He took one look at the two different flag patterns on my feet and gasped at Ren. "Oh my god, why haven't we done that?"

"And he got me a teapot with the Union Jack on it as well," I said.

Gunter smiled warmly. "That's really sweet."

"He is."

Hamish was already googling socks with the Australian flag when his phone beeped with a message. He opened it and gasped so loud it scared me.

He put his hand to his mouth and began to bounce in his seat. He turned the phone around to show Ren. "It's from Jayden," he said, still covering his mouth. His eyes were now glassy.

Then he showed me and Gunter. It was a photo of two left hands. Jayden and Cass's hands, I could guess, and there on Jayden's ring finger was a silver diamond band.

Hamish took his phone back and dialled, squealing into

the phone as soon as they answered, and all we could hear was Jayden's laughter.

"Christmas Cupid," Gunter said to me, smiling. "Without fail."

I leaned in and whispered, "I thought it was a Cupid-Santa tag team?"

He laughed. "You've been spending too much time with Hamish."

"This is probably true."

His smile was easy, and Gunter had a peacefulness about him that I really liked. "So have you thought about work options?"

I shook my head. "Not yet. It's really not like me to not have a plan and I don't like the unknown, but what I *do* know," I said with a shrug, "is that staying feels right."

Gunter grinned and I noticed then that Clay was listening. "If it's meant to be, it'll work out," Clay said. "It might feel like a huge leap of faith, but it's really just a step in the right direction."

I liked that.

I really liked these guys. All different, each with their own quirks and traits, and not one thing I'd change.

I hugged them all and bid them farewell, wanting to get home.

Home.

Colson's home, where I now lived.

And my other home, on a video chat with my family back in England.

The screen filled with familiar faces and voices, all saying hello and Merry Christmas. My nan's sweet smile, the way my nephews laughed, and I could almost smell Mum's kitchen.

I missed them, sure.

But the whole time I chatted with them, I knew my heart was happy right where I was.

I told them I was staying in Hartbridge a little longer. I figured the more serious conversation could happen when Colson was with me and I could introduce them.

He was my boyfriend, after all.

And when I said goodbye to my family and ended the video chat, there was no sadness. No wishing to be anywhere else.

Sure, I wished I had secure employment, and there was the whole issue of the visa to sort out. Colson and I would need to have that whole discussion at some point. Yes, I was staying in Hartbridge. That was decided, and I felt good about that.

But my visa was not a permanent one. And in eighteen months, we'd need to make harder decisions. It wasn't lost on me that I was already thinking long term with him. That I'd only known him for a matter of weeks, yet there I was thinking about forever . . .

But that felt right too.

As night fell, the only lights in the room were the flickering fire and the soft glow of the Christmas lights. I sat curled up on the sofa with my book as a gentle dusting of snow fell outside.

It couldn't have been more perfect.

Until it was.

Just after eight, Colson's cruiser pulled into the drive and he came through the door brushing snow off his coat. He was hours early and I stood up, wondering if something was wrong.

"You're home early," I said. "Is everything okay?"

He grinned and came around the couch. He hadn't even taken his boots off, but he tossed his hat on the couch and threw his arms around me. "Better than okay," he said, beginning to sway us. "Everyone was at work when I got there; they all clapped as I walked in. A hero's welcome, they called it. Little Bailey was there with his family. He's fine, he wanted to say thank you. His mom cried when she hugged me. We swapped Secret Santa gifts, and normally I don't go in it, but I did this year, and I got a neat little wooden puzzle box. It's kinda awesome."

Our swaying had become rocking, dancing almost, and he still held me tight, his lips at my neck.

"Anyway," he went on. "It was quiet and not much was happening, and Charity could tell my mind was elsewhere, so she told me to go home and see you. She'll radio me if I'm needed and I'll go back, but she said she was sick of me smiling and watching the clock. She told me to come see you before I drove her crazy."

I laughed and pulled back a little so I could see his face. "To see me?"

He nodded and took my face in his hands. His eyes searched mine, and he was nervous and determined, a little scared and very happy. "I love you, Braithe."

Oh my . . .

My heart pinballed against my ribs.

He swallowed and licked his lips. "I know it's probably too early to be saying that, but it's true. You came into my life, speeding, actually. Eight miles over the speed limit, and like a ray of sunshine, you changed everything for the better. Every single thing about my life is now better because of you."

"Oh, Colson," I whispered.

He shook his head, not done speaking. "I kept telling myself it wasn't you. It wasn't you, exactly. It was what you stood for, what you represented. The dream boyfriend. Someone to live with and laugh with. Someone to share my bed with, to hold, to care for. After all these years of loneliness.

The dream that I couldn't possibly have in real life." He smiled then. "But now I do have it. All of it. And he came into my life in the form of blond hair and an English accent and a wicked laugh. And I don't know how or why he smells like honey, but he does. And he finishes work covered in paint and glue, his laugh gives me butterflies, and he makes me so incredibly happy. And I fell in love with him, and he chose me. And I'm not sorry for falling in love so fast because how could I not love you?"

I put my hand to his face, tears in my eyes. "I'm not sorry either, because I did choose you, and I chose you, Colson, because I fell in love with you too."

He cried, instant tears of disbelief and hope. "You did?"

I nodded, teary and laughing. "How could I not love you?" He hugged me again, lifting me off my feet and twirling me around like a Disney princess, before he put me down, took my whole head in his hands, and kissed me in a way that made my whole body react.

There was nothing Disney about this kiss.

And just when I was getting ready for whatever he wanted to do to me, he broke the kiss with a groan. "God, I wish I could stay," he said, swiping my bottom lip with his thumb. His eyes were dark, his lips wet and swollen.

"I'll be here when you get home," I said, trying to catch my breath. "Every night."

He closed his eyes and inhaled deeply, as if he were breathing in my words. "I love you," he whispered.

I leaned up and captured his lips with mine. "I love you too."

He took my hand and placed it over his heart. I could feel it thumping under my palm. "Every time I'm with you," he murmured. "Every time I see you."

I smiled at the thrill his words gave me. "You're such a romantic."

He ducked his head. "You might need to get used to that."

I laughed. "I'll get very used to it." Then I remembered something. "Oh, Jayden and Cass got engaged today. He sent Hamish a photo of his hand with a ring on his finger. I'm surprised no one called in the blood-curdling squeal that Hamish let out."

Colson laughed. "That's awesome. I'm happy for them."

"They're all convinced it's some Cupid and Santa tag-teaming thing for the gays at Christmastime in Hartbridge. I thought it was a joke before," I said, sliding my hand down to his arse. "But now I'm not so sure."

He was grinning. "Are you a believer?"

I looked at the Christmas lights, the warm fire, the snow falling outside, and the incredibly gorgeous man in my arms. The sweet man who loved me. "I think I am."

I WENT to work early on Thursday morning to finish cleaning up after the concert day and to make sure the classroom was in perfect order. It was my second to last day, and I planned to take a cake in tomorrow as a farewell and thank you, so I wasn't sure how much free time I'd have.

I plastered on a smile that I didn't particularly feel as I walked down the hall. "Morning!" I said to Raeleen.

"Good morning," she replied. "You're in early."

"Much to do," I said, pushing the doors open to my classroom. The familiar smell of paint made me smile.

I was going to miss this so much.

With a heavy sigh, I began putting things in their place and was carrying the tub of craft supplies back into the storage room when there was a knock at the door. It was Sandra. She poked her head in. "Nancy wants to see you."

"Oh."

I put the tub down and went to the principal's office, feeling very much like a student about to get lambasted, which was silly considering I was a teacher.

But I was nervous, and when I saw Emily sitting across from Nancy, I knew the shoe was about to drop. The beginning of the official goodbye.

Until Emily turned and I saw her face.

She was crying.

"Oh my heavens," I said, rushing in. I sat in the spare seat beside her and took her arm. There was no pram, and I'd never not seen her without her baby. "Are you okay? Is everything okay? Did something happen?"

Emily laugh-cried, dabbing a tissue to her eyes. "You are just so sweet. No, nothing's wrong. Well, kind of. I don't know . . ."

I looked to Nancy for an explanation. Her face softened. "Emily is unsure about returning to work so soon."

Emily began to cry again. "I don't want to leave my baby. I thought I could, but then after Christmas . . ." She shook her head. "My husband and I talked it over and we thought maybe I could take some more time."

My gaze shot to Nancy's. I mean, I didn't want to get too excited, but my hopes weren't just up; they were in the stratosphere. Even though I felt like I was swooping in and taking the win while poor Emily's life was falling apart.

"I . . . I'm happy to stay," I said, trying to quell the urge to jump up and down. "In fact, I'm already staying. In Hartbridge, that is. I declined the offer for the position in Spokane yesterday. I'm staying with Colson for the foreseeable future, so I have a place already. And I'm happy to stay on for as long as you need." I patted Emily's arm. "Kindergarten will always be yours. I'm happy to sub until you're ready to come back."

She cried again but she spoke to Nancy. "He's just so sweet!"

Nancy nodded and her eyes met mine, smiling. "Emily actually proposed a job-share situation.

I looked between them both, not sure what they meant.

Not daring to hope it meant what I thought it meant . . .

Though it was too late. Because hope began to rise in my throat.

Nancy took pity on me. "Where you would teach three days a week, and Emily would do two. This would allow her to keep her medical insurance and hopefully would suit your visa requirements. I hoped it would be a perfect solution for both of you—"

"Are you kidding?" I asked. I was so excited, so happy, I could barely stay seated. "That's brilliant. It would be perfect." I looked at Emily. "Are you sure you're okay with that?"

She nodded, dabbing her eyes. "Ignore my tears. I'm just . . . Hormones."

I barked out a teary laugh and plucked one of the tissues from the box, needing to dab my eyes too. "Ignore mine. I'm just . . ." I was going to say gay but decided it wasn't the place. "Happy."

Emily laughed and even Nancy smiled. "I'll put a proposal together for the board and the department."

She went through some details and formalities, and everything going well, our new arrangement could be implemented as early as next week, starting the new year.

Everyone was so impressed with me at the school Christmas concert, and the kids clearly took a shine to me, Nancy said.

"And young Bailey Brown will have a story to tell in class

today, I hear," Nancy said. "Saved by a very brave deputy at the light festival."

"I wasn't there," Emily said. "We left early. But we heard all about it. So relieved that everyone was okay. And so grateful for Colson."

I flushed with pride. "Same."

Nancy smiled at me. "Did you want to call him to tell him the good news? Before the children arrive?"

I nodded quickly. "Can I?"

"Of course."

I gave Emily's arm a final squeeze. "Thank you. For suggesting the split rotation. I can never thank you enough. We're going to have the best kindergarten year ever."

She smiled wide, her tears gone. "I think so too."

I ducked out of Nancy's office and went back into my classroom, my phone to my ear. It was still early and Colson was probably still in bed. He'd worked until almost one this morning.

"Hello?" His voice was gruff. "What's up?"

"I'm sorry for waking you," I said. "But I have news."

It sounded as if he sat up. He definitely sounded more awake. "You do?"

"They're proposing a job share between Emily and me. I'd work three days and she'd work two. She's not ready to leave her baby yet and Colson, it's perfect. It really could not be more perfect. What if they give me Mondays and Tuesdays off? Those are your days off. We would have two whole days—"

"We won't be leaving this bed," he said. "I can tell you that much right now."

I laughed. "Could it really be this perfect?" I asked, still not believing it. "It's not approved by the school board yet, but Nancy said there shouldn't be a problem."

Colson laughed. "You know why she said that?" he said. "Because Ronny's the chairman."

I snorted and covered my mouth with my hand. "Of the school board?"

"Yep."

I shook my head, my eyes burning. My mind was spinning, my heart racing. "Can you believe this is happening?"

He laughed again. "Yeah. I think there might be something to those jokes about Santa and Cupid making dreams come true."

"I think the term was tag-teaming, but making dreams come true also works."

He chuckled. "I wished for you," he said, his voice warm. "I wished for a boyfriend when I was younger. A man I could love, and who would love me. I had to wait a while, but Santa delivered him this year."

I smiled with a happiness I felt right down to my core. "Next year we should leave him extra cookies and milk as thanks."

He hummed contentedly. "Deal."

Epilogue

BRAITHE

Colson wasn't kidding when he said the view from the top of the mountain in spring was even prettier than it was in winter.

Hartbridge was gorgeous in the springtime. Green grass and flowers and a sea of green trees for as far as the eye could see.

We'd driven up that firebreak road to the lookout not many people knew about, the one he'd shown me months ago on our way home from Mossley.

"You ready?" he said, his grin wide.

It was lunchtime on a Monday. We did, in fact, end up with the same two days off. Well, I technically had four days off and worked three days at the school. But I also helped Gunter one day a week with the charity start-up he was getting off the ground, and I also helped Jayden and Cass at the B&B on the weekends if they had a full house.

But my two days off with Colson were magical. We slept in, we made love, we did domestic stuff.

We kept the teabag / condom tally going until it was a

non-contest. The teabags never stood a chance. And then we stopped using condoms, so it was moot anyway.

I was busy, and I'd never been happier.

But today was a special day.

"I am so ready," I replied.

We jumped out of the cruiser and carried the two heavy pots to the tree line. Well, Colson carried the pots, I carried the shovel.

Today was the day we were replanting Conifer Aniston and Spruce Willis.

They were outgrowing their pots and now that the ground wasn't frozen solid, we decided it was time.

Colson dug two holes a few metres apart and I freed the little trees from their pots. We stuck them in the ground and filled the dirt back in.

And then we stood back and admired them in their new homes. I slid my arm around Colson's waist. "We should do this every year," I said. "In fifty years, we'll have planted a forest."

He kissed the side of my head. "Fifty years, huh?"

I sighed. "Yep."

"Sounds about right."

"Oh, before I forget," I said, turning around. "Selfie time. Mum wants a pic with us and the trees."

"You told her we were replanting them?"

"Of course I did." Me telling my parents everything was such a strange concept for Colson. I made him pose for some selfies, then took a few scenery shots. "I'll send these to Mum and Dad too. You know they'll want you to bring them up here when they visit."

He gave me that nervous smile he did every time my parents talked about meeting him.

I laughed. "They already love you, so don't worry." They really did. Mum thought he was the sweetest and Dad liked that he was in law enforcement. Poor Colson had been so nervous the first time we'd FaceTimed them, which I understood. He'd needed my family's approval to validate his own family's failures, and while I could appreciate his concern, it was unfounded. My parents adored him.

Colson slung his arm around my shoulder and together we looked out across the view to the valley below. "I'll never get tired of this," he murmured.

"The view?" I asked. "I can't wait to see it in autumn."

"Not just the view. But getting to stand here with you."

I smiled and leaned into him a little, taking in the patchwork of greenery as far as the eye could see. "I hope you don't get sick of it, because we just agreed to planting our little Christmas trees for the next fifty years."

He smiled and let out a happy sigh. "Fifty years and I still won't take a minute for granted."

He was such a romantic. "Next year, I think I'll call my tree James Frond."

He laughed. "Is that right?"

We walked back to the cruiser. "Yep. What will you call yours?" He had a think while he started the engine. "Uh, Chris Pine."

I snorted. "But that's not punny."

"No, it's pilarious."

I groaned, trying not to laugh but failed. "Promise me one thing, Colson."

"What's that?"

"Never change."

He reached over and took my hand. "I'll remind you that you said that in fifty years."

I grinned at him. "Deal."

The Merry End

Hartbridge Christmas Series

WANT TO READ MORE IN THE HARTBRIDGE SERIES?

HARTBRIDGE CHRISTMAS SERIES

About the Author

N.R. Walker is an Australian author, who loves her genre of gay romance. She loves writing and spends far too much time doing it, but wouldn't have it any other way.

She is many things: a mother, a wife, a sister, a writer. She has pretty, pretty boys who live in her head, who don't let her sleep at night unless she gives them life with words.

She likes it when they do dirty, dirty things... but likes it even more when they fall in love.

She used to think having people in her head talking to her was weird, until one day she happened across other writers who told her it was normal.

She's been writing ever since...

nrwalker.net

Cronin's Key IV - Kennard's Story

Exchange of Hearts

The Spencer Cohen Series, Book One

The Spencer Cohen Series, Book Two

The Spencer Cohen Series, Book Three

The Spencer Cohen Series, Yanni's Story

Blood & Milk

The Weight Of It All

A Very Henry Christmas (The Weight of It All 1.5)

Perfect Catch

Switched

Imago

Imagines

Imagoes

Red Dirt Heart Imago

On Davis Row

Finders Keepers

Evolved

Galaxies and Oceans

Private Charter

Nova Praetorian

A Soldier's Wish

Upside Down

The Hate You Drink

Sir

Tallowwood

Reindeer Games

The Dichotomy of Angels

Throwing Hearts

Pieces of You - Missing Pieces #1

Pieces of Me - Missing Pieces #2

Pieces of Us - Missing Pieces #3

Lacuna

Tic-Tac-Mistletoe

Bossy

Code Red

Dearest Milton James

Dearest Malachi Keogh

Christmas Wish List

Code Blue

Davo

The Kite

Learning Curve

Merry Christmas Cupid

To the Moon and Back

Second Chance at First Love

Outrun the Rain

Into the Tempest

Touch the Lightning

EWB - Enemies With Benefits

Finders Keepers

Galaxies and Oceans

Nova Praetorian

Upside Down

Sir

Tallowwood

Imago

Throwing Hearts

Sixty Five Hours

Taxes and TARDIS

The Dichotomy of Angels

The Hate You Drink

Pieces of You

Pieces of Me

Pieces of Us

Tic-Tac-Mistletoe

Lacuna

Bossy

Code Red

Learning to Feel

Dearest Milton James

Dearest Malachi Keogh

Three's Company

Christmas Wish List

Code Blue

Davo

The Kite

Learning Curve

Merry Christmas Cupid

To the Moon and Back

Second Chance at First Love

Outrun the Rain

Into the Tempest

Touch the Lightning

SERIES COLLECTIONS:

Red Dirt Heart Series

Turning Point Series

Thomas Elkin Series

Spencer Cohen Series

Imago Series

Blind Faith Series

Missing Pieces Series

The Storm Boys Series

FREE READS:

Sixty Five Hours

Learning to Feel

His Grandfather's Watch (And The Story of Billy and Hale)

The Twelfth of Never (Blind Faith 3.5)

Twelve Days of Christmas (Sixty Five Hours Christmas)

TRANSLATED TITLES:

ITALIAN

Fiducia Cieca (Blind Faith)

Attraverso Questi Occhi (Through These Eyes)

Preso alla Sprovvista (Blindside)

Il giorno del Mai (Blind Faith 3.5)

Cuore di Terra Rossa Serie (Red Dirt Heart Series)

Natale di terra rossa (Red dirt Christmas)

Intervento di Retrofit (Elements of Retrofit)

A Chiare Linee (Clarity of Lines)

Senso D'appartenenza (Sense of Place)

Spencer Cohen Serie (including Yanni's Story)

Punto di non Ritorno (Point of No Return)

Punto di Rottura (Breaking Point)

Punto di Partenza (Starting Point)

Imago (Imago)

Imagines

Il desiderio di un soldato (A Soldier's Wish)

Scambiato (Switched)

Tallowwood

The Hate You Drink

Ho trovato te (Finders Keepers)

Cuori d'argilla (Throwing Hearts)

Galassie e Oceani (Galaxies and Oceans)

Il peso di tut (The Weight of it All)

Pieces of You - Missing Pieces 1

FRENCH

Confiance Aveugle (Blind Faith)

A travers ces yeux: Confiance Aveugle 2 (Through These Eyes)

Aveugle: Confiance Aveugle 3 (Blindside)

À Jamais (Blind Faith 3.5)

Cronin's Key Series

Au Coeur de Sutton Station (Red Dirt Heart)

Partir ou rester (Red Dirt Heart 2)

Faire Face (Red Dirt Heart 3)

Trouver sa Place (Red Dirt Heart 4)

Le Poids de Sentiments (The Weight of It All)

Un Noël à la sauce Henry (A Very Henry Christmas)

Une vie à Refaire (Switched)

Evolution (Evolved)

Galaxies & Océans

Qui Trouve, Garde (Finders Keepers)

Sens Dessus Dessous (Upside Down)

La Haine au Fond du Verre (The hate You Drink)

Tallowwood

Spencer Cohen Series

GERMAN

Flammende Erde (Red Dirt Heart)

Lodernde Erde (Red Dirt Heart 2)

Sengende Erde (Red Dirt Heart 3)

Ungezähmte Erde (Red Dirt Heart 4)

Vier Pfoten und ein bisschen Zufall (Finders Keepers)

Ein Kleines bisschen Versuchung (The Weight of It All)

Ein Kleines Bisschen Fur Immer (A Very Henry Christmas)

Weil Leibe uns immer Bliebt (Switched)

Drei Herzen eine Leibe (Three's Company)

Über uns die Sterne, zwischen uns die Liebe (Galaxies and Oceans)

Unnahbares Herz (Blind Faith 1)

Sehendes Herz (Blind Faith 2)

Hoffnungsvolles Herz (Blind Faith 3)

Verträumtes Herz (Blind Faith 3.5)

Thomas Elkin: Verlangen in neuem Design

Thomas Elkin: Leidenschaft in klaren

Thomas Elkin: Vertrauen in bester Lage

Traummann töpfern leicht gemacht (Throwing Hearts)

Sir

THAI

Sixty Five Hours (Thai translation)

Finders Keepers (Thai translation)

SPANISH

Sesenta y Cinco Horas (Sixty Five Hours)

Los Doce Días de Navidad

Código Rojo (Code Red)

Código Azul (Code Blue)

Queridísimo Milton James

Queridísimo Malachi Keogh

El Peso de Todo (The Weight of it All)

Tres Muérdagos en Raya: Serie Navidad en Hartbridge

Lista De Deseos Navideños: Serie Navidad en Hartbridge

Feliz Navidad Cupido: Serie Navidad en Hartbridge

Spencer Cohen Libro Uno

Spencer Cohen Libro Dos

Spencer Cohen Libro Tres

Davo

Hasta la Luna y de Vuelta

Venciendo A La Lluvia

En la Tempestad

El Toque del Rayo

Corazón De Tierra Roja

Corazón De Tierra Roja 2

ECB (Enemigos con Beneficios)

CHINESE

Blind Faith

JAPANESE

Bossy

PORTUGUESE

Sessenta e Cinco Horas

Want another Christmas story?

REINDEER GAMES

Chapter One

REINDEER GAMES

Russ Quarrington sat in his office, gazing out over the view of the small city of Vintage Ridge, staring into that space between past and present, not really seeing anything at all. His mind had wandered. Again. His heart was heavy. He told himself it was the time of year—winter, Christmas—that affected him this way. Melancholy settled over him much like the blanket of cold that settled over the city outside his window.

He was thirty-four and had every physical thing in his life that he could ever need. He'd built a business and real-estate empire with a portfolio people only dreamed of. He had a fleet of great staff, had a mansion, cars, expensive suits, watches, a wine cellar, and a budding art collection.

Material things, he conceded. No emotional attachments, no personal relationships.

He was alone, and once upon a time, he'd thrived on that. He'd used it as the driving force to propel himself forward, to succeed. To be everything he was today. He'd refused any human interaction that might distract him from his goals. *Succeed at all costs* had been his mantra for sixteen years.

But now the loneliness was a pool of inky-black water lapping at his feet. Well, it began at his feet. Now he waded waist-deep in it.

It's just the time of year, he told himself. *Christmas is never easy.*

He had no family, no close friends, no boyfriend, no lover. No one.

It was his choice. Well, the absence of family wasn't his choice. When given the ultimatum of being a part of his family or being gay, he chose the truth. His only truth. If he had chosen his family, it would have killed him anyway, to not be true, to not be his true self. So he chose honesty and integrity. He chose life.

He didn't regret it.

After sixteen years, he didn't miss them anymore.

Except at Christmastime.

Like now.

December and winter always hit him hard, right in the solar plexus, under his sternum, and inside his ribs. It felt like a lump of hot concrete. Heavy, and hard to ignore.

It was always worse this time of year, and each year it got a little harder than the year before.

There was a quick knock on the door before it opened, and Caleb walked in with his eyes glued to his iPad. Russ didn't need to check the time. Caleb said he'd be here at 2:00 p.m., so Russ knew it would be precisely 2:00 p.m. Everything about Caleb was precise. His appearance: impeccable suit, short and neatly styled hair, defined eyebrows, and square jaw. He was angular, sharp, and incredibly efficient. He'd been Russ's PA for five years and knew every facet, every detail, every schedule, every appointment.

He was also the closest thing Russ had to a best friend. Which Caleb would probably find horrifying and incredibly sad because Russ was sure Caleb wouldn't even think of him as any kind of friend, let alone a good friend. Least of all a best friend.

Christ. I need to make some changes in my life . . .

Caleb sat in the seat opposite Russ's desk and had still barely looked up from his iPad screen. "Okay, so we have a few things to go over before Friday. City planning meeting for the rezoning of Providence Street is tomorrow at ten, meeting with the bank and insurance broker tomorrow at two. I've sent both appointments to your calendar. We should close on the metro apartment if the real-estate attorney does his goddamned job, deeds and covenants pending, and the final preparations of the masquerade ball are all but done. I've requested the final marketing proofs by five o'clock today. Oh, and we still need to find a designer for the loft. I sent you a shortlist, just some recommendations . . ."

Russ heard everything Caleb had said but didn't exactly need to reply. In fact, Russ was seriously beginning to wonder if he needed to be here at all. Caleb had everything under control.

"Okay, what's wrong?" Caleb asked, clipped and to the point.

"Nothing's wrong," Russ replied, his voice hoarse from disuse. God, how long had it been since he'd spoken to someone? This morning's barista had spoken, and Russ was sure he'd replied out loud . . . He'd meant to. Christ. "Sorry. I've been distracted. There was nothing wrong with any of what you said. In fact, you're so good at what you do, I was just wondering if I needed to be here at all."

"That doesn't sound like nothing's wrong."

Russ looked back out over the city, shrouded in winter. "Maybe I need to go sit on a beach somewhere. Or buy a new car. Or a motorcycle."

"A motorcycle?" Caleb's eyes went comically wide. "Uh, I can think of things that are less likely to kill you . . ."

"What about a boat?"

"Yes, because crashing and drowning is better than crashing and skidding along gravel."

"Or maybe I should take a cooking class," Russ added, then shook his head at how ridiculous he sounded. "God, I hate cooking. Maybe I should volunteer somewhere. In a soup kitchen or for the Pride festival."

Caleb's sigh was long and knowing. "Those are some great ideas, Russ. But just answer me this. How long have I been telling you to take a vacation?"

"Years."

"And have you?"

"Well, I've been busy . . ."

"Which is why you need a vacation."

"I need to stay here," Russ countered, though it was hardly with an ounce of conviction. "My businesses—"

"Your businesses are prime examples of effective and efficient management." Caleb had his serious face on. "Your teams are well-structured, well-balanced, and well-versed in procedure and protocol. You could leave for a month and there wouldn't even be a blip on the radar."

Russ stared at him. Because feeling unnecessary and unwanted was just what he needed to add to his loneliness. "Gee, thanks."

"That's not what I meant," Caleb added apologetically. "What I meant was, you're so good at what you do, your entire business model is perfect. You could have a month's vacation and the wheels will not fall off; every cog will turn, just as it should. You *should* have a month off."

A month? Russ almost broke out in hives at the thought.

"A month?" He shook his head. "Yeah, not ever gonna happen."

"Take a week. Hell, take a weekend."

"I know, I try to, but then something comes up."

"Something that one of your teams can fix, or it can wait until you get back." Caleb raised an eyebrow, then looked at his iPad. "I can book you something right now. It'll be a complete surprise."

"No, please don't. I can't . . . I need more time . . . and I need to know where I'm going. I can't just do some mystery vacay thing." He shuddered at the thought.

Caleb stared at him for a long, uneasy moment. He tapped a finger on the side of his iPad, the way he did when he was thinking. "Okay, a compromise. You need a change of scenery, agreed?" Caleb asked, not giving Russ the time to reply. "The masquerade ball next weekend, you're going."

"Well, yes, of course I am. It's the Quarrington Annual Christmas Charity Gala at *my* nightclub. I have to go."

"No, you're *going*, going. Not as the owner or organizer or benefactor. As in, attending with a masquerade mask on, having a few drinks, maybe talk with a guy or two. Find some festive cheer."

"Festive what?"

"Exactly," Caleb said seriously. "That is exactly my point." Then his face and his tone softened. "I know this time of year isn't easy for you, but perhaps you should make new memories. I think volunteering your time at some local shelters throughout the year and not just at Christmas is also a great idea, and I'll see what I can find out for you on that front. But for now, let's agree that this year you'll at least try and have some fun."

"Caleb, I don't know . . ."

"It's the perfect opportunity," he countered quickly. "Complete anonymity with the mask. You can have some fun without the added pressure of anyone knowing it's you."

Russ opened his mouth to object.

"Great. It's settled," Caleb said, standing up. He was already tapping and scrolling on the screen of his iPad. "I'll organize your mask and whatever else you need. Leave the details up to me."

He started for the door. "Caleb, wait," Russ called out. Caleb stopped and turned, and Russ had every intention of telling him there was absolutely no way he was going to dress up for his Christmas gala night. But when he tried to form the words, when he tried to refuse, something stopped him. *Did he want to do this? Could he do this?* The truth was, he had nothing to lose. So instead of saying no, he sighed. "I want classy and sophisticated. You make me look like a candy cane or a Santa's Helper and you're fired. I mean it."

Caleb laughed. "No jolly Santa or naughty elf outfits. Got it. Oh," he added, his hand on the door. "One suggestion . . ."

Russ resisted rolling his eyes. "Yes?"

"You're familiar with Ace's Wild? It's a specialty—"

Russ put his hand up. "I know what it is. Or rather, who they are."

Caleb grinned. "I have it on good authority that's where a lot of the guys are getting props for the gala night. Maybe you could stop in and see them." He had a wicked gleam in his eye, almost a wink. "Tell Ace I said hi." And without another word, he disappeared and the door closed quietly behind him.

Great. Just fucking great. Russ spun to gaze out across the city again, this time wondering what the hell he'd just agreed to.

❄

WANT TO READ MORE?